Praise For Eric Red

"Eric Red gifted us a beauty with *It Waits Below*. This one has a little bit of everything, but the claustrophobic nature of the tale, and the balls-to-the-wall conclusion help push it into near uncharted territory. Red is a beast!" [One of Top Ten Horror Novels of the Year]
    —Horror Novel Reviews

"In our mythos of the Old West, there are bad guys and even badder guys. But Eric Red's are the biggest, baddest guys of all..."
    —Jack Ketchum on *The Guns of Santa Sangre*

"A fun and exciting read that no horror fan should miss."
    —Famous Monsters of Filmland on *The Guns of Santa Sangre*

"Eric Red's *The Guns of Santa Sangre* has all the elements of a classic. It is an almost filmic rendition of the time-honored traditions of the Western, with a deftly handled incursion of the unnatural, with the two blended into a single, intriguing story."
    —Hellnotes

"An old-fashioned, well-made dime novel, doing Louis L'Amour, Elmore Leonard and Richard Matheson proud. The book begins at a gallop and never lets up. Once again, Red delivers the pulp goods. And it'd make a helluva film."
    —Bookgasm on *The Guns of Santa Sangre*

Look for these titles by Eric Red

Now Available:

The Guns of Santa Sangre
It Waits Below

White Knuckle

Eric Red

SAMHAIN
PUBLISHING

Samhain Publishing, Ltd.
11821 Mason Montgomery Road, 4B
Cincinnati, OH 45249
www.samhainpublishing.com

White Knuckle
Print ISBN: 978-1-61922-978-5
Digital ISBN: 978-1-61922-588-6

Editing by Don D'Auria
Cover Formatting by Scott Carpenter
Cover by John Gallagher

First Samhain Publishing, Ltd. electronic publication: June 2015
First Samhain Publishing, Ltd. print publication: June 2015

Dedication

To my father, Cornelius Gerard Durdaller. I love you, Dad.

Chapter One

Thwap, thwap, thwap.

Gusts of rain swept her windshield and the slashing wipers did nothing to stave off the deluge as Carrie Brown drove home on the lonely night Midwestern Interstate. The water came on in gusting waves. Tired as she was, Carrie had to struggle to see through the blurry glass but was used to these road conditions this time of year. The weather wasn't the problem.

The commute would be a breeze if it weren't for those damn big rigs.

At this hour, there was nobody but her and the endless succession of late night truckers on the road. The eighteen-wheelers surged past in galaxies of crimson taillights and Christmas-tree configurations of colored lights webbing the trailers and cabs. The rolling dinosaurs hurtled by her, one after the other.

They drove like Carrie didn't belong there—like it was their road and she was in their way, an inconvenience.

With each truck that overtook her, a huge *whoosh splat* of wind and rain bombed her car. She winced from the ache in her tired eyes as yet another explosion of blinding headlights assaulted her in the rearview mirror. A rumble like thunder as a gigantic tractor-trailer overtook her little car in a wall of spray and afterblow that shook her dwarfed vehicle and sent it hydroplaning across the white lines. She felt the warning rattle of the plastic bumps on the divider—roadway braille. Then the truck was gone up ahead, red taillights receding in a curtain of wet. Those bastard truckers had no respect or caution for regular drivers.

It was 3:01 AM according to her watch. Carrie was alone in the vehicle. Her shift had just ended at County General Hospital. The RN was exhausted, struggling to stay awake behind the wheel of her drenched Prius. In another forty miles, she would be home under the covers. But she had to get there first. The commute was bad enough when it was dry, but intolerable when it rained. She rubbed her eyes and squinted through the drenched glass at the three-lane gloom ahead, a watery blur of blacktop and broken white lines. The relentless metronome beat of the wipers made her drowsier. Rubies and diamonds of refracting taillights and headlights kaleidoscoped in distortion through the soaked glass. The effect was hypnotic and lulling. She blinked to stop seeing double.

Her hands were gripped, rigor-mortis tight around the steering wheel, and Carrie noticed how tense she was. The confines of her car closed in on her. Always skittish of the trucks on the highway, she routinely clenched in fear when they barreled past, the huge wheels and transoms seemingly close enough to scrape her door. She forced herself to picture the mangled bodies from the auto wrecks she saw weekly in the ER to scare herself into wakefulness, but drowsiness descended moments later like a druggy fog. She knew the statistics that driving tired was the largest cause of car crashes next to DUIs.

She had to resort to emergency measures to stay alert.

She opened her purse and pulled out the Jalapeno chili she had in the little plastic baggie. A friend once told her taking a bite out of the raw hot pepper was the one sure way to stay awake when you were driving tired. Popping it in her mouth, she bit down, and felt the searing acid heat a white-hot agony against her tongue and palate. Her jaw swam with pain, but it did the trick.

Carrie was wide-awake all right.

The rearview mirror burned blinding white as four headlamps of two big rigs fast approached, one in the left passing lane and one in the right truck lane. The eighteen-wheelers surged forward and bellowed past her, rocking her vehicle back and forth in the wet hurricane of their afterblows. The nurse whimpered and gritted her teeth against the terrible noise of the rampaging diesels rushing by, sandwiching her car between a hundred and forty tons of wheeled steel. She decelerated to aid in their departure ahead, shaking like a leaf as she did so. *Assholes!* Within moments they were red-jeweled pinpricks of taillights twinkling out in the watery darkness up the road.

Blacktop and broken white lines unfurled.

Thwap. Thwap. Thwap.

Her mouth seriously smarted.

A greenish blob floated out of the inky murk ahead in the windshield. Reflective words became discernable. "Johnstown. Next exit." She passed the sign.

Fifteen minutes would bring her to her exit.

Twenty minutes and she'd be pulling into her driveway.

A few minutes later, she'd be safe in bed.

Please God, just get me home.

Mouth hurts.

The radio. *Turn it on.* Static. *Flip up the dial.* Static. Static. More static. *Ugh. Turn the fucking thing off.*

Thwap. Thwap. Thwap.

The blackness ahead was melting like oil in the smear of the windshield wipers. A glance into her mirrors showed only darkness behind.

Twinkle.

Headlights.

Coming on fast.

Two big saucer eye headlamps inflated in her back windshield, filling her car with stark illumination that violated her safe confines like a kind of rape. The front grill was vaguely outlined and resembled a grinning demon. *Oh c'mon, just get past me,* she thought. The rig must have had its high beams on because her rear and side view mirrors were a white-out of blinding triangular reflection that made it impossible for her to see or move her eyes anywhere. *Just get past me!* The trembling thunder and low register vibration of the tractor-trailer shuddered her vehicle as it hauled itself up alongside on the right. Carrie held on to the steering wheel for dear life, waiting for the truck to pass.

But it didn't.

The monster eighteen-wheeler, a towering shadow silhouette on the passenger side, just hung there—as if it sensed her anxiety on some animal predatory level and was toying with her. It had slowed to her speed as she was nose to nose with the cab. *Asshole,* she thought, and decelerated to get behind the speeding big rig.

Its taillights flared and hellish red light inflamed the inside of her car.

The truck had slowed, too.

Neck and neck again.

OK, fine fucktard! The nurse stepped on the gas and her Prius shot ahead up the unfurling blacktop and broken white lines of the highway that was now empty except for she and her seventy-ton unwelcome companion. Carrie felt her car hydroplane on the unsafe wet tarmac and she struggled to wrest the vehicle back under control.

A throaty diesel engine roared behind her and the cough of smokestacks, jutting up like twin chromium steer horns on the cab in the sopping back windshield, belched smoke that sinisterly wreathed the truck. It heaved forward, easily pulling up alongside her again and now she was scared shitless.

Carrie threw an anxious glance at the cab and driver door window of the big rig keeping pace beside her. Through her rain speckled passenger's window an empty seat away, she could see nothing but the lower edge of the driver's window. There was a shadowy silhouette of a head with a cap on the trucker inside. A light went on inside the cockpit of the flanking truck, and now she could make out that the blurry oval of his face was Caucasian and male. The rain on the window glass made his distorted features look like melted candle wax. Fear jolted her body like sparking jumper cables and she decelerated down to 30 mph, but without missing a beat, in a hydraulic hiss of brakes, the truck slowed too, so that his window and the face beyond hovered over hers. The driver was looking at her, staring at her—she could feel it, if not see it, beyond the walls of glass and rain.

Suddenly a bright light exploded in her car, lighting her up and she heard herself scream. It was coming from an industrial flashlight the stalking trucker shone out his window, aiming it right in her face. Terror flared as she realized he was trying to make her out. Then, just as quick, the flashlight switched off.

And the tractor-trailer edged inwards to impact the side of her car!

CRANNN-NNNG!

Now Carrie screamed and screamed, releasing the steering wheel. The truck veered like a gigantic rattlesnake and hit her passenger side again. Metal buckled and glass cracked as she skidded out of control, sideways. She was going to die. He was going to kill her. *But why?* Seizing control of the rotating steering wheel, she wrestled it into alignment with both white-knuckled fists and somehow kept her wits enough to steer into the skid, regaining traction as she pumped the brakes and slowed as fast as she dared, coming to a near standstill on the shoulder of the fast lane.

The eighteen-wheeler could not stop as fast and didn't try, just plunged on ahead. As her little vehicle came to rest on the bad side of the road, Carrie watched the red taillights recede up the highway. The maniac was picking up speed and getting the hell out of there, his lethal prank over. No question, he was speeding off and that must mean she was safe. The truck was gone, thank God and blessed Jesus.

Sitting, sobbing and shaking behind the wheel, the nurse found her jeans were soaking and at first thought it was rain but then realized she'd pissed herself. Was still emptying her bladder all over the vinyl car seat. Her breath and heart were sledgehammering in her chest as she sat paralyzed and alone. The inside of her car stank of urine.

The front and back windshields were black as melting onyx in the muddy rain. The highway was otherwise deserted, and it was just her. Carrie couldn't move, frozen in place with indecision. No way she was going to get back on the road after that close shave, even though the exit was a mile away. The mad trucker might be waiting for her. But she couldn't stay here, could she? What to do. *Gotta do something,* her mind raced. What?

Fumbling her cell phone out of her purse, the nurse punched in "911."

The phone rang. "Police emergency." A man's voice.

"H-H-H—"

"Ma'am, this is police emergency. I can't understand you."

Shit, her mouth wasn't working. *Use your words*, like her mother always told her as a child.

"Ma'am, this is an emergency line. Are you hurt?"

Once Carrie spat out the first syllable, she couldn't stop talking. "Help me, please! A big truck just ran me off the road! He smashed into my car on purpose! Tried to kill me! Help! Please! Send the cops!"

"Where are you now?'

"I'm in my car. I'm on the 80 about a mile north of the Johnstown exit." Good, her RN training was coming back to her and she was lucid and articulate. It was going to be all right. *Give the 911 dispatcher the information. Be calm.* "My name is Carrie Brown. I'm a nurse at County General and I was driving home from my shift and this big rig just came up on me and knocked me off the road." She heard the sound of a keyboard tapping on the other end of the line as the 911 dispatcher took down her information.

"Are you injured?"

"No, just shaken up."

"Stay in your car, Ms. Brown. Lock your doors. Do not leave your vehicle. We have a Highway Patrol unit in Johnstown and he is on his way."

A flare of headlights in her windshield came from the oncoming lanes on the other side of the road and her brief rush of expectant relief that it was the authorities turned into a chill as she saw it was yet another truck, hurtling in the opposite direction. Then there was red glow in her car as the big rig disappeared behind her and all was dark again.

"Can you hear me, ma'am?"

"Yes, I'm sorry, yes. Stay in the car. Lock the doors." She pressed the master plunger lock button and heard the locks on all four doors all drop with a soft *thunk*. "Don't worry, I'm not getting out."

"We have a unit on his way. Should be there in ten minutes."

"Thank you."

"Sit tight."

The call disconnected. Carrie put the phone in her pants pocket. She lay in her own water on the driver's seat, gasping for breath. The body heat of her wild fear was fogging up the windows. Outside, the night highway was desolate and empty, barely visible in the thrashing sheets of torrential rain. Blackness embraced her. The nurse waited, counting the seconds, then switched on her blinkers. A yellow pulsing glimmer broke the black void outside that was broken only by her headlights, which seemed so weak. Wiping snot from her face with her shirtsleeve, she smelt the acrid tang of her pee filling the car and permitted herself the luxury of embarrassment worrying about the state trooper discovering her in this condition. That was the least of her problems, she decided. As the moments passed, listening to the *thwap thwap thwap* of the wipers and the *click click click* of her blinkers, she grew restless and felt her skin crawl, trapped in her car like she was out on the great big scary empty Interstate. Fear spread.

Then stygian darkness brightened.

Two white pinpricks to her rear.

Somehow, Carrie knew two things right away.

It was not a police car.

And the trucker was back.

Now she knew why the big rig had picked up speed after it had run her off the road. It had been in a hurry all right.

The exit was a mile ahead.

The trucker wanted to take that exit so he could cross the overpass, turn around and come back the other way, then take the next exit and come back for her—it was the truck she'd seen speed past in the opposite direction a moment before.

The two humongous headlights of the gargantuan tractor-trailer grew and slowed in her back windshield as the twin saucer eyes of the truck eased to a stop on the side of the road directly behind her, the high beams blasting into her car and spotlighting her. A twisted shadow fell over the nurse as the silhouette of the driver stepped out of his cab and partially blocked his lamps.

In those few desperate seconds, Carrie Brown put up a fight. Managing to turn over the ignition and step on the gas, she knew as her car didn't budge—tires squealing in protest despite her revving the engine to ninety—that the wheels were stuck in the slippery mud of the road shoulder and she wasn't going anywhere.

Then her window exploded.

The wipers stopped.

Chapter Two

FBI Special Agent Sharon Ormsby looked out at the faces of the police officers sitting in the chairs of the Ramada Inn conference room. Most were in uniform except for a group of detectives in suits and what appeared to be undercover agents who were dressed casually. Sharon made a mental head count of thirty-seven. Glancing at her watch, the SA saw it was time for her to take the podium and begin conducting the session.

As the cops chattered and took out their notepads, the agent glanced out the window. The long stretch of Denver, Colorado I-76 Interstate passed a mile away and that's why she was here.

Today was a regional training session she conducted with police forces around the country that operated near freeways.

Sharon began with a warm smile. "Thank you all for coming. I'm here today to brief you about the FBI Highway Serial Killings Initiative, acronym HSK, in order that our departments might better interface. In 2004, an analyst from the Oklahoma Bureau of Investigation detected a crime pattern: the bodies of murdered women were being dumped along the Interstate 40 corridor in Oklahoma, Texas, Arkansas and Mississippi," she continued. "The analyst and a police colleague from the Grapevine, Texas Police Department referred these cases to VICAP, our Violent Criminal Apprehension Program, where our analysts looked at other records in our database to see if there were similar patterns of highway killings elsewhere. Turns out there were. So we launched an extensive effort to support our state and local partners with open investigations into highway murders."

A hand went up. She nodded and pointed.

"Did you catch the killer?"

"Yes, we did."

Sharon was thirty-two. The fresh-faced agent had graduated from the FBI Academy in Quantico eight months earlier, still in her regulation two-year probationary period until final review before becoming a full-fledged SA. She had not anticipated when she was assigned to HSK that she'd find herself ending up lecturing other officers like a Mary Kay cosmetics salesperson, which was the way she felt right now. While Sharon knew she'd be assigned to some small to medium-sized field office, she'd hoped for more challenging first assignments than her current analyst position at HSK. Other agents she graduated the academy with were already posted to FBI white-collar crimes or counterterrorism units. At least she hadn't been assigned to FBI applicant or White House employee background checks with the endless neighbor interviews and poring over banal financial records. The SA yearned to be in the field, weapon drawn, busting suspects, and that would come soon. But for now, this was her assignment and she was under constant scrutiny and evaluation during her probationary period. It was her job and she did it.

She went on with her lecture before the attentive faces of the various law enforcement personnel. "First, some background. The victims in these cases are primarily women who are living high-risk, transient lifestyles, often involving substance abuse and prostitution. They're frequently picked up at truck stops or service stations and sexually assaulted, murdered, and dumped along a highway."

The rustling of papers had stopped, and she could see the interest in the eyes on the faces in the audience. Sharon cleared her throat, took a sip of a Dixie cup of water on the podium, and continued.

"The suspects are predominantly long haul truck drivers. But the mobile nature of the offenders, the unsafe lifestyles of the victims, the significant distances and multiple jurisdictions involved, and the scarcity of witnesses or forensic evidence can make these cases tough to solve.

"Enter VICAP, part of our National Center for the Analysis of Violent Crime and a national repository for violent crimes. Most of you are already familiar with it. The database—which contains information on homicides, sexual assaults, missing persons, and unidentified human remains—is available to law enforcement throughout the country over a secure Internet link on our Law Enforcement Online, or LEO. VICAP analysts have created a national matrix of more than five hundred murder victims from along or near highways, as well as a list of some two hundred potential suspects. Names of suspects—contributed by law enforcement agencies—are examined by analysts who develop timelines using a variety of reliable sources of information."

The lecture lasted an hour. Afterwards she answered questions, took and gave cards, said her goodbyes and got out of the Ramada Inn like her pants were on fire.

Sharon was at the Denver International Airport an hour later and caught a commuter flight back to Washington, DC. Her plan was to shower and change at the Georgetown apartment she rarely had a chance to use, and then be at the Hoover Building FBI headquarters offices of the HSK right after lunch. The agent had a pile of work to do. She caught a small nap on the plane and reliably woke right as the 727 was in its final descent to Dulles. Putting her seat back up, she gazed out the porthole of her window seat. The intricate circuitry of the 66, 95, 395 and 495 Interstate highways surrounding the airport stretched on in every direction as far as the eye could see.

It was her beat.

When it was safe to switch her cell phone back on as the jet taxied to the gate, Sharon saw she had two emails from Frank Campanella, the Supervising Special Agent in charge of the FBI's Critical Incident Response Group and her supervisor at HSK. He wanted to see her when she got into the office. The SA emailed back a quick reply that she had just landed and disembarked with the other commuters.

Home at her small, functionally furnished apartment, after a quick shower, Sharon studied herself in the bathroom mirror. Blonde hair, freckles, sharp features. Skin clear. Body fit. Beyond a small white chip on her brow from a childhood bicycle accident, she had no scars. Yet.

The agent drew her fresh dark jacket over her clean, white, button-down shirt and dark pants, the picture of the Bureau's traditional clean cut and professional presentation.

She picked up her regulation black Glock Model 23 .40 caliber semiautomatic handgun, checked the magazine, holstered it and put it on her belt beneath the jacket. Then took a moment to admire and feel pride in her hard-won FBI badge. It was gold, with a squared shield topped with an eagle. The embossed words "Federal Bureau of Investigation" were above a blindfolded figure holding scales in the right hand and a sword in the left between a "U" and an "S" above the words, "Department Of Justice." It gave her a charge holding it in her hand. Closing her FBI ID badge wallet, she slid it into her pants.

Time to get to work.

Her cell phone had two texts from the office. Alabama DMV had found the registered owner of the license plate she had them run. North Dakota HP wanted her to call them about a roadside body they needed an I.D. on. Sharon would get to it when she was at her desk.

Twenty-five minutes later, Sharon got out of her Honda Accord in the parking garage of the J. Edgar Hoover building FBI Headquarters in DC, the largest of the fifty-one field offices of the FBI in the United States. It was where she was presently assigned by the Bureau and where she got her orders.

Walking through the courtyard, she looked up at the imposing cement building that spanned the entire block, rowed with red, white and blue American flags on poles drifting in the breeze. The seven-story complex was gray with dull uniform rows of square windows, designed to blow out rather than in on personnel in the event of an attack. A Hoover quote on the rounded, brown, ivy-topped wall in the entrance read, "The most effective weapon against crime is cooperation. The efforts of all law enforcement agencies with the support and understanding of the American people." It sat across from a circle of wooden benches. Sharon passed the tall bronze statue of a man standing with his arms protectively over two huddled figures in front of a metal unfurled flag on the dark gray cement pedestal with the words, "Fidelity Bravery Integrity."

She entered the glass door and walked past the office locator on the wall.

HSK, The Highway Serial Killer Initiative, was on the third floor.

Using her key card, the SA entered into the nondescript and modest one-floor arrangement of offices, cubicles and computers. The eight SAs and five support personnel who comprised the staff were at the desks. For now, it was home.

SSA Frank Campanella walked up and said good morning with a firm handshake. Her boss was in his mid-forties, clean cut and fit with sharp brown eyes that didn't miss anything. He wore a black suit, white shirt and pressed maroon tie, as he usually did.

"Morning, sir."

"Hi, Sharon."

"You emailed you wanted to see me."

"I've been going back and forth with the Omaha field office today. They think they're narrowing down on a trucker suspect who may have been involved in the Nebraska killings, and might be sending up his information today. They want us to run it through NICS and VICAP, and if we get a hit put an APB out on the national wire tonight. The information so far is all on your desk."

She nodded. Good.

"How was Denver?"

Sharon smiled agreeably. "Had about thirty officers show up. They were happy to have our resources to access, and of course now they know how to reach us."

"Nice job. I think they're more receptive getting the information from an attractive female agent. Thanks for doing all this traveling, and welcome back. Check on the faxes we got this morning from the crime lab. And don't make any dinner plans; if we put out the APB it may be a late one."

"Will do."

She went to her cubicle.

There was a killer preying on truck stop hookers and bodies had turned up in three states.

All the evidence pointed to a deranged big rig operator.

Sharon knew the US Interstate Highway system had over 46,800 miles of interconnected highways and there were two million tractor-trailers driving those roads. Finding a killer truck driver was like finding a needle in a haystack. But certain factors increased the odds of apprehension. One half of the drivers drove local routes. That meant less than a million drivers were long haul truckers driving interstate routes who were the likelier suspects in interstate killings. Most truckers worked for freighting companies and by law had to file precise transportation logs with the authorities, making their movements relatively easy to track.

She stood and walked into the operations room to regard the forty-foot map on the wall of the continental United States. Pins and length of colored string delineated where victims had disappeared and their bodies were later recovered.

There had been a recent string of truck stop hooker murders on the I-10 corridor over the last two years. Six of the sex worker victims—Lot Lizards or Pavement Princesses in trucker jargon—had disappeared. Three of the bodies had been discovered dumped on the side of the highway, or on adjoining roads. They had all been stabbed. The killer had not been making any great effort to conceal the murders and the body disposal seemed to have been hasty. These appeared to be crimes of opportunity. The profile they had worked up was of an impulsive and brutal long distance trucker.

The actual number of killings could be far greater, Sharon knew—the dangerous transient lifestyle of the Lot Lizards, who haunted many of the thousands of truck stops around the country, made them tough to track. They often hitched rides with their long hauler Johns to the next truck stop and often covered many states within days, slipping past local law enforcement. Communication between interstate agencies was less than ideal, and that was one of the reasons that the FBI Highway Serial Killings Initiative had come into existence. A few hookers had cell phones—this made tracking their movements occasionally possible by getting the coordinates of cell towers they had used for the calls and pulling phone company records—but as often as not the girls used disposable phones or phone cards. And few went by their real names.

Sharon had spent the last three weeks running exhaustive Federal Transportation Authority log checks. Every licensed trucker driver in the United States was required to write and turn in logs to the FTA records of their pickup and drop off points on every haul, including dates and routes. This was entered into the national database. Sharon was looking for all drivers who had been driving the I-10 route during the dates of the disappearances.

Over 17,000 truckers were registered as having driven the murder highway. Half of those had regular routes; others were just driving the route for a specific haul. Gathering all that information was a daunting task. Sharon had narrowed the search to drivers who had a criminal record, flagging those who had served time for violent crime such as assault and battery. Being a trucker was one of the few jobs an ex-con could secure without undue discrimination for having done time. Even multiple DUIs and a crash on their record did not mean that truckers could not work, because even though some of the major freight concerns might not hire them, they could always work independently, as long as they had a CDL-A license.

She was getting a fax. The agent took a look. It was a criminal record sent from the Omaha field office. The driver's license photo of a burly, bearded, good-looking trucker stared back at her. His name was Rudy Dykstra. Age thirty-two. Home address Arizona. Ten years before he had been convicted of second-degree manslaughter for knifing a truck stop hooker outside New Orleans. He'd served eight years of a fifteen-year sentence in Angola Prison in Louisiana. He was now an independent owner/operator of a big rig. License 894RFT. Arizona plates.

Rudy Dykstra's FTA travel logs showed that he had been in the area where three of the Lot Lizards later found knifed had reportedly gone missing.

He clearly had tendencies.

Sharon walked into Campanella's office and he signed the authorization.

They put out an APB on Rudy Dykstra and it went out over the wire to law enforcement agencies nationwide.

Chapter Three

Montana was getting cold this time of year and Candy Dolowitz was thinking in a few days she would hitch south for a couple months. It was chilly in the shabby 76 ladies room off the I-38. The seventeen-year-old redhead was shivering in her fishnet stockings and hot pants, and pulled her fake white fur parka tighter around her low-cut tank top over her firm young tits. Her left boob was bruised from where she was bitten by the overenthusiastic John in the eighteen-wheeler last night. The crystal meth was wearing off and she was crashing big time. Her nerves were raw and she smelled the last Latino trucker she was with a half hour ago on her body. She brushed her teeth in the smelly gas station bathroom and spat toothpaste, returning it to her purse—if it was a good day she would use the bathroom another seven or eight times.

She checked her plastic purse and pulled out a crinkled piece of tin foil. She unfolded it and cursed when she saw there were just a few grains of white powder left. She licked it off and tossed the foil in the trash can.

Candy didn't remember having those lines and dark circles around her eyes she saw staring back at her in the mirror, but she figured she was probably just tired.

Fixing her face and applying lipstick in the cracked bathroom mirror, she smoothed her hair and saw the red dye was coming off at the brown, flaccid roots.

The girl had seen a lot of the country in the last six months since she ran away from home in Mississippi. Her stepfather had beaten the shit out of her when she finally ignored his threats to kill her if she ever told her waitress mother that the fat psycho fuck had been sticking his uncut chubby in her since she was thirteen. To her surprise, her mother sided with her husband—Candy knew it was because the forklift operator was paying the bills and her useless Mom had nowhere else to go—and kicked her teenaged ass out.

So Candy had hit the road.

She walked right out the door of her trailer park with the clothes on her back and her plastic purse and stuck out her thumb on the stretch of Route 51 that ran outside the gate.

It had started while she was hitchhiking on Interstate 55 with the first trucker she got a lift with. He hadn't forced himself on her, just offered her a hundred dollars for a blowjob. The first time she had dick in her mouth for money was hard, but it was over in a few minutes and she could buy her next few meals.

Candy learned her first lesson in the rulebook of The Life—always carry a toothbrush.

Drugs were easily found out there on the open road. Many of the drivers had them and she was raking in the dough. Once she began giving head, it was a small step to let them feel her tits or between her legs, and a week later, when a trucker offered her five hundred dollars to fuck her in the back of his rig, she was working for a living.

The meth kept her flying.

On the best nights, the highway rolled by like a trip through outer space, the broken white lines and headlights of the traffic like stars and galaxies. On the best days, the sunsets were like a video game.

Her iPod drowned out the sound of the diesels and she soared through the country like a beautiful flying bird on her angel wings that spread like her legs. The truck stop hooker tried to be safe, and always used a condom, except when she didn't. It wasn't going to be for long, she told herself, just until she got on her feet, although she admitted she was spending most of her time on her back these days.

Candy had always wanted to travel. Now she had been to California and New Mexico and Michigan and she was blasting like a missile, fueled by crystal meth and jizz and her shaved moneymaker between her legs that these truck-driving cowboys couldn't get enough of.

Everything had gone fine until she took the fifty from the Dade County undercover cop and been arrested for soliciting. She called her mother Janice, the only person she knew, and was released into her Mom's custody. There were lots of hugs and tears and drunken bonding back at the double-wide in the homey trailer park in Mississippi— Mom told her she had thrown out her stepfather a few weeks after Candy split, but the teenager knew the freak had dumped her drunken parent's sorry ass once he couldn't stick it in her daughter. For a few days it was good, until her mother pushed her to get a job at the local bowling alley and the teen realized the pathetic women just wanted her to pay the bills. Candy worked that magic tongue of hers and swallowed some of the manager's load and made herself a quick two hundred and she was gone, baby, gone.

The road called her.

This time she'd made up her mind to do some hard hooking and Candy had turned pro before her eighteenth birthday.

Oh God, it hurt.

The girl came to in shearing ripping anguish from unseen wounds in her body. Candy knew she was naked from the cold she felt on every inch of her bare flesh. Her wrists and ankles were handcuffed, and she was spread eagled and wet everywhere with what she knew was her own blood. The first thought that went through her mind was that her pretty face would be ugly now because she could feel her peeled cheek hanging off over her exposed gums.

It was chilly inside the back of the truck's cab from the wind blasting through the open passenger window up front. Candy was tied and bound on the bunk bed in the back. She could see the naked centerfolds of nude chicks taped to the walls and roof above the mattress. Turning her head, she saw the front seats and the driver's hulking shoulder and back of his bald head beyond the headrest. Night highway peeled away through the windshield.

She tried to scream, oh did she ever.

But the electrician's tape was wrapped around her mouth and jaw, and her screams were swallowed in her throat.

Jumbled memories in a mental jigsaw of terror, trying to piece together what happened but the pieces didn't fit.

The Dakota truck stop on I-29.

The Texan trucker that had given her the lift all the way from Des Moines. Friendly. The joint shared and songs sung. He dropped her off at the Fargo depot.

The blowjob she gave the fat guy in the Peterbilt that had gotten her the fifty she used to pay for dinner at the diner.

A burger with bacon and cheese.

Tractor-trailers pulling in and out of the isolated truck stop. Behemoth dinosaurs with headlights like big eyes in the night under the neon of the overhang.

Where was she on her way to?

What was her name?

That one rumbling big rig parked in the darkness. The glow of the driver's cigarette, as he watched her in his cap. She came toward him down the tarmac, shaking her ass.

He had a decal on the side of his trailer. What was it?

White something.

White Line Fever. Yes, that was it, like the old flick she used to see on late night TV.

His door opened.

Another hundred, easy.

Then there was a blur and the lights went out and Candy woke up in screaming pain and she was here and it was a nightmare beyond comprehension and it was real.

Chapter Four

The call came in at 3:46 PM.

Special Agent Sharon Ormsby picked up and it was Nevada HP Commander Don Harrison. She immediately recognized his gravelly voice. They'd gotten a hit on the APB the HSK had put out on the trucker suspect Rudy Dykstra and his men had picked him up at a truck stop in Prim. He was in custody at Nevada Highway Patrol headquarters on Sunset Road in Las Vegas.

The agent did some quick mental calculations and told Harrison she and her SSA could be there in six hours.

The Highway Patrol interrogation room was sweltering. The whippet thin, gray-haired sergeant apologized for the air-conditioning being under repair as he led Sharon and Campanella into the viewing area. There were two chairs and a telephone in the darkened, olive-green, drably painted room. A six-foot, two-way mirror looked into the interrogation cubicle and the solitary man sitting hunched by the table, staring at his hands.

The trucker looked to be in his forties, hefty and red bearded, with a florid face and tattoos on his muscular naked forearms jutting out of the rolled-up sleeves of a checkerboard shirt beneath a worn denim jacket. His trucker's cap sat on the table before him, and he toyed with it nervously in sausage-thick, calloused fingers—working man's hands.

"That's him?" Campanella asked.

The local cop nodded. "That's Dykstra. Independent owner operator. Arizona license. Drives a Mack Cruiseliner cabover. He was running a load to Arkansas when we pulled him over. Truck's impounded. The forensics team is going over it right now. No outstanding warrants on it, though."

"Has he asked for a lawyer yet?" Campanella asked. Like cops, the FBI were not required to have a lawyer present for questioning if the subject were not in custody, and Dykstra wasn't yet.

"No. We haven't told him why we brought him in. This is interstate and it's Federal, so the ball's in your court. I'll let you handle the questioning."

Sharon felt a surge of excitement. A big part of every agent's academy training was interviewing and interrogation and developing active listening skills. The Bureau considered these skills essential for every agent in gathering information, a prime directive of the FBI.

"You want to handle the questioning?" Campanella said to her and she nodded right away, knowing she was under the microscope and he would be evaluating her skills, stepping in if necessary. Most of her duties at HSK had been as an analyst and spokesperson, and from the day she joined the FBI Sharon had itched to be a field agent. Accompanying Campanella on an interrogation made her feel that she was in the action. He boss had been slowly increasing her field duties, testing her, easing her into it.

Sharon studied the rugged, rough-hewn but kind face of the driver in the holding tank. His puffy eyes raised to meet hers, but she knew he didn't see her, only his own reflection in the two-way mirror she was concealed behind. The look of naked distress in his unguarded glance struck her, then his gaze traveled away from the mirror and around the room, lost and hopeless.

"Can we talk to him?" she asked.

The sergeant nodded and opened the door for the two agents.

The smell of fear lay in the room.

Dykstra looked up at the two FBI agents as they entered, his eyes going cottony with caution. "I didn't do anything," he managed in a gravelly voice with a lilt of twang.

"Hello, Mr. Dykstra, I'm Special Agent Sharon Ormsby and this is Supervising Special Agent Frank Campanella from the Washington FBI Field Office. We're sorry about this and we'd just like to ask you a few questions." It has been hammered into her in training. *Treat everyone with respect; those who have something to hide will eventually let their guard down and tell us what we want to know.*

The trucker nodded agreeably. "Sure, ask away."

"Mind if we sit?"

"Be my guest. Mi casa su casa." Dykstra gave a wry glance to his surroundings and Sharon let a smile slip. The sergeant stood by the door. The agents took seats across from the detained trucker. She watched his body language—arms uncrossed, shoulders tense, but gaze direct in hers.

Okay.

Sharon observed the trucker carefully, routinely looking for nonverbal signals in his posture or gait, but while the big redneck was tense, he stoically looked right in her eyes. "So, how long have you been a truck driver?"

He shrugged. "Twenty years, give or take."

"You must enjoy it," Sharon said warmly. "I have an uncle who's a long hauler"—it was true, she did—"and he always tells me he can't wait to get back on the road."

The prisoner nodded. "Yeah, trucking's like that. Most drivers don't want to do nothin' else."

"I always wanted to try it. Nothing but you and the open road. Is the feeling of freedom what you like best about it?"

Dykstra's eyes lit up. "Nothin' like getting behind the wheel and hearin' the scream of them diesels, putting the hammer down on a thousand miles of hard asphalt. I guess most truckers'll tell you pretty much the same thing."

Through interviews, the SA knew agents learned about their subjects' personal and psychological makeup. *Interview questions should be open-ended, giving subjects the opportunity to tell something about themselves. Closed-ended questions tend to elicit "yes" or "no" responses. Create a rapport that builds trust that leads to disclosure.* "My uncle used to say exactly that."

"There you go." He gave the thumbs up, seeming to relax.

Sharon turned on the charm. "But my Uncle Jack didn't get into long hauling until his thirties. Wow, you started young."

"Yeah, I been a gearjammin', double-clutchin' fool since my teens." He grinned, friendly if nervous. "'Cept for a break in Angola Prison, but I figure you already know that, which is why I'm here and you're here." The humor went out of his eyes but his gaze remained steady and, Sharon thought, honest.

Time to ask the real questions.

"Can I be honest with you, Mr. Dysktra?"

"Sure."

"You seem agitated. I was watching you through the mirror before we came in and it seemed you were pretty worried about something."

The trucker sat up rod straight and now looked back and forth evenly between both agents. "Yeah, I'm being held by the HP for ten hours and now the FBI has come down from Washington to interview me. I'm just an independent owner operator and I'm already late delivering my load to Albuquerque and I'm going to have to eat the cost. Got an ex and a little boy and support payments to make and I ain't no big outfit, it's just me. I lose my license or word gets out the FBI was grillin' me, the freight companies'll drop my sorry ass. Will too if I'm late delivering the load. So yeah, I'm worried."

She observed, mentally collated. *No angling of body away from interviewer, no shifting of eyes or avoidance of eye contact, no text bridges...*

No obvious signs of lying, in other words, not yet.

"Do you recognize her?" Sharon laid a snapshot on the table in front of the prisoner. The SA's guts clenched. The woman, what was left of her, had been nineteen, an African American lot lizard. She had been found naked and carved up with a knife on the side of the road forty miles outside of Bismarck, North Dakota. Her mouth, wrists and ankles were bound with electrician's tape. She was the fifth victim of identical prostitute killings over the last two years whose bodies had been dumped and recovered on the sides of the highway around the country. The trucker eyeballed the photo, shook his head side to side, confused and rattled.

"No, I never seen her. Who is she?"

"Her name was Keisha Solomon. She worked as truck stop hooker."

"Pavement Princess."

"Yes, same thing." The SA nodded, and then produced another photograph of the girl's bashed in face at the crime scene. The side of her face was a livid eggplant of black and purple bruising where the cheekbones had been caved in. The agent set it on the table.

Rudy winced squeamishly and for the first time dropped his gaze, and Sharon registered that. His revulsion was real. "Never saw her in my life."

"Are you sure?" Sharon leaned forward and observed Rudy Dykstra hard, reading the verbal and non-verbal cues in his behavior—posture, the tone of his voice, which could indicate he was lying. Behind her, she felt Campanella doing the same. Active listening was considered one of a Special Agent's primary weapons. So far, there weren't any tells Sharon could see. The man seemed truly upset and horrified.

"Yes, I'm sure. That poor kid."

"Did you kill her, Rudy?" Sharon's voice was flat.

Dykstra's face fell. "You got the wrong guy. I didn't kill her. Listen, I'm sorry what happened to this kid but I never even seen her before."

"You did pull an eight year stretch in Louisiana for second degree manslaughter." Campanella interjected for the first time, going on the offensive, and Sharon noticed the reticence in the sergeant's face over the direct line of questioning, but it was jurisdictional and he was staying out.

"Yeah, that was fifteen years ago."

"You killed a prostitute in a truck stop in Oklahoma."

Rubbing his reddened eyes with his handcuffed wrist, Dykstra sighed. "It was self defense. Listen, I was dealing then and I did my bit for it, but that crazy cracked-up whore tried to steal my stash and went at me with a knife. I was trying to take it from her and she got the wrong end of it. I'm sorry about that; I was high then, but I did my time and paid my debt to society. I got rehabilitated. I changed my life when I got out. Got sober and been off the booze twelve years now. Still go to AA meetings. Have a regular job. Bought my own rig. Rebuilt my life. Keeping it together. I'm not that guy anymore." His eyes were tearing, Sharon noticed, and his voice quaked, and as far as she could sense he was being sincere, genuinely remorseful and torn up about his past. "I was just a kid, man."

"You want to call a lawyer?" Campanella asked.

"I don't need a lawyer. I got a higher power. I'll cooperate any way I can."

Sharon thinking, *No way he did it*, when they got the call.

Chapter Five

The helicopter banked north over the low trees and neat fields of the Tennessee farmlands in the gathering dusk.

Sharon stared out the bubble glass at the drab checkerboard quilt of landscape. The chopper traversed the unfurling stretch of the Interstate Highway several hundred feet down below, intermittent red taillights of the rush hour traffic beginning to back up and cluster. The vibrant red pulse of the assembled police cars by the bridge span ahead below signaled their destination was approaching.

The pilot set the bird down in a hurricane surge of rotor wind that swept the grass by the ten clustered TPD squad cars and Highway Patrol vehicles. Sharon unbuckled and followed Campanella as he ducked out the cockpit door, both of them covering their heads against the rotor wash of the slowing chopper blades.

The SSA flashed his badge to the first HP they encountered by the patrol cars, yelling over the clamor of the helicopter that was so loud she could barely hear him. The officer gestured toward the bridge, and then Sharon was following Campanella down a steep embankment toward the river under the steel arches of the span.

Night was closing fast and the gathering darkness was grimly ignited by the garnet blossoms of the red party lights of the cop cars on the bridge. Yellow crime scene tape was strung along the pinion below the overpass, and a dozen law enforcement personnel were gathered around, Sharon making uniforms of HP and TCP officers scattered among the raincoats of local detectives.

The dead girl's naked body was dumped in the gloom of the shadowy underpass. Sharon was trained in basic forensics and guessed the young woman had been dead for about a day, her pale body bluish with lividity and beginning to stiffen with rigor. The carcass was caked with dried blood and punctured with numerous jagged stab wounds. Her mouth, wrists and ankles were bound with electrician's tape.

A man with a county coroner's cap kneeled by the body and looked up at Campanella as the SSA flashed his credentials and asked, "What can you give us?"

"A driver pulled off to take a leak three hours ago and discovered the vic. She was bludgeoned to death. Won't know if she was raped until we do an autopsy."

A thin police lieutenant walked up to them. "We think we have an ID on the vic. A truck stop hooker named Candy Dolowitz. One of my officers had picked her up a few months ago and recognized her."

The SAA fixed the local officer in a firm stare. "This slaying looks almost identical to several recent interstate killings of women the Bureau is actively investigating. Please have your men stand down, Lieutenant. Don't move the body or disturb the crime scene. This is a federal case and the FBI is assuming jurisdiction and control of the crime scene. I'm going to call in an evidence response team to collect, identify, manage and preserve the evidence here."

The lieutenant nodded and seemed relieved for the help. Sharon watched as Campanella took out his cell phone and called the Knoxville field office to deploy their ERTs.

The SA crouched and ran her eyes up and down the corpse, noticing a crescent of cuts on a bluish nipple. "Is that a bite mark on her left breast? " she asked.

The coroner nodded. "Your crime lab should be able to get a dental imprint from that indentation."

Standing up, Sharon watched as Campanella finished his call and walked over to the police lieutenant, his face pulsed by the red police beacons in the air. "The Knoxville ERTs are on their way," he said. The local cop was waved over urgently by one of his men to a police car where he took an important radio call.

Sharon took her boss aside, a few steps away from the immediate crime scene and milling police. "The cause of death looks exactly like Keisha Solomon and those other girls."

"I agree, and soon we'll know for sure."

"We got the wrong guy back in Nevada, sir. That trucker Rudy no way could have dumped this body because they had him in custody at the time."

Campanella nodded.

The lieutenant hurried over to them. "Looks like we got a break. A passing driver saw a big rig pulled over on the bridge a few hours ago and thought it was suspicious so he took down a plate number. We called the local truck stops and a tractor-trailer with those plates got made thirty miles from here at a truck stop. SWAT already has a tactical unit in position and has the place surrounded."

The FBI agents were already on the move.

The truck was pulling out.

It was all going down at the exact moment Sharon and Campanella drove into the parking lot of the truck stop where the Tennessee Police Department staking out the suspect's big rig were moving in.

Sharon was pumped with adrenaline—she was getting all the action she could stand today. This is what she signed up for.

The cop cars scrambled around the pavement of the lot. Uniformed officers were grabbing their weapons and diving into the vehicles. The two FBI agents parked and leaped out of the car, but not for long.

"He's on the move!" a police loudspeaker squawked.

Tractor and trailer twisting like a gigantic snake, the big rig aggressively accelerated out of the truck stop, whiplashing again as it slithered onto the freeway. Unmindful of passing traffic, the driver was making a run for it and trying to escape. Cherrytops blazing, six blue and white TPD cars hurtled out of the parking lot access ramp after the fleeing eighteen-wheeler.

"C'mon!" Campanella yelled as he and Sharon ducked back into the black Crown Victoria. She slammed her door and buckled her seatbelt but the vehicle was already in drive and he had his foot on the gas, spinning the steering wheel hand over hand as he gave pursuit to the squad cars. The SA watched breathlessly out the window as the view of the truck stop rushed out of her field of vision and then the freeway filled it, the SSA dodging the car sideways around a surprised RV as they hurtled into the median lane.

Ahead, the sparkling ruby gems of the rooftop lights of the police cars swung in and out of traffic after the swaying trailer tailgate of the fleeing tractor-trailer. It was the only big rig in the immediate area and hard to miss as it towered high above the roofs of the surrounding cars and buses. The air was rent by a cacophonic chorus of sirens and screeching tires. The chase was on.

"Are they going to shoot out the tires?" Sharon yelled over the roar of their car engine.

"Too dangerous," Campanella shouted back, straining to concentrate on the road as he steered behind the police cars ahead, the speedometer climbing past eighty. "They flatten the tires, the truck could flip and there's too much traffic around."

"Where the hell does he think he's going?"

The police radio on the dashboard was alive with transmissions from the squad cars ahead of them. "—Driver is hauling it up I-30. He saw the units, jumped in his truck and fled. We're giving pursuit—"

"—Roger that, 945. We have six units coming your way about three miles ahead. The entrance ramps behind you are now closed to traffic."

A mile ahead, the eighteen-wheeler was picking up speed, barreling at 90 mph up the busy highway. Cars and RVs saw it coming up behind them like a bat out of hell and swerved into the slow lanes or passing lanes as the big rig surged past them, honking its horn. Strips of shorn tire rubber from the back wheels of the trailer—'gators in trucker slang—flew like falling leaves past the mudflaps on the skidmarked blacktop behind. Noxious clouds of black exhaust belched from the chromium horns of the twin 'stacks on the tractor, drifting a smoke screen around the entire length of the rig.

A slow Ford Impala was not paying attention as the tractor-trailer battering rammed it out of the way, sledgehammering its rear end with the front bumper of the cab. The hood of the other car flew up, crumpled, and it spun out in a 360, getting sideswiped by a Toyota pickup in the next lane. Both cars flipped and somersaulted in explosions of mangled metal, flying glass and jagged debris.

The cars behind the accident slammed on their brakes to avoid collision with the decimated vehicles, and now traffic was actively decelerating in the wake of the truck. The pursuing police cars plunged on ahead after the rig, now having the road to themselves.

Choppers appeared on the scene.

Back in the Crown Victoria, Sharon leaned forward to peer over the top edge of the windshield as a police helicopter swung past overhead and sped ahead toward the truck. Looking out her passenger window, she saw the clustered mosquito formation of three news choppers already covering the high-speed pursuit. For the moment, the TV crews stayed out of the path of the law enforcement aircraft, but she worried that the news helicopters were so tightly bunched they were going to knock each other out of the sky. That wasn't her problem. Focusing her gaze ahead, she saw Campanella was now a few car lengths behind the closest police chase car and they were all gaining on the rampaging tractor-trailer.

There was nothing but freeway straightway for miles, as far as she could see.

A half mile ahead, around a bend in the freeway, two police cars pulled to a stop on the median far ahead of the oncoming truck.

The radio squawked. "—We're laying the spikes."

The cops in those distant cars, small as ants, leaped out in the briefly deserted tarmac, dragging a long, armored, interlinked chain laden with tire buster spikes they draped across the four lanes. Then they ran for it as the hurtling big rig came on straight for it.

The big rig slammed on its brakes front and back, tires burning rubber and pluming smoke. *SSCRRREECCHH—EEECHH-EEEECHH-EEECH!* The acrid stench of hot tire came back at Sharon as she saw the brake lights flare red and the trailer fishtail sideways— the eighteen-wheeler was going too fast to stop.

All those many wheels rolled right over the chain of spikes.

There was a machine gun staccato sequence of loud pops as the tires all blew out and the rubber turned to ribbons. The big rig dropped on its wheel rims and sent firework showers of sparks up as the steel scraped the asphalt.

A police chopper roared deafeningly overhead of the FBI Crown Victoria as it banked, a police sharpshooter crouching in the open bay with his high-powered rifle.

Sharon heard the screeching tires and looked over to see Campanella stomping the brake as she felt the seatbelt snap taut around her bosom. The SSA was coming to a sudden stop behind the truck.

The big rig was tipping over.

It all happened in slow motion—the angle of gravity too steep on the trailer slinging sideways at the sudden stop and then lifting off its six right wheels, ravaged tires hanging in rags of rubber on the spinning rims. Slowly, inexorably, with a terrible inevitability, over it went.

As the trailer slammed on its side, it whiplashed the cab right off all six flattened wheels and flipped it onto its roof, crushing the steel chrome smokestacks like aluminum foil on the tarmac.

Then everything was quiet and still. The totaled big rig lay on the road like a slain dragon.

The police cars quickly mobilized into position and the red cherrytops in the air flared on the pooling oil and gas on the ground. The cops were already getting the people and cars back in anticipation of a major explosion.

Sharon leaped out of the car as Campanella slammed to a stop a few hundred feet from the overturned, decimated eighteen-wheeler. The agents ran up the middle of the freeway as several more patrol cars screamed to a stop and surrounded the wreck, the officers running forward with pistols aimed in a two-hand grip at the mashed cab. As she and Campanella advanced toward the spectacular wreck on the pavement, Sharon could already see the splashed blood all over the exploded windshield of the mangled tractor and see the twisted body of the driver within, a pile of meat.

"Case closed," Campanella said quietly. "Let's go home."

Dykstra blinked in the bright Nevada daylight as he was released from custody and stepped out of the police station. He was very shaken.

Sharon and Campanella stood outside, wearing their shades against the bright sunlight. The trucker averted his eyes as he walked past them.

"Can we give you a lift?" Sharon felt like all kinds of shitheel.

Amazingly, he regarded her politely, eyes downcast. "No thank you, ma'am. Impound yard is a few mile from here. Think I'll walk, take the air, get my truck, be on my way."

"I'm sorry." It came right out of Sharon's mouth. Campanella glared at her like it was sign of weakness.

Rudy looked her in the eye appreciatively and touched the brim of his cap with a tattooed hand. "Thank you. Shit happens. I know you were just doing your job. Glad you caught the guy. Let me know any way I can help you guys in the future." Then, with the deprecating gait of an ex-con, he turned and walked away toward the highway. The trucker had a three-mile hike through the office parks in the humid day toward the yard, but was smiling as he breathed the free air.

The SA watched the hulking bear of the man's body language as he trundled off up the side of the road. He wasn't bad-looking in a rugged, redneck way. She'd grown up with a lot of guys like him in rural Pennsylvania. There was something trustworthy about Rudy Dykstra, and she was surprised at the tinge of regret she felt to see him go.

"He's fine," her SSA said. "The Bureau called his freight company and told him he had been detained by mistake, so he won't get in any trouble."

"Glad you caught the guy," Sharon recalled Rudy had said as she got in the car with Campanella. As the air-conditioning cooled her and the smell of vinyl filled her nose, the agent looked out the passenger window as they overtook the trucker hiking up the side of the road. He gave her a little wave.

She knew he couldn't see her as they drove away, because the windshields were tinted.

But she waved back anyway.

Chapter Six

Carrie Brown drifted in and out of consciousness.

She was in some kind of enclosure.

It was pitch black and she smelled the fuel and tried to scream and when her mouth finally worked, she did scream, loud enough to rip her lungs out. But the rumbling roar of the diesel engines splitting her eardrums drowned out her voice and the woman knew she was in a big rig.

There was total darkness but the ceaseless noise was terrifying—a roaring, rumbling, bumping, *hissing* din echoing in a brutal sonic assault on her nervous system in the stygian gloom.

The woman had no idea where she was. She had lost track of time since the truck had run her off the road and she had been knocked out and captured. Carrie was not sure how long she had been unconscious, but when she awoke she was imprisoned in a steel locker—a compartment of some kind. It was cold. It reeked of rust and dried blood and old fear—and death. As a nurse, she immediately recognized the fetid, rotten stench of clotted blood that assaulted her nostrils.

Her hands and wrists were shackled with steel manacles to the frigid, vibrating metal floor. Her mouth was loosely gagged. The enclosure was dark and crypt-like—as if she were buried alive.

Except Carrie wasn't under the ground.

Her tomb was on the move.

The roar of engines was deafening and horrific, and she felt every shift of gear and thrust of acceleration and stall of brakes. The hard metal surface she was trammeled to trembled and shook.

Right away, to her horror, she knew whose truck she was in.

His big rig.

The truck was highballing, because Carrie felt the agonizing vibration of the steel plates under her trapped body, the scream of the diesels punishing her eardrums in the rolling coffin that held her.

She was very cold.

Relief came in waves between the terrible pain, as weakness from loss of blood and her system's natural morphine made her euphoric, a dream state she floated in and out of in the darkness.

Now the truck was slowing, lurching sideways.

She heard *hisses* and *chinks* and felt the whole monster shutting down.

The engine turned off.

Then it was silent and still and dark.

Somebody save me.

She screamed into the gag but no sound came out.

Then the waiting began.

For something to happen.

Let it be over, please.

And that was, by far, the worst part.

Chapter Seven

The pins had been pulled out of the big board back at the HSK offices at FBI Headquarters in Washington.

The hooker killings along Route 10 had been solved and the case was closed, buried in the wreckage of the homicidal trucker's eighteen-wheeler in the fiery pileup back in Tennessee. Now, the only file activity would just be the addendums made if or when the dead bodies or human remains of dead prostitutes turned up to be identified as additional victims in the coming months or years.

Sharon wished they'd been able to get the trucker alive—it would have made her job easier, because now his lips were permanently sealed and they would never know his exact body count.

His name was Sam R. Harper. Twenty-nine. Served in the army with an honorable discharge. A domestic violence charge by ex-wife, later dropped, was his only criminal history. After the autopsy, his system was found to be loaded with drugs—cocaine and meth—and the idea of him being on the road was terrifying in and of itself. When he had gotten the taste for killing roadside prostitutes they would never know. Harper was just a brutal thug, not a serial killer—he didn't torture the girls, didn't keep trophies. He was an opportunity killer, taking out his violent urges on victims who were easily procured and rarely missed. A banal, cheap, vulgar murderer.

Now out of the picture.

Sharon poured herself a fresh cup of coffee and turned her attention to the dozens of other pins on the board, correlating to the photos of a dozens of men, women and children on the other wall.

Some of the photos were old.

Very old.

Thirty years, some older.

Sharon listened to the air-conditioner's hum in the quiet office and the muffled sound of DC traffic out the windows. She tried to get past the nagging disappointment she felt being back behind a desk after the shot of adrenaline her field sojourn had provided the last few days. The regular part of her current job was straight analyst work, and she felt benched and officebound. Yearning to distinguish herself as an agent, she knew all that depended on powers beyond her control—on where the Bureau assigned her, on luck and being in the right place at the right time. Every agent knew full well that major cases may only come along once in a career, or never. It all came down to fate.

Fate.

Being in the wrong place at the wrong time accounted for the photographs of the victims piled on her desk in anonymous folders or on her computer hard-drive.

She fingered the early 80's photograph of an attractive blonde woman. Rebecca Pratt. Her remains had been found buried in the desert outside of Albuquerque, New Mexico last month. She was just a skeleton and all her teeth had been knocked out by her killer, preventing identification though dental records. Pratt's bones had been analyzed by forensics at the FBI crime lab in nearby Quantico, Virginia. Her deoxyribonucleic acid, or DNA, was identified by a lab technician using an AirClean 600 chamber and a bone hammer to extract the Mitichondrial DNA, or mtDNA, which was then analyzed. The information on the case was included in the forensic profiles FBI National DNA Index system, or NDIS, because the killing had involved interstate transport and was a federal crime. Death was determined to have been caused by a large knife or blade-like weapon that had broken three ribs in the upper left chest upon entry. The FBI crime lab had suspected that the blade was serrated, given the striations on the bone. The weapon used may also have been an axe, judging by trace elements of rust on the rib cleaves. The kill was clean, efficient. One powerful blow. The body not cut up.

But it had been buried deep. Animals couldn't get to it and it was only when a housing developer's bulldozer had cut into the ground did the skeleton of Rebecca Pratt, gone missing three decades before, turn up.

Once identified, Pratt was identified as a missing person from the New Hampshire area back in 1986, when her sister submitted a saliva swab sample to the FBI for analysis. The sample was entered into the combined DNA index system for use in the FBI's national missing persons DNA database. The New Hampshire crime lab and the FBI's nuclear DNA lab got a hit between the sister's nuclear DNA and the remains, showing a likely biological relationship. There had been no leads as to who had abducted her or why, and she had been last seen at a gas station mini mart near Portsmouth. The body had been transported over a thousand miles. So much time had gone by that when the authorities tried to notify the other next of kin, most of them had passed.

Absently, in the subconscious way her mind worked, Sharon free-associated a bit. There was something about this case that was familiar, some aspect of it that she'd seen before, in the mental file cabinet of case files between her ears.

An itch she couldn't scratch.

What was it?

Carrie had no idea how much time had elapsed in the black and silent steel tomb before the engines suddenly roared on and the enclosure shook violently, surprising and startling her so badly that she almost had a heart attack.

Please, oh Lord, please give me a coronary and take me now.

The air was cloying with a smell like copper pennies and the nurse recognized it was clotted blood. Not hers.

A *hiss* of brake lines, muffled by inches of steel.

The chamber lurched to the right, sending shooting pains up her manacled wrists as she felt the box accelerate.

The truck must be getting back on the road.

She realized they had been at a rest stop, the driver getting some sleep. They had been there for hours. While the total darkness had made it hard to keep track of time, she'd counted the minutes to herself to keep her mind clear and maintain her sanity—*fifty-eight, fifty-nine, sixty, one, two*—a minute at a time trying to collate the hours going by.

A stab of fear struck Carrie as she realized her prison must be very secure for this bastard to have the balls to pull into a public rest stop area. She didn't know anything about trucks, but had already figured she was in some sort of holding area inside the trailer of the big rig, because there would not be room in the cab.

This couldn't have been the first time he'd done this.

She wasn't his first victim.

Carrie could literally smell it.

Her fingers explored the rusty grated surface of the welded steel box in the complete blackness. Poe's story *The Pit And The Pendulum* had come back to her. The man who awoke in the pit in total black, feeling around, trying to find out just what type of torture chamber he was in, using just his sense of touch, feeling over the edge of the terrible drop, the unimaginable horror of the swinging pendulum...

Her in this rolling diesel and steel casket.

Someone must be looking for her by now, wouldn't they be?

Carrie figured she must have been gone forty-eight hours and the hospital would have reported her missing. Somebody would have gone by her apartment and discovered she wasn't there.

Her car.

The police would have found it by the side of the road. Put two and two together. A search would be underway. Nothing else made sense.

Unless the car was stolen, or picked up by the trucker's accomplice, if he had one. The keys were still in it. It couldn't have been taken from the scene by her captor—he had been driving her—but who knows who else he had working with him.

And this wasn't about Grand Theft Auto—the smell of old blood in the stash hold made that perfectly clear.

They—the police or hospital staff—probably would have called her sister Mary Beth by now. She was a soccer mom who lived in Omaha, Nebraska. The sisters weren't close, but Mary Beth's name was listed as her emergency contact in her file. And on many other official records like the DMV and her medical insurance.

Mary Beth would have been called.

And she would have called their mom.

My God, her family must be worried. And what could they do? How could they find her? Carrie knew she was inside one of a million trucks on the road and unless this guy made a mistake...

But he didn't make mistakes.

He'd been doing this a long time, with many victims.

Stop it.

Don't let exhaustion and pain and terror make you weak minded, not when keeping a clear head and thinking is what will keep you alive.

I'm sorry, Mom.

I'm sorry, Mary Beth.

It wasn't my fault.

I didn't mean to let you down.

I didn't mean to die.

And not tell you I loved you.

Stop it.

Be calm.

You will survive this.

Not.

It was then that she heard the crackly radio voice in the total gloom.

"Howdy, Honey."

She must have imagined it.

"Wakee wakee. Hope you're enjoying your accommodations."

No, somebody was talking to her. There was some kind of speaker inside the compartment and a folksy speaking voice was on a radio. The voice was male, husky, had a twang. A cheerful, jolly, jocular, good ol' boy lilt.

"Special-made. My box. Just for purty things like you. Scream if ya want. It's six inches 'a solid steel. I could get pulled over by the cops, go through a weigh station, folks could be three feet away from ya, and y'could be screaming your fool head off and nobody would hear a thing. Trust me, lotsa gals have tried."

Oh God.

Oh God.

Kill me now.

Make it quick.

Get it over with.

Lucy Elizabeth Tuttle. Twenty-six. Disappeared in Lodi, California in 2010. Waitress. Car abandoned in the bowling alley parking lot where she worked. Body discovered three weeks ago in Wichita, Kansas, buried in a cornfield, five years after her murder. Cause of death was determined as an axe wound to the chest. All of her teeth had been knocked out of her skull by her killer to impede identification. When the Nebraska crime labs brought the body in for forensic analysis, her breasts were discovered to be surgically enhanced and the silicone implants were identified by serial number and tracked to their owner. That information had been entered into the FBI's computers.

A series of photographs at the cornfield showed the grisly toothless corpse caked with dirt and dried blood, its decayed face contorted in a hideous rictus of terror. The knife or axe wound in the left breast was savage and powerful, with bruising lividity apparent from the force of the stab that drove the blade through flesh, bone, and finally heart. The crime lab photographs were taken by local Nebraska crime lab technicians and lacked the precision of the Bureau Evidence Recovery Team crime scene photographers. Sharon could tell the difference, since the FBI laboratories provided all new SAs with six hours of basic and crime scene photography.

Putting the two print outs of the crime lab reports for Lucy Tuttle and Rebecca Pratt side by side on her desk, Sharon Ormsby compared the details.

Both women abducted, killed by a probable knife or axe, teeth removed, corpses buried after being transported interstate.

Pratt disappeared in 1986.

Tuttle reported missing 2010.

Over twenty years apart.

The SA took that in, leaning back to sip her coffee in her office cubicle at the HSK. It could be coincidence—two unrelated murders with marked similarities done by two separate killers. There was no definitive similarities between the separate forensic profiles, but she got a twitch in the pit of her stomach, like a Spidey Sense.

There was something here.

She needed to speak to her supervisor, Campanella. Gathering the files and printouts, Sharon left the office, took the elevator up to the Critical Incident Response Group offices and knocked on his door.

Campanella templed his fingers as he sat back in his office chair, listening. After his SA finished her report, he sat up and spent a few minutes poring over the Tuttle and Pratt coroner reports while she waited patiently.

Her eyes traveled around the room, taking in the commendations and family photos on his desk. On the wall was a framed photograph of the SSA standing with FBI director Robert S. Mueller and other Section Chiefs and Supervising Special Agents involved in the JTTF, the Joint Terrorism Task Force—it was where Campanella had been assigned prior to the CIRG. Sharon knew that reassignment was a fact of life for Special Agents. Unlike other law enforcement agencies, it was intrinsic to the FBI infrastructure that the broad training Special Agents received allowed them shift almost seamlessly from one type of crime to another, as the needs of the Bureau dictated. Whether it was terrorism, white-collar crime, or espionage, all FBI Special Agents could be instantaneously deployed to any crisis and to work any program effectively, without standing down for new training.

Sharon knew she would have many reassignments over her career, if she lasted.

The SA saw her boss's mind working, carefully and methodically as it always did. Sunlight streamed through the windows showing a view of the stately Washington skyline outside.

Finally looking up, Campanella spoke thoughtfully. "We need a positive match. Our crime labs needs to pull up the forensics and run a detailed work up on the wounds of both victims, checking the width of the weapon and any other possible similarities. Pratt is skeletal remains but the point of impact of the weapon on the bone of the chest cages should be measurable. I hope they have enough information in the computers."

Sharon felt a twinge of excitement that was maybe a little wrong to feel, and her conscience nagged her. "Or bodies have to be exhumed."

"Yes." Campanella nodded. "Let's see if the labs have enough forensics information first. But I think we have sufficient cause for me to file an exhumation request with the Bureau, if the labs don't have what we need. Bear in mind, one or both women may have been cremated by now."

"What do you think we are dealing with?" she asked, knowing full well what she herself suspected they were dealing with, but being deferential to her superior.

He regarded her with a *don't bullshit me* curt glance. "Same thing you are. Two murders crossing state lines twenty years apart, possibly the same killer, probably the only two of his victims we have connected yet. We could be dealing with a serial killer, and one who has been around for a long time, at least two decades."

"That's what it indicates to me. Plus, these women don't fit the usual pattern of highway slayings. Tuttle was a secretary and Pratt was a stay-at-home mom."

"That's true," Campanella brooded. "They don't fit the classic profile of truck stop hooker murders by truckers, do they? Neither were likely abducted from a truck stop. Both disappeared driving to the market or driving home from work."

"We need to check if those women knew each other or had any relationships in common. The killer could be somebody they both knew."

"Could be. Check it out. They may also have been random victims. If they were transported across state lines to hide identification and discovery, the killer could have hidden them in the trunk of a car."

"Or truck."

"Yes. Or a truck."

From the jump, both FBI agents suspected they were dealing with a trucker killer. The interstate routes that long haulers drove and rootless lifestyle provided opportunities for them to do a killing in one state and dispose of bodies in another, which made them logical suspects for this. Most of the killers that the newly formed FBI Highway Serial Killer Initiative dealt with were truck drivers.

But this was different.

Most of the truckers they had apprehended to date had done one or two slayings, generally transient prostitutes, usually over a short time span.

This subject had committed two murders twenty years apart.

What had he been doing during all that time in between?

Sharon had a queasy feeling they were going to find out that he had been killing more people.

A lot more.

This subject potentially had been on the road a very long time, decades, murdering with a deliberate and methodical procedure.

She began reviewing all the open cases on her desk, looking for the same causes of death and related details.

The bad news was the crime labs did not have the detailed forensics evidence the agents needed on Pratt and Tuttle.

Campanella faxed the exhumation requests to his Section Chief an hour later.

Chapter Eight

The FBI laboratory in Quantico, Virginia loomed ahead as Sharon decelerated her car toward the parking structure. The new, state-of-the-art facility occupied almost 500,000 square feet of space and had a 900-space parking garage. The complex was composed of four seven-story, high-tech buildings with walls of blue reflective glass windows rimmed by tan stone. A narrow steel and glass atrium sat between one double row of buildings and the other. Nine tall white ventilation ducts on the roofs of each building, in three rows of three, resembled modern art industrial smokestacks. The place looked neat and pristine, surrounded by a sedate office park with pathways. The sky above was a picture-postcard-perfect slate blue with cottony clouds reflecting off the windows of the structure.

After she parked her vehicle, Sharon entered the complex through the courtyard, passing a rough-hewn white granite plaque with a gray steel FBI seal above the inscription. "Behind every case is a victim — man, woman, or child — and the people who care for them. We dedicate our efforts and the new FBI laboratory to those victims. April 25th, 2001."

The SA walked into the building and headed for the forensics wing down labyrinthine, clean, white corridors containing various labs. It never ceased to impress her. She passed the sprawling chemistry lab, a 150 million dollar facility that contained over three million in high-tech gear, including infrared spectrometry equipment. Professional support employees of the FBI labs—scientists, cryptologists, and engineers—walked past her in the hallway. One of the most comprehensive forensic laboratories in the world, the FBI laboratory provided forensic and technical services to federal, state, and local law enforcement agencies at no expense to them.

Luckily, neither the Pratt or Tuttle human remains had been cremated.

For the last three days, Sharon and Campanella had followed the progress of the exhumation of the two bodies in New Hampshire and California where they had been buried locally near where they had originally been abducted. There was some resistance from Tuttle's husband and her father on religious grounds, but when the Bureau explained how it might help catch her killer, they relented.

The original coroner's evidence for Pratt had been kept in New Mexico and Tuttle's was in Nebraska, so those materials were flown to Quantico, where the FBI crime lab was now analyzing the bodies.

It was why Campanella had sent her down from Washington today to check on the progress.

Rounding another corner, Sharon glanced through a window into a room where lab technician from the firearms and tool marks unit was testing a submachine gun involved in a crime. The tech wore a blue full-body suit, purple rubber gloves and ear protection. He stood in front of a stainless steel bin with an open six-inch spout of a pipe to fire the barrel of the weapon into. The tank had gauges, valves and tubes on it. The tech fired seven rounds into the water tank, then began recovering the rounds for later microscopic examination.

Arriving at the forensic lab she had been sent to, Sharon peered through the big steel-rimmed windows that overlooked a large white room completely sealed and sterilized. Blue hoses and ducts with metal seals extended from the ceiling pipe to the walls. There was a roll-up gray metal gate that led to an outside loading bay. Rows of rectangular, soft, white lights were built into the white ceiling and the whole place was brightly lit, radiating cleanliness and precision. Three forensics personnel wearing white lab coats and latex gloves stood around two steel tables with the browned remains of a skeleton beside a decayed female corpse.

Tuttle and Pratt, Sharon knew.

One of the forensics team opened the door and let her in, and after greeting the personnel, Sharon walked over to the skeleton and the corpse. Seeing the remains of the long dead women in front of her, it suddenly became more real for her.

Sharon looked up at Campanella looking over her shoulder to her computer, which had a photo of a Toyota Camry taken on the side of some highway near the Everglades. Both agents had been poring through twenty years of highway related missing person and homicide reports on VICAP. "The Dade County Sheriff found this abandoned car on the side of the road two years ago. It belonged to a waitress named Tracey Scrubbs who had been returning from her shift at Denny's. Yesterday, cops in Spokane found a severed arm in the woods and the fingerprints matched Scrubbs'. We presume the killer was trying to bury the body, but got alarmed and took off, misplacing the limb. The decedent's wrist showed severe contusions from what looks like handcuffs or metal restraints. It appears she may have been run off the road and abducted, then murdered and dismembered, and her body dumped in Washington state. The killer drove her clear across the country, alive or dead. And he crossed interstate lines, so it's federal, and it's ours."

"Any DNA on our perp?"

"No prints or hair follicles, and no skin under the fingernails; she didn't scratch him with the hand they found. The lab apparently found a few fibers from industrial type workmans' gloves."

"We should be looking for those fibers on other bodies, besides the blade imprints. How many bodies like this one have been discovered?"

"Checking."

And so it went for the next seventy-two hours. The two agents searched open cases where bodies that turned up in one state were found to be people abducted from other states. Particularly women.

"About ten years ago an unidentified woman was found buried in Montana in the middle of nowhere, think it was near Billings. She'd been cut into pieces and had shackle marks on her wrists. Her teeth had been knocked out. The forensics are inconclusive, but there are indications she may be a waitress reported missing near Anchorage."

"Do we have the file on that?"

"What are we looking for?"

"Glove fibers."

"Let's run the DNA against that any other similar cases, going back years."

The map of the United States filled the entire wall of the main office. The veins and arteries of the major highways crisscrossing the country from state to state were highlighted in red and blue. Sharon had gotten a box of rainbow stickpins and now the pins were stuck all over the map with the colors corresponding to the location the victim was reported missing and the state where the body was found. Photos of the victims were pinned to the map.

"There's no rhyme or reason, no apparent connection to the victims, except that they are young women," said Campanella. "Franklin disappeared in Utah. Turned up in Maine. O'Reilly went missing in Oregon and what was left of her was discovered in Michigan. If the same person is responsible for the slayings, he has no set route. "

"Three of them were hookers who worked the truck stops."

"If the same killer did these, he obviously has nothing to do but drive around."

"Which could be his job."

"A long hauler who does runs all across the country. That should narrow the search because we're not dealing with a local trucker."

"We still don't know it is a trucker."

"No, we don't."

"But a trucker is the perfect cover. Kill in one state. Bury them across country. Probably keeps the bodies in his truck."

"He's been doing this for twenty years."

"Or more."

"Right. Or more." Sharon was curious. She had never heard of anything like this. "Have you ever had a truck driver serial killer who fit this specific profile?" she asked Campanella.

The SSA shook his head, no. He sipped coffee, staring holes through the map, looking troubled. "Those two girls were killed seven years apart, but this was one was two months from the other. If this trucker is a serial killer, he may be doing them at the rate of twelve a year. That could be a hundred and twenty kidnapping murders under his belt. And that's assuming that the one twenty years ago was his first. What if he's been driving for forty years? We would have a rolling serial killer on our hands."

"One thing we know for sure is our trucker has to be at least forty years old, in all probability, for his age to link to the timeline of the murders. And he drives a nationwide route. Some truckers just do the same runs so that wouldn't be him. And I'll lay odds he's an independent, not a fleet driver."

By end of the day Thursday, Sharon Ormsby and Frank Campanella had flagged fifty-two homicide files that might be tied to their suspected serial killer. But right now it was all conjecture; they had no certifiable proof the deaths were the work of the same truck driver, or a trucker at all. The agents had put in twelve separate requests to forensics at the crime lab for glove fiber and axe wound analysis, trying to connect the dots.

The break came two days later.

Forensics came up with a match on Pratt and Tuttle.

The size of the blade wounds and approximate force of impact was identical.

But it was the traces of the exact same metal rust from the blade that had been found in the splintered bones of the two skeletons that sealed the deal.

They had a bona-fide Jack the Ripper on the road.

Chapter Nine

The darkness closed in on Carrie Brown in her rolling torture chamber.

She had no idea how much time she had been imprisoned there—the days and nights flowed together. It was all a hopeless black abyss she tumbled and tumbled further down into.

Her best guess was two days had passed because twice the big rig had pulled over and shut down for what seemed like several hours—at a rest stop, the woman figured.

Each time the truck ground to a halt, Carrie clenched in terror that her number was up—but only hours of relative stillness and silence followed. The muffled occasional traffic somewhere outside hummed through the steel walls. Or the intermittent creak of the tractor-trailer settling on its suspension.

When the rig stopped it was a relief of sorts, because the constant hammering and jarring of the suspension while it traveled sent relentless shooting pain through her back and trammeled limbs.

The worst hurt was the back of her skull, which hammered repeatedly against the floor. For hours, the nurse had tried to lift her head but finally an excruciating muscle spasm cricked her neck and she had to drop her head back on the floor to be pummeled by the punishing vibration. God, her headache was excruciating.

She could feel the blood oozing from the raw flesh beneath the sharp, rusty shackles on her wrists and ankles.

Her pants were soaking wet and the stench of urine filled the foul chamber. It had been many hours since she could hold her water no longer and just let go. It didn't matter anyway—anyone who saw her soil herself would not pass judgment given her situation. And the smell of piss was bad but at least it covered up the nauseating stink of dried, rotted blood in the metal box.

Right now, they were driving. She heard the cars and trucks outside, a lot of them, so it must be day.

Kill me now was yesterday.

Fear was days before that.

Now all was numb.

And along with numbness came clarity.

Three words ran around her brain, like a mantra…

I will survive.

Think.

Bitch, think.

She had known it was there all along, the hard lump in her hip pocket.

Her cell phone.

Carrie had just not figured it was an option because her hands were shackled by the sharp iron manacles, so she couldn't reach it. She wouldn't be able to dial with her feet like a monkey either, because her ankles were clamped, legs open.

She'd given up on the phone, too terrified to consider it an option. But now she was so tired that fear was going into remission and she started to obsess about the salvation her device might offer.

It was a lidless model with the keyboard on the outside.

Shifting her thighs, she had spent the recent block of time infinitesimally adjusting her hipbone to sandwich the phone against the floor.

She felt the plastic grind.

Careful, don't break it, she told herself.

That would be bad.

Using all her focus, she felt the obstruction of the keypad. *Not those buttons, though, not yet, don't worry about those yet.* One thing at a time. The phone was off. Wriggling, just a fraction of an inch at a time, she wormed her midriff so that she finally barely felt the single button at the top of the cell between her hip bone and sticky metal floor.

Careful.

You can do this.

She twitched her thigh.

Depressing the power switch.

A faint glow of illumination suddenly emanated from her pants pocket.

It was the most beautiful light she had ever seen.

Carrie Brown bit her lip, adrenaline surging.

Her cell phone was on.

It was a half an hour later when she was able to use her hipbone to press the single keypad button for her sister's number on speed dial…

"No news yet, Mom. I called the police again three hours ago and nothing about Carrie...Yes, I know how the odds of finding a missing person drop after seventy-two hours missing—I saw that TV show too...Yes, I told them that...*Yes*, I asked them that, too."

The house in Omaha, Nebraska had been quiet as a funeral home since Mary Beth Waters had taken a leave of absence from her sales job and worked out of her home in the week following her sister's disappearance. The family—their mother and grandfather, and her two children who loved their aunt—were devastated. Mary Beth's mother Agnes called ten times a day at all hours, and she was whom the sister was on with now. The saleswoman's professionally chipper voice was ragged from strain and exhaustion.

Mary Beth was a year older than Carrie and had the same brown eyes and heart-shaped features, but her face lined with stress from raising a family was now haggard with worry about her missing sister. "I told you the police said there was no blood in the car, Mom, we've been over all that."

Her cell phone was ringing, distant, muffled.

Mary Beth sat up like a shot. She had kept her cell right beside her the whole last week—even in the bathroom—in case she got a call from her sister while she was on the toilet or in the shower. Where the hell was it?

"Will somebody get that?" she yelled, only to remember that her husband and children were at the market.

"Mom, I'll call you back!" She slammed down the receiver of the landline she had come upstairs to answer and searched the bedroom. No cell phone.

Ring.

Throwing open the door, the woman heard the phone going off downstairs in the living room.

Oh shit I left it down there!

Bolting into the upstairs hallway, Mary Beth raced around the turn of the banister to the staircase, tripping and falling over one of her five-year-old boy's toy trucks left on the carpet. Mary Beth tumbled halfway down the carpeted stairs before righting herself and staggering with a twisted ankle into the empty living room.

Ring. Ring.

The blue Nokia cell phone sat on the coffee table where she left it, vibrating. *Ring.*

Snatching it up desperately in her hand, she saw the caller ID was Carrie!

Just as it stopped ringing and went to voice mail.

The Crown Victoria's windshield displayed block after block of bland Omaha suburb.

"It's a left turn here," Sharon told Campanella as she read off directions from her smart phone GPS. The agent hardly needed to navigate since the cluster of Nebraska police cars were plainly parked in front of Mary Beth Water's house. The SSA steered to a stop.

It was almost three hours to the minute from when the HSK had gotten the call from the Omaha field office about the voice message from Carrie Brown—the SA and SSA had choppered in from Washington, requisitioning one of the helicopters kept available for Bureau use, and the car was waiting for them at the airport.

From Carrie Brown's personal profile and the circumstances of her abduction, the evidence was persuasive, though not conclusive, that she was the latest victim of the truck driving serial-killer that SA Ormsby had recently uncovered. It was why the new agent was in the field today and why her supervisor was along with her.

"At least we know she's alive," Sharon said.

"From what they are telling us, the call was cut off like her abductor discovered her making it, so she may not be all right." Campanella looked grim. "Her sister's married name is Mary Beth Waters, by the way."

They both stepped out of the vehicle into the humid sunny air. Neighbors were standing on the neighboring lawns watching the activity around the Waters house.

A heavyset detective in a suit and tie walked over to block their way and the agents flashed their badges. "FBI. I'm Supervising Special Agent Frank Campanella. This is Special Agent Sharon Ormsby."

"What are the Feds doing here?" the abrasive, portly cop asked.

"Ms. Brown was transported across state lines, so it's federal."

"We don't know that. Have you located her?"

"No."

"So you don't know exactly where the missing woman is, so you don't know if she was transported across state lines, so you have no jurisdiction at the present time, and this is our investigation."

Sharon glared at the asshole cop defending his turf and wanted to punch his face.

Since the HSK dealt with interstate killings, they had to deal with countless tiers of local law enforcement around the country. While most of the police were more than happy for their help, every so often HSK butted heads with some provincial flatfoot trying to cockblock them. "Jackass," she muttered.

The detective heard her. She meant him to. "What did you say?" he bristled.

Campanella simultaneously shot her a stern glance and jumped in. "We have reason to believe that this abduction matches a series of kidnapping killings around the US so, yes, we do have jurisdiction."

"File a complaint. I got work to do." The Omaha PD detective was getting ready to turn his back on them. Sharon shifted her gaze from the recalcitrant cop to a distraught, pallid woman with short hair and humane brown eyes standing on the lawn who had to be the sister. The woman's eyes met hers and Sharon held her gaze sympathetically—female to female. That did the trick.

Mary Beth pushed away from the crowd of cops and walked across the pavement to where the FBI agents were standing, her face full of questions, worried and hopeful.

"Ms. Waters, we're from the FBI," Sharon interjected before the local detective could get a word in edgewise. "We'd like to hear the phone message."

"Help me. Please help me."

The diesel rumble was unmistakable in the background.

"I don't know where I am. It's a compartment in a big truck, I think. I don't know who took me. Oh God, I'm hurt. Please help me."

Carrie's voice was raw, weak, a whisper.

"BITCH! YOU GOT A PHONE?"

A gruff, rural accented male voice boomed, so loud and distorted through some kind of speaker as to be virtually unidentifiable.

Sharon and Campanella shared an electric glance as they sat at the kitchen table listening the cell phone play the message on the speaker phone back for the tenth time. A small army of police crammed around the room, all eyes on the device.

Mary Beth stood, tears soaking her face, shivering as she listened in terror.

"No, please!"

Carrie again.

The sound of gears grinding and air brakes engaging turning everything into canned, incomprehensible static.

"This is where he is pulling over," said Frank, listening intently.

"That's where he stopped and went after her," said Sharon.

The rest was jumbled...a rusty metal creak like a heavy door opening...Carrie's hysterical scream...a violent struggle. Then the phone went dead.

"Do you want to hear it again?" Campanella meant his agent but when Sharon saw Mary Beth shaking her head vigorously back and forth, she shook her head no.

Chapter Ten

"Sir, I wanted to talk to you about something."

"Permission to speak freely," Campanella replied with a sarcastic smile to Sharon. He had sensed his SA had something she wanted to say for the last ten minutes.

They were sitting at an Omaha truck stop watching the tractor-trailer eighteen-wheelers pulling in and out to refuel, and both agents had much on their minds.

They had an hour to kill before they headed to the Eppley Airport to catch the next available flight to DC. The FBI chopper and pilot had to be released to the Omaha field office, who had pressing use of the electronic surveillance equipment the aircraft was outfitted with to pursue a court-ordered listening device placed in a drug dealer's car.

The Carrie Brown voice mail had already been sent back to the crime lab in Quantico where sound engineers would analyze it with their high-tech equipment—the technicians would try to cull some kind of background audio details from the data that could provide a clue to where the call had been made. Even sounds of the truck that could determine the make, model and year would help narrow the search for the subject.

Neither Frank nor Sharon verbalized what they both feared, which was Carrie Brown had been killed not long after her abductor had discovered her on the cell phone—murdered or worse.

But that was not what the Supervising Special Agent guessed his Special Agent had on her mind.

"I have an idea about how I could best be used to work this case, but it's irregular." She stirred her coffee cup.

"Go on."

Sharon sat up in the chair, eyed her boss across the booth firmly. He could see she'd decided to come out with it. "I'd like your authorization to go undercover on this case."

He held her gaze. "UC? As what?"

"I was thinking as a truck driver."

"What would be the exact purpose of this?"

"To be on the ground."

"And then what?"

"Look for the killer. Track him down on the road. His turf."

He raised an eyebrow. "You're telling me you hope to just drive around and somehow stumble on a clue, or even less probably run into the killer?"

"I suppose I am, yes."

Campanella didn't blink. Didn't say anything. So she went on. Made her pitch. "I feel if I can be on the road for a few weeks, maybe a month, covering the killing ground where we know he's been, I might be able to get close to the truck drivers and truck stop staff and weigh station operators and possibly get information we can't access through VICAP."

At last he spoke. "Can you drive a truck?"

"You mean a tractor-trailer?"

"That's what I mean."

"No."

"So is your intention to learn, go to a truck driving school?"

"No. I was thinking I'd do a ride along. This trucker we brought in, Rudy Dykstra, he said he wanted to help the Bureau. Maybe I could tag along with him and we can pursue the investigation from the road. I'm sure he can teach me things about operating a truck if I'm in the field. I could pose as his wife, and he could handle the driving. I think, I really feel, that he wants to help us on this case."

Frank Campanella shook his head and couldn't suppress a smile. He felt Sharon Ormsby's steady gaze on him. This wasn't a plan she was proposing, it was a Hail Mary. But it was also out-of-the-box thinking, and that was encouraged in the Bureau. The SSA didn't say anything for a few moments, looking out the window and doing some mental calculations on logistics. Finally he looked at her. "To the best of my knowledge, we've never had an agent do anything like this before."

"Respectfully, sir, we've never encountered a killer like this before."

Campanella looked at Sharon. He respected his new agent, liked her a lot. She was a superb analyst, dedicated and smart, and she had been the one who had put together the leads that helped them uncover the monster they were up against. Also, he knew how she wanted to distinguish herself. The SSA had seen that drive in so many SAs during his years in the Bureau. But there was the danger she could overreach, get in over her head.

Get dead.

Her eyes hadn't blinked the entire time, sitting across from him, holding his gaze surely and hopefully. She meant business, knew this was a shot she wouldn't get again.

And she might be right about her instinct that they could pick up information on the ground. Sometimes, you just had to call it.

The senior agent broke his junior agent's stare and sighed.

"Let's talk to that trucker."

Sometimes you just had to go with your gut.

Rudy Dykstra looked plenty nervous when he arrived at the J. Edgar Hoover building after driving up to Washington in the tractor of his big rig, Sharon observed. He'd parked his truck in the lot and come into HSK wearing a hangdog *what did I do this time* look on his face. She felt bad for him as she observed his slumped body language through the window of her office while he waited in reception. The trucker looked like a man walking into a firing squad, probably thinking they were going to lock him up or at least take his license. The agents had not given him any information on the phone about why the Bureau wanted to see him, wanting to keep him off balance. Sharon felt it was better to have him at a disadvantage, to have the edge. The SA was getting tougher-minded. The job did that to you.

Ten minutes later, they were all sitting in Campanella's office in CIRG. The trucker's leg shook nervously. His handsome rugged face was stoic, but a sweat stain was spreading in the armpits of his denim jacket, and his fingers were damp on the STP cap he gripped in his lap.

Sharon reassured Rudy several times that he wasn't in trouble but that did little to eradicate the tight caution in his large brown eyes and apprehensive tension in his shoulders and posture. She reflected that once men had done time, those not of a recidivist nature lived with that fear of being arrested again the rest of their lives. She offered him coffee; he took it but didn't drink, and it wasn't until five minutes later when she finished her pitch that he finally took a swig and flashed a big 'ol grin. "You asking me to work with the FBI?"

"Yes. We think you can help."

"I'm in."

She said they would make sure the Bureau reimbursed him for his fuel.

Not just gas, as it turned out. In order for Rudy to take a month off long hauling, he said flat out that the FBI had to cover his nut. That included fees for lost hauls, permits, repairs, and more. It surprised Sharon how many operating costs were involved in being a truck driver, figuring it was one of many things about over-the-road trucking she was about to learn.

Rudy had called from the road and told her he would be three quarters of an hour late—a construction mishap on the highway had caused a bottleneck out of Houston—but he was driving straight from Texas to Georgetown to pick her up in his tractor-trailer.

They would set out from her place.

Sharon had never spent much time in her apartment—when she was not in the office she was traveling around the country—and now she was going to spend a whole lot less time in it. A month in a tractor-trailer eighteen-wheeler, unless they caught the killer sooner.

Her suitcase was open, half-packed on the bed.

Three pairs of jeans.

Two T-shirts.

Underwear and socks.

Sweaters, a jacket—it got cold some of the places they would be going.

A Glock .40 pistol.

Three boxes of .40mm ammo.

A Remington Model 870 pump shotgun in its carry case.

Three boxes of 12-gauge ammo.

Sunglasses.

A trucker cap she had purchased the at local 76 station mostly as a joke. It had a smiley face on it.

An iPad.

A MiFi portable wireless hot spot.

Packing her blue agent cap and windbreaker with FBI in white stenciled letters on them in her suitcase, she pocketed her badge.

Last, she packed her toothbrush and the rest of her toiletry kit and zipped up the suitcase, traveling light.

The SA looked at her watch. 3:30 PM and Rudy would be pulling up in the big rig outside anytime now.

She had butterflies in her stomach, not so much from her assignment as from the prospect of spending all those long miles over the coming weeks with a strange man in thirty square feet of space. She wasn't frightened of him physically exactly. For one, she was heavily armed—plus with her extensive Bureau hand-to-hand combat training she could drop the biggest adversary by simply grabbing his wrist and twisting. Her unease was an intangible. She would have to be close to this man, ride with him, eat with him, share a sleeper and bathroom facilities, and it was going to be invasive.

Strange the stuff you were scared of.

Gazing out the apartment window at the distant Potomac River beside the long stretch of I-66 heading off to places west, she studied the endless succession of cars and trucks on the interstate.

He was out there.

The monster she was after.

The parking area was still empty. No Rudy.

She better call him and get an ETA.

Then as she turned to grab her iPhone, there was a blast of a steam horn and a thunder of diesel engines and escaping brake pressure, and when she turned to look out the window, there the big white rig sat.

His hand waved out the open driver's window.

Time to go.

"Watch your step."

Sharon felt Rudy's beefy hand grip hers as he helped her up the ladder on the transom of the thirteen-foot-high truck. "Catch hold of one of those grab handles," he said. The trucker stood on the pavement beside her luggage. She stepped through the open door into the cool air-conditioning of the surprisingly spacious and luxurious cab of the tractor. It was like being in an airplane cockpit. She felt giddy.

"What kind of truck is this?" she asked, impressed and curious. The nose of the tractor was high and flat, grill flush with the windshield. It was unlike others she had seen on the highway with the long hoods in front of the windshield.

"My rig is a Mack Cruiseliner. Standard three-axle—your basic tandem. It's a cabover, CEO for short. That means the cab is built on top of the engine. Them other trucks that you see on the road with the engine out in front of the cab, that square-cut look, those're called a conventional."

"Which is better? I guess your cabover is, right?"

"There is no better. Depends on the driver's needs." Rudy handed Sharon up her suitcase and shotgun case. "Throw your stuff in the back. You can use the closet. We got a double sleeper. You get the top bunk."

"This is nice." She smiled admiringly, checking out the interior of the cab

"What were you expecting?"

"Don't actually know what I was expecting."

"Gotta spend thousands of hours and cover millions of miles in one of these, so you best make it like home. It's got all the amenities."

The truck driver wasn't lying. The agent stepped past the huge plushy bucket seats into the long compartment in the back. There were two bunks, one above the other. Carpeting. A fridge. A TV. A nice LG stereo and speaker system. No ashtrays.

"Few rules. No smoking in the truck. You'll have plenty of opportunities to have a cigarette when we pull in to gas up or take a break."

"I don't smoke. What are the other rules?"

"I make 'em up as I go." Rudy chuckled as he climbed into the driver's seat, turning over the ignition.

Below Sharon's feet, the floor rumbled with the huge power of the engine diesels of the idling truck.

She set down her bag on the carpeted floor in the back of the cab and stowed her shotgun in the locker. Then the agent eased her ass into the comfy passenger seat. The swivel bucket seat enveloped her like a sofa. "Comfortable," she admitted.

The trucker smiled over at her, eyes twinkling. "Air suspension seats, makes the ride smoother. It can get bumpy. Mess up your kidneys."

The SA sat and studied the vast tractor dashboard, eyes sliding over the numerous rows of switches and gauges and multiple stick shifts, as complex to her as a plane cockpit. Dashboard switches were designated *Head Lts, Cl Lps, Load Lp, Lt Fuel, Pwr Mirror. Below, Engine Brake*, two switches for *on/off, high/low, Ether, Eng Fan, Hi Mirror*. Below them, *wiper* button and *Panel Lps* button. A switch with guard for *lock/unlock shift at any speed even if a wheel is spinning. 5th wheel unlock/lock cab control. Dump valve deflate/ normal*. Dashboard alert lights for *mirror heat, engine fan, load light, check engine, oil, stop engine, diff lock, brake air, water, fifth wheel*. A red octangular thick button *Trailer Air Supply. Pull to evacuate. Push on starting truck.*

"Wow," she marveled.

"Got everything?" He gave her a friendly grin.

She shrugged and smiled. "Good to go."

"Buckle up," he said.

Sharon Ormsby *snicked* closed her seatbelt.

The smokestacks snorted and the big rig surged forward out of the parking area onto the street. Minutes later they were on the westbound I-66.

As they shot up the Interstate, the SA saw all the cars far below their cab; the first time she had seen the highway from this high vantage point. It was a powerful feeling of floating above it all. The air-conditioning was comfortably cool. Sharon's eyes passed over the dashboard gauges and controls of the cab as she idly watched Rudy shift, trying to familiarize herself.

The trucker asked her what the plan was, where she wanted to start.

Sharon gave him the address of where Lucy Tuttle's body was found in Kansas, said that they would start there and backtrack to where she disappeared in California, following the serial killer's likely route. The remains of both Tuttle and Pratt had only recently been discovered and their cases only just been upgraded from missing persons cases to open murder investigations. The SA wanted to speak to the local police departments regarding their progress on the investigation, share information, and see what they knew. She also wanted to reinterview any witnesses. Driving the serial killer's probable routes, Sharon planned to detour at truck stops and diners and other places Rudy thought might make sense along the way. There, they would interview drivers and staff. See what information they could find. Hopefully somebody might remember something about an unusual or suspicious trucker from many years ago.

After that, they would drive the possible routes from where Pratt's remains were discovered to where she had disappeared, talking to local police departments, reinterviewing witnesses, questioning trucking and service personnel, and see what they could turn up.

Truth was, that was the extent of her plan at the moment.

It wasn't much of a strategy, she knew, felt the vagueness of it as the words came out of her mouth, but it was a start. Sharon's gut told her this was right where she should be, and how the FBI would pick up the monster's scent.

She was determined not to fail at this.

Now she was in the truck, the operation was real. The sheer hopelessness of her mission disquieted her. The odds of success appeared insurmountable. Nearly fifty thousand miles of interconnected highways on the continental US Interstates. Two million tractor-trailers. It was a needle in a haystack. She remembered her SSA's words, *"You're telling me you hope to just drive around and somehow stumble on a clue, or even less probably run into the killer?"* Sharon felt overwhelmed. She looked across at Rudy behind the wheel, and that reassured her. It had to be an advantage for her to be in the field, she believed that—of that one small thing at least the agent felt certain. Having started this, she now had to follow through and finish it.

As Sharon sat in the passenger seat and looked out the window, the rows of long haulers moved like assembly lines in both directions on the highway, reflected in the tall West Coast Side Mirror.

Boy, she thought absently, there sure are a lot of trucks on the road.

But only one I'm interested in.

Chapter Eleven

Frank Campanella got a text on his cell phone.

On the road.

Good luck, he texted back, sighing to himself. Moving over to his desktop computer, he began typing a memo to his Section Chief to update him on the progress of the investigation.

For now, he would keep his doubts to himself about the viability of the operation. Worst case, it was only going to be a few weeks and if Special Agent Ormsby turned up nothing, he'd pull her back to desk duty and all they would have lost is a little time and some expenses. Even so, he felt a twinge of unease at the base of his spine.

What was the worst that could happen, he asked himself.

Nothing to lose here.

He hoped.

And remembered his parting words on the phone to SA Ormsby earlier that day before she left in Dykstra's truck. Words to live by.

"Don't get killed by being stupid."

Seventy-two hours in thirty square feet of space.

Sharon was not going to make it.

The tractor was incredibly confining and her ass hurt from all the seat time in the bouncing cab, despite the air ride cushioning. No way she was going to cut it as a long distance trucker. The tedium was indescribable. They had traveled through eight states. The novelty had worn off. The man Rudy was a machine. How long could he drive without taking a break? He had the bladder of a camel. Endless blacktop and broken white lines rolled past as the terrain changed from urban to rural and back again, the flats turning to grades, the only thing changing being the boring restaurants and gas stations they traveled past.

The citizen's band radio buzzed and crackled as Rudy talked into the hand mic. "You got a copy on me, Mongoose? This here is American Iron. I got the hammer down from Wichita to Lodi and I been listenin' to you modulate about that bear trap on the I-Five."

"This is Mongoose. Got my ears on you American Iron, for sure, for sure. Just hit the speed trap on my way out of Stockton. Smokey's roundin' up the swivel jockeys."

"Thanks for the heads up. Catch you on the flip flop, Mongoose. Keep it out of the ditches." Rudy hung up the mic.

"I didn't understand a word you guys were saying," Sharon quipped.

"Gearjammers got their own trucker speak. Mostly, we talk on the CB at night just to stay awake."

The agent tried to work on her iPad tablet and collate the information on the investigation.

Something was unnerving her.

She had been thinking of her mother, and the long distance drives from Pennsylvania to Ohio they used to do to visit her grandmother those long years ago. She had not been on the road for this duration since then.

Her mother.

"I'll be back in a minute, honey…"

Distracted, she turned her gaze to Rudy's hand enveloping and working the heavy stick shift of the tractor, watching him step on the clutch and go through a complicated series of gears as he negotiated an upgrade. The engine rumbled and brakes hissed—*damn,* this rig was powerful.

He saw her watching him and gave her a cracked grin. "Ain't like driving an automatic, is it?"

"How many gears does this truck have?"

"It's a high-geared twelve-speed transmission with a sweet overdrive. It's got ten forward gears. Two for reverse."

"And two brakes right? You brake the trailer first and then the cab so the truck doesn't jackknife."

He popped gum. "Done your homework."

"Saw it in a movie once," she shrugged. "That must be tricky."

"It's like anything. Once you know what you're doing, it's all second nature."

The SA looked at the odometer and noticed for the first the mileage was in the seven digits. "You have a million miles on this rig?" she asked incredulously.

"Yes, ma'am, I do. That's pretty normal for a good truck. Maintain and rebuild the engine like I mean to, should get another one to two million miles more out of her before putting her out to pasture. Got a 600 horse V-12 Cat engine under our butts. Good power train."

Sharon was fascinated. "This is your truck, right?"

"You betcha. Lock, stock and barrel. Bought her six years ago. Cost as much as a house, 'cept they give you three years not to pay it off, not thirty. Anyways, she's served me well. I worked for a company for ten years, but you don't pull down the pay you do as owner operator, though you got more paperwork hassles. Us independents is always squeezed between government regulations and bureaucracy on one hand, and the sheer burden of the cost of operation on the other."

"But you're your own boss."

"Nobody telling me where to go but the man that owns my load, like the song says. And now you, I reckon." He looked over at her. "So, this killer…"

"What about him?"

He regarded her with cautious eyes. "You want to tell me about him or her?"

It was time she did.

Up until now, Sharon had only told Rudy that the killer was a suspected male truck driver, not the grisly details.

When she finished a half hour later, his face was white in the green dashboard lights—not a pretty visual. He didn't say anything for a long time, so she broke the ice. "Second thoughts?"

"Nope."

"This guy, or girl I suppose, sound like any trucker you heard of?"

"Nope."

"Sure?"

"Yeah, real sure."

"Can you tell me anything you think might help us build a profile?"

Across the seats, the bear of a man just drove staring through the windshield. "Jesus."

"I know."

"Twenty years on the road you figure?"

"Maybe more. Those are just the five killings we tied him to so far. Anything you can think of we should be looking for?"

He shrugged, spooked. "Hell if I know."

It was three in the afternoon when Rudy's cabover lumbered across the county line into Lodi, California. It was where Lucy Tuttle had disappeared five years before. Sharon looked out at the steady succession of fields of crops under plastic covers passing in the bright dry sunshine. They had driven all night from Kansas.

Sharon had all the witnesses' addresses in her iPad tablet, and just hoped they still lived there and were alive. She tried calling on the road and found many of the numbers had been disconnected over the years, which wasn't encouraging.

The FBI agent had her trucker companion park in a warehouse parking lot a few blocks away from the workplace of their first witness on her list. She changed out of her road gear in the back and put on slacks, a shirt and a jacket.

"I'm not good enough to be seen with you now, huh?" Rudy quipped.

Sharon brushed her hair in the rearview mirror. "This is an FBI questioning session and it wouldn't do for me to climb out of a truck credibility-wise. Plus I'm undercover, remember?"

Pocketing her badge, the SA looked to see the coast was clear and climbed out of the truck.

It was a several block walk to the Hi Lanes Bowling Alley. At the front desk she asked the cashier to see Bertha Kibble. There were a few bowlers in the facility at this hour, and a janitor swept the polished wood floor as Muzak warbled. Sharon felt she was in a 1960s time warp.

A moment later, a heavyset woman in a floral dress came out and shook hands with Sharon. She had a friendly, saddened attitude. "I'm Bertha Kibble."

"I'm Special Agent Sharon Ormsby. We spoke on the phone."

"Yes. How do you do?"

"I'm sorry about Lucy Tuttle. I hear you both were close."

Bertha nodded somberly, her triple chinned jowls jiggling. She showed Sharon to the back office and they both took seats, the SA politely declining a coffee. The big woman heaved a huge sigh, thick with bronchial wheeze from smoking. "At least I know now. At least there's that. Lucy was such a nice girl. We was besties, then she took off, up and gone missing one day, no card, no nothing. Wasn't like her, but I never thought nothing like this, never…" She trailed off.

"Ms. Kibble—"

"Bertha, you can call me that."

"Bertha, I need to know if you remember seeing anybody suspicious on that day when she disappeared. I know this has just become a murder investigation the last few months and the police have already asked you questions, but maybe there's something they missed or you forgot. Did you see anything out of the ordinary that day?

"The police already asked me that. Didn't see no strangers that day that come to mind. Just our regulars. We mostly just get the usuals around here."

"Please try to remember. I know it's been a long time. But was there anybody strange, maybe driving a vehicle that you might have noticed…"

"It was years ago." The cashier shrugged. "The cops asked me all this last week."

"I know."

"Well, let's see. The last time I actually saw Lucy, she was—yes, that's right she was taking a smoke break and she'd left the coffee shop what was right over there where the restaurant is now—" Bertha helpfully pointed through the glass windows of the café inside the bowling alley. "She went out into the parking lot."

Sharon thinking *this is a waste of a trip; the woman doesn't know anything,* but asking anyway. "Were there any vehicles that perhaps stick out in your memory?"

"Now you mention it, I remember there was a big 'ol tractor-trailer in the parking lot that day…"

From: Sharon.Ormsby@ic.fbi.gov
Subject: Lucy Tuttle
To: Frank.Campanella@ic.fbi.gov

Sir,

For the last two days Rudy Dykstra and I traveled from Wichita, Kansas to Lodi, California primarily along Interstate 70, the killer's logical route. Along the way, we interviewed various truck drivers and truck stop employees, and in Lodi, re-interviewed the last people who saw Ms. Tuttle the day she disappeared.

Two witnesses, Bertha Kibble and Hank Robeson, recall seeing a tractor-trailer in the area the day Ms. Tuttle went missing. Both of them differed in the color of the rig. Kibble said it was black. Robeson thought it was gray. Kibble's memory appeared good for somebody remembering a five-year-old incident and recalls that the truck had Tennessee plates. Neither remembered any other distinctive markings. At this point, they have been unable to provide further details.

I have contacted Tennessee DMV records to pull up all commercial trucking registrations during the period of 1980-2010. Additionally, we should check trucking companies, DOT and FTA logs during that period to track which long haulers had a scheduled delivery on their books driving that route.

SA Ormsby

Chapter Twelve

The calloused, sinewed hands held the newspaper open to the third page.

The newsprint photograph of Rebecca Pratt was a black-and-white high school yearbook picture. It occupied the top of the third column just below the headline…

"THREE-DECADE-OLD MURDER VICTIM EXHUMED IN NM INDENTIFIED."

The gnarled fingers shook in recognition, just slightly, on the paper.

Below the photograph the story was a single paragraph.

"Previously unidentified skeletal remains found buried last month in Albuquerque, New Mexico were identified this month as belonging to local twenty-one- year-old Rebecca Pratt. The area woman disappeared in 1986. The FBI, using VICAP, linked the DNA and made a match."

The story went on about the surviving mother of the victim and her brother holding a quiet funeral ceremony. The man reading the paper wasn't concerned about that, just the face in the newspaper photograph.

He remembered the eyes.

Had seen the life leave them.

Trashing the paper, moving now with a surly energy, he returned to the big black Kenworth conventional eighteen-wheeler parked at the curb of the McDonald's. On his way, he splashed the dregs of his coffee on the sidewalk, crumpling and tossing the cup in the gutter before swinging up into the cab.

The door slammed shut.

There was a little traffic noise in the area from the cars passing on the cross street.

Another sound could be heard also, coming from the depths of the truck.

A woman's screaming, heavily muffled behind thick iron and steel—a faint echo emanating under the shadowy darkness below the chassis between the big double radial tires.

Then the diesel engines roared on in a shuddery thunder-like rumble, drowning out any trace of the screaming that went on and on.

With an exhaust brake *hiss* and a lurch of suspension, the eighteen-wheeler pulled out.

The driver turned his rig onto a side street he knew led to the freeway without having to consult a map.

He remembered this town.

It was where he'd picked Rebecca Pratt up so long ago.

Chapter Thirteen

From: Frank.Campanella@ic.fbi.gov
Re: Tuttle/Pratt investigation.
To: Michael.Robertson@ic.fbi.gov

Yesterday, SA Ormsby visited the area in Los Lunas, New Mexico where Rebecca Pratt was buried. She visited the local police department, spoke to Sergeant Raymond Navarro, who handled the ongoing investigation, and reviewed the files. Bear in mind that the body was only recently discovered and it is a new case for the local PD. During the approximate time period our crime lab estimated the body was buried, an Indian reservation cop had reported seeing an unmanned black tractor-trailer parked off the road. Based on his description, SA Ormsby said Mr. Dykstra believes it to be a Kenworth conventional model of that era. We are running record searches on owner/operated Kenworths known to have been hauling along that route during that time period.

Unfortunately, there have been no additional cell calls received from Carrie Brown or any further information on her whereabouts.

I have not informed SA Ormsby yet of our intention to cancel the operation in two weeks if it yields no significant results.

"If I were him…"

Sharon looked up as Rudy trailed off, wheeling the diesel around a curve and fighting with the gears as he topped a hill. The SA was working on her iPad, making notes in her profile file on Documents To Go application. The mighty Mack Cruiseliner was following the white line through New Mexico, making ground on the continually retreating horizon. Outside the wraparound windshield, the mesas and buttes of the desert floated majestically past as they rumbled up I-40 East. She kept watching the trucker as he gathered his thoughts.

"If I were him, meaning if I were a serial killer trying not to get caught…man, there's no way I'd do the deed on one of my trucking routes. Too easy to track." He nodded to himself, convinced.

"So what then?" the SA asked, taking a sip of dead 7-11 coffee.

"Me, I'd detour to the places I did the killings. A big detour. Then go the long way around the barn to where I'd dump the bodies. This guy has been careful for thirty years not to get caught, or even made. He'd have to know that the first thing the law is going to investigate is who was long hauling on the corridors where the people went missing. If it were me, hell, I'd do the murders three, four states away."

She nodded. Made sense. "But don't the trucking companies keep tight schedules?"

"Course they do, but the cross country runs allow time for sleep. There's a twelve or even twenty-four hour grace period. It's federal law so the drivers don't black dog and wind up in a ditch. But I know guys pop bennies or dexies like candy; they drive five days without a break, sharp as a tack but speeding out of their brains. This guy, this freak we're after—"

"We don't know it's a man—"

"But he is probably."

"Okay, probably."

"—This killer, they could easily be cranked up and use that time to cross three state lines, do his pickup, then double back, deliver his load with time to spare. Nobody the wiser."

"He could also be doing the killings on his days off."

The affable, bearish trucker shook his head. "I don't think so. They could track that too, like who wasn't working the day of the disappearance."

Tapping on her tablet, Sharon made notes. "That sounds right. To never have been caught for twenty, maybe thirty years." She set her tablet on her lap and leaned her head back on the seat. The SA checked off a mental list, thinking out loud and talking mostly to herself. "So what the hell do we know about this guy so far? First, he's old, probably sixties to seventies."

She held up her index finger.

"Second, he's a long-distance, rather than a local, trucker. Has to be a highly experienced and capable truck driver, likely a long hauler."

A second finger. Rudy nodded.

"And he's probably an owner/operator, because he's carrying human cargo inside his truck."

A third finger.

He has been doing it for a long time.
And lots of people on the road know him.
Just not what he is.

Discouraged, she sat back in the plush seats, the diesels rumbling under her butt, gazing hopelessly out of the glass at the endless succession of big rigs rolling past and stretching on ahead on the highway disappearing into the vanishing point. Any one of them could be their boy.

A needle in a damn haystack.

"He has a stash hold."

It was the first words Rudy had uttered in a while as they rode through the Texas panhandle—he'd been lost in thought, and his brow had been furrowed the last few minutes.

"What's that?" she asked.

He nodded to himself. "It's a secret compartment, usually built under the trailer. Drivers rig 'em up illegally. You see a lot more of 'em nowadays with all the drug smuggling and running Mexican illegals across the border some truckers do. But stash holds go back decades. Drivers started using 'em to run whisky during prohibition. Bet your boy keeps his victims in one of those, that'd be my guess."

Sharon smiled. "Swell, thanks."

Why didn't we think of that?

Right away, she began typing an email memo to her boss on her iPad.

The stash hold actually sounded like a legitimate lead to Frank Campanella, who for the first time thought this undercover operation might yield some fruit. Maybe SA Ormsby's instincts were good, as they had been so far on this case.

After receiving Sharon's memo tip he emailed back thanks and made a few calls. The first was to one of his people in the DEA, who was out of the office and would have to call him back.

Then he put in a call to the Border Patrol, which handled records relating to border activities and spoke to a cheerful agent named Joe Helms. "Hey, Joe, Frank Campanella here. Can you pull any records for me you have on US truck drivers arrested for smuggling illegals where, and this is important, a stash hold or custom built secret compartment was discovered in the truck?"

"Sure, we've had a few of those."

"Great, thanks."

"Let me check with our impound yards. Have some info to you this afternoon. Did a few migrants get killed?"

"No, we got a serial killer out there, a trucker, who's been preying on US citizens, mostly female we think."

"Jesus. Still out there, huh?"

"Unfortunately, yes. Has a woman captive now. We don't know if she's still alive, but are trying our level best to get to her in time if she is."

"I'll get right on this. Bear in mind, all the drivers we have on record are probably mostly still serving time. They'd be on the inside, so probably wouldn't be your guy."

"All of them?"

"Maybe not. Some could have been released. Let me check."

"We'll want to interview them anyway. Maybe they know something about our perp."

"Or they might know the people who built the compartments, who may have built your guy's. The drug cartels have teams of custom car riggers in Mexico right now who are specialists in building secret compartments in vehicles to smuggle narcotics. They're making a cottage industry of it."

"Right, but you're talking about smuggling people, and the cartels don't really deal in that, and they don't usually put those kind of huge shipments in trucks because they get weighed. I think we're dealing with a smaller group of suspects."

"You'd be surprised the stuff we find these low-lifes put in trucks."

"No, I wouldn't."

Frank hung up, getting a promise he'd have some names on his desk that afternoon.

The DEA got back to him an hour later, and he had pretty much the same conversation with them, this time focusing on trucks with compartments built to smuggle contraband and arrests pertaining to that.

He was figuring he should try Homeland Security as well.

HSK would take anything they could get at this point.

Chapter Fourteen

"Are we there yet?"

She has just turned five years old.

The little girl still remembers when she had to sit in the uncomfortable child seat but right now feels all grown up wearing the seatbelt in the front seat of her mommy's car.

Her mother smiles over at her from behind the wheel. It is just the two of them and the little girl feels very happy on the long drive to Grandma's house in Pennsylvania.

Even though the drive is so long and boring.

"Are we there yet?" the child asks again.

"Another three hours, honey," her mom replies with that voice she has when she is trying to be nice that is not really nice at the same time. "Try to sleep."

"I can't sleep."

"Do you want me to turn on the radio?"

"Okay."

Her mother does but it is just talk, talk, talk and no music so she turns it off.

The blue handkerchief her mother has wrapped around the back of her long yellow hair and how that hair always looks like wheat will always be a perfect memory in the little girl's mind as they drive that day. The sun is shining from the other side of the car and it makes her mother's hair seem to glow like an angel, like there is a light inside.

The little girl forgets every time. It is always such a long drive to Grandma who Mommy says lives in another state and the child has no real sense of direction but sometimes she remembers the restaurants like Howard Johnson's they drive past.

It seems like they are never going to get there. The little girl shifts in her seat and studies her fingers. She tries to read her Dr. Seuss book but it makes her tummy want to throw up and her mom calls that carsick.

Looking over at her, her mother smiles with those big white teeth with the one sort of cute bent one, the freckles in her face crinkling, and says, "I know, how about we play Punch

Buggy?"

    "Okay," the child replies. It is something to do.

    The little girl can barely see over the dashboard and it blocks her view of the road so she sits up as straight as she can and is just able to see the highway and passing cars out the window.

    No punch buggies.

    Just a lot of cars.

    There are trees and hills and a few office places passing by.

    There.

    A blue Volkswagen Beetle.

    "Punch Buggy!" the little girl shrieks happily and punches her mother in the arm, not too hard, and makes her mom giggle.

    "Ow! How did I not see that?" Her mother ruffles her hair. "You're so observant."

    "What does ob-ser-vant mean?"

    "It means you notice things."

    Smiling, the child knows it is a compliment and she feels happy and for a little while forgets about the boring drive and she keeps a sharp lookout for Punch Buggies and sees two before her mother does.

    Sometime later her mother says they need gas.

    There is a sign with a yellow seashell coming up and her mother says we'll stop there and makes the turn.

    They park by one of the things you get gas that made the car go from.

    Her mom asks her if she has to go and she says no and then her mother asks if she wants a snack and the little girl says sure and her mother says great come in with me while I pay.

    Unbuckling her seatbelt, all grown up, the child opens her door by herself and steps out, watching for other cars like she was told.

    Her mom takes her hand and they walk toward the building where you pay for gas and get snacks.

    There sure are a lot of trucks.

    Sharon woke up with her throat tight. She lay in the darkness on the cramped upper bunk under her sheets, eyes wide open, staring at the metal ceiling of the back of the truck cab.

    In the bunk below her, Rudy snored, and the sound comforted her. The air was close and cozy from the heating unit that quietly droned in the stillness.

The agent's eyes traveled forward past the rear double sleeper compartment of the tractor, to the empty driver and passenger seats by the dashboard. Faint yellow light from the rest stop mercury vapor lamps framed the edge of the windshield and absently she counted the bug splats on the glass.

In a few minutes she sank below sleep's dark and silent gate into a different dream.

Chapter Fifteen

The tractor-trailer barreled on through the night.

The Mack Cruiseliner was somewhere out on the I-44 corridor, eastbound for New Hampshire where Pratt had disappeared. Darkness thundered at the windshield.

Rudy drove, gearing down and sipping his coffee. Sharon was listening to the CB radio. For a few days now, the agent had been memorizing trucker lingo during hours of listening to it over the airwaves in the cab. Turning to her partner, she pointed to the citizen's band radio. "Can I try it?" she asked.

Rudy shrugged jovially. "Knock yourself out." Eagerly, Sharon picked the CB microphone off the cradle.

"You're gonna need a handle," he reminded her.

"I got this." She winked, already thinking one up. Finally, she put the mic to her lips. "Breaker breaker, this is Hot Patootie, come back." Rudy rolled his eyes as Sharon tried to keep a straight face and talk trucker. "That's a big ten-four to all you gearjammers," she transmitted. "Over."

Soon, a driver on the CB replied over the airwaves. "You got a copy on me, Hot Patootie? This is Jolly Roger. Come back."

"I got ears on you, Jolly Roger. I'm putting the hammer down. Come back."

Another trucker voice came over the transmission. "Roger that, Hot Patootie. This is Hairy Sasquatch, come on. Hot Patootie, we got nothing but eights for you and my box has rubber-to-road on eye-one-o in Kansas right now. "

Before long, Sharon was enthusiastically talking smack with the long haulers on the CB, although she didn't have the faintest idea what she was talking about. Rudy was laughing so hard he had tears rolling down his cheeks while his partner improvised, "I was pedal to the metal on this good 'ol boy down pulling logs on the dirty side and he had an eyeball on my truck. I saw his bucket of bolts in a chicken coop outside of Dayton and he tried to give me pursuit but lost him near Columbus—"

"That'll do 'er," Rudy said at that point, taking the CB mic from Sharon and hanging it up. "Not bad for a tenderfoot."

Once they stopped laughing, Sharon sat back and absently listened to the different conversations coming in over the *crackling* citizen band, the disembodied voices like phantoms in the air. It was a lot of extraneous chatter on the CB. A lot of colorful handles. Mostly questions and answers about road conditions. The lingo was a lot less colorful than in the movies.

"...The bridge is out by Breckinridge and the detour will add about twenty minutes to your run..."

"...The new diner by the Shell station makes a nice apple pie but the coffee is mud..."

"...Copy that..."

And so forth.

Then all of a sudden she was on the CB with a trucker out there who went by the handle White Knuckle. He was bragging with some other asshole late-night long haulers about his female conquests and his descriptions were getting graphic.

It pissed her off, so she grabbed the mic and spoke up.

"Keep it clean, good buddy. This is a family channel."

"Hey, honey, what are doing out on the road this late?"

"Working for a living," the SA quipped, looking over at Rudy grinning at her.

"I got something you can work," the CB voice chuckled.

"I'm not your type, from the sounds of things."

"You sound like just my type."

"What is your type?"

"Feisty."

"I don't know, White Knuckle, you sound pretty old for me."

There was an abrupt pause and sudden palatable tension on the other end of the line, and Sharon exchanged glances with Rudy. Behind his bearish grin, she could see he picked up on it, too. "I'm more than you can handle," the rough but high-pitched voice on the other end of the line growled defensively.

The FBI agent pressed the CB mic to her lips and taunted him. "How old are you?"

"Old enough to make you call me Daddy."

Sharon roared with laughter. "Good one. So you were going to tell me what your type is."

"Since you asked, honeypot, I like 'em all shapes and sizes. Like me blondes, brunettes, big ass, little ass. But I like quality. Don't go for none of that truck stop trash."

"So you where do you meet these ladies?"

"Hell, I meet 'em all over the damn place. Florida. Michigan. New Mexico. Why I had me a real fine piece of trim out of Omaha just last month."

Sharon's lips pursed and her brow knitted. Her mind worked behind her eyes. "She work a pole did she, cowboy?"

"No, ma'am, she was a nurse, pretty as you please."

The SA felt her blood run cold.

"How did you meet her?" she asked.

"Found her broke down on the highway and gave her some roadside assistance."

Chills ran up her spine. "What was her name?"

A low chuckle. "Now that's getting a little personal. I want to know about you, sweetcheeks. What's a nice sounding girl like you doing in a job like this?"

"Actually, I weigh three hundred pounds and barely fit in my truck. Don't let the voice fool you."

"I can be a chubby chaser, depending on the mood I'm in. You're getting me in all kind of mood."

"Maybe you can buy me a drink."

"I'd like that honey. Where are you now?"

Sharon sat bolt upright in her seat, feeling like there was a steel rod in her back. "Well, I'm on I-44, twenty miles west of Oklahoma City."

"I'm close by."

"Where are you?"

"Michigan. Seven hundred miles. That ain't too far."

She exhaled.

He had a cold, vicious humor in his tone. "Actually, I was wrong. I'm in Dallas. Could be where you are in say—no, no, must be tired, looks like I'm in Cody, Wyoming on my way to Boston. Been driving so long I'm asleep at the wheel of my big beautiful truck."

The trucker on the CB was toying with her. She grit her teeth. "I hope we get a chance to meet up."

"No, reckon you wouldn't."

"Why's that?" No answer. "I said, why's that?"

"I'll see you soon. That's a big ten-four."

White Knuckle disconnected.

"Son of a bitch." Sharon punched the dashboard, holding the dead mic.

Her partner shook his head, smiling. "You had yourself a bonafide Bucket Mouthed Ratchet Jaw there." When he gauged her expression, the smile fled. "You think that was him?" Rudy's warm brown eyes flickered with caution.

"What do you think?"

"I think he sounded all kinds of wrong."

"He was going by White Knuckle. Can we run a vehicle description on his handle?"

Rudy shook his head. "I doubt it. They change their handles all the time and some people have several ones, even made up ones. White Knuckle is pretty unusual, I'll give you that. Don't make too much out of it, though, there's lots of assholes driving rigs who get on the CB."

"There was something about that guy."

She felt it in her sphincter.

"You ever heard of a trucker goes by the handle White Knuckle?"

The two redneck drivers sitting at the counter of the "Truckers Only" section of the Texaco truck stop shook their heads. Nope, they sure hadn't.

Neither had the fifty or so drivers, waitresses and gas jockeys Sharon had asked that very same question to the last three hundred miles from Missouri to Ohio. Now she was sitting with Rudy, wolfing down a burger, and so far nobody they talked to had heard of White Knuckle.

Nobody except that one guy in Indiana who said he'd heard the handle, and the other long hauler out of Fresno who said he hadn't—the flash of fear in his eyes making her know that was a big fat lie. In fact, both men—two truckers of different ages from different states—had reacted nervously at the name.

That was why she was still asking questions.

That funny tingle in her stomach when her spidey sense kicked in told her she was onto something.

"White Knuckle sounds like an Aryan Brotherhood," Rudy offered after a sip of coffee, sitting next to her.

"We ran it. No dice." And indeed Sharon had—over the last twenty-four hours running the moniker through the Bureau's National Crime Information Database, or NCIC, but getting no hits on any organizations or individuals tied to the name other than a ski shop in Aspen, Colorado.

So the SA was resolved to personally ask a whole hell of a lot of truckers if they recognized the handle, White Knuckle.

Over the next three days she did.

Ten truck stops.

Three bars.

A hundred blank faces.

She became convinced she was pissing in the wind.

Until Morris DeGraw.

She and Rudy were filling up in Wisconsin at a Chevron truck stop. Her partner was doing the spot checks around the rig, checking tire and brake pressure and filling out his FTA form. Even though he wasn't pulling a load, Rudy was keeping the log and keeping his nose clean for the government. Sharon was over by the pumps, watching the digits turn over, gallon by expensive gallon.

"How much fuel does this truck hold?" she asked.

"You're not really interested in all that crap." He chuckled.

"I am."

"It's got a two-hundred gallon tank, which works out to about eight hundred miles a tank. That's 1,000 pounds of fuel, which factors in when you're hauling because the average weight of a loaded truck is 73,280 pounds, and when I say 73,280 pounds, that's what I mean, 'cause 73,281 pounds and you're fined."

That's when she noticed the spindly, gray-haired, denim-clad old long hauler standing by the grassy plot beside the tall steel pole with the Chevron sign that displayed gas prices atop. He was walking his burly German shepherd on a leash.

Rudy kept on talking, on a roll once you got him started. "The weigh stations check that. You drive through Montana in a blizzard and pick up another five or six hundred pounds of snow. You have to pay for the snow. You pull up on the scale and they say you're overloaded. You can explain that it's because of the snow and they'll say, 'Take it up with the Almighty.' Poor God gets blamed for a lot of things."

On a hunch, and with nothing better to do, Sharon wandered over to the trucker walking his dog.

"What's his name?" she asked casually, indicating the canine sniffing around for a suitable patch to do his business.

The old timer was friendly. "That there's Flynn."

"He ride with you on hauls?"

"He drives the truck." Both people laughed. "Everywhere I go, Flynn comes with. He's my best pal. Sometimes I let him do the night drives. Everybody knows dogs got better night vision." Sharon smiled as the trucker winked at her.

"Good behind the wheel, is he?" she joked.

"Has a problem reaching the clutch sometimes, but we're working on that."

"Do you know a trucker uses the handle White Knuckle?"

Everything stopped.

His gray eyes narrowed, grew dull with caution—and she knew right then he did. "Come again?"

"You heard me."

"Who wants to know?"

"A woman who got sexually harassed the other night over the CB. That would be me."

The elderly trucker's whole body language had tensed up, and he stared at his pet squatting on the grass, eager for the animal to finish what it was doing. "You ought just forget about some things, let 'em roll off your back."

"You know who White Knuckle is, don't you?"

"I know you should drop it."

"But you know him."

"Not personally. Just by name. And reputation. He's some bad business, a real piece of work."

The SA stood and stared, her eyes burning through the old man's head as adrenalin surged through her body. Out the corner of her eye, she registered Rudy hanging up the pump spigot and heading her way, but her own gaze was fixed on the trucker. The old man sighed, feeling pressured to continue.

"I knew this guy once. Maybe fifteen years ago. Long hauler out of Miami. He had some unfortunate dealings with this White Knuckle fellow, ended up with his legs run over and on Disability."

"Do you remember his name?"

"Fact I do."

Chapter Sixteen

The drive to Fort Lauderdale took them straight on through morning. They pushed the diesel down to Florida taking the 40 to the 65 to the 10. Sharon reviewed her notes on the iPad and sent a few emails to Campanella as Rudy double-clutched and drove, tirelessly chasing the white staccato of the centerline south. The miles rolled by. The rumble of the engines and a succession of country stations eased the monotony. As the sun rose over the Everglades, Sharon took a moment to enjoy the view of the sprawling swamps along the I-75—a new place she had never been.

If this were a regular case, her SSA would have assigned Florida field office agents to do the questioning, saving the SA the thousand mile trip, but it wasn't a regular case. Campanella had trusted Sharon's instincts in granting her request to conduct the interview herself.

Pulling into the tree-shaded estuary of the Kincaid Nursing Home outside of the Fort Lauderdale right after breakfast, they parked the big rig by the curb. She and Rudy were both stiff when they disembarked the cab and each stretched into the fresh Florida air. *What I wouldn't give for a few days in the gym*, she thought. The SA figured she'd better start taking breaks every day to do some running, sit ups, and pull-ups to maintain her physical conditioning. The FBI had a long-held belief that physical fitness ranked equal with mental preparedness.

"Let's do it," she grunted, and they went through the wrought iron gate. Both entered the manicured grounds of the Teamster retirement home, walking up a stone path through well-tended lawns whizzing with sprinklers.

Inside, the SA flashed her badge at the front desk. Within moments a pert, stern, Asian nurse came down the hall. She took them through the cool antiseptic hallway to a large door to the recreation room. For Sharon, the place felt like old people and death, and it depressed her. The nurse stood aside and showed them into the bare area populated by a dozen of the elderly and infirm. A TV was playing quietly in the corner. Nobody noticed them.

"That's Mr. Goines over by the window." The nurse pointed. "Please keep your questions brief and try not to upset the other residents."

The broken old man was hunched in his wheelchair. He was rolled into a corner of the nursing home, facing away from them. Sharon thought he was dead at first.

The Asian nurse spoke quietly so as not to wake some of the other sleeping residents sitting on couches. "Fifteen minutes. He has his good days and his bad days."

Sharon thanked her and walked politely across the linoleum floor toward the old paraplegic trucker. Rudy followed obediently behind. Flat, overcast sunlight poured through the white curtains onto the puke green floor.

The agent pulled up a chair and sat across from Bobby Ray Goines.

His bald head was down, parchment pale face lined with years of pain and fear, and his eyes closed. He seemed at peace.

"Mr. Goines?" She spoke softly.

Those heavy lidded eyes opened, revealing cataract-clouded brown orbs. Fear stabbed in the elderly man's gaze as he blinked in confusion and alarm. "Wh-who are you?" he mewled.

"I'm Sharon Ormsby, Mr. Goines. We spoke yesterday on the phone. You said I could come to see you."

"Who are you?"

"I'm with the FBI, sir." She flipped open her wallet and displayed her badge. "I'm a Special Agent."

Special Agent. She always liked saying that.

"You don't look like no G-Man." The cripple squinted at her jeans and denim shirt.

"I'm undercover."

He nodded. "I see. He undercover too?" Goines was eyeballing Rudy.

Her partner stepped forward. "No sir, I'm a long haul man, just like you."

"What d-do you want?" the old man shuddered. Sharon was shocked at how fragile Goines' once-massive bulk now was, horribly shattered years ago and atrophied in the wheelchair.

The SA touched his hand gently, brushing hair from her eyes and putting on her most tender and gentle expression, like a concerned granddaughter. "May I ask you a few questions?"

"What about?"

"About an incident years ago when you were a truck driver. There's somebody we're trying to find, who we think maybe you might be able to give us some information about."

"Somebody who?" he asked suspiciously. "What's their name?"

"He was another truck driver. We don't know his name, only his handle."

Goines was just listening.

So she said it—"*White Knuckle*"—and when those two words escaped her lips, the crippled old man's reaction was so extreme Sharon jumped back, and even Rudy stood up straight. Bobby Ray Goines shrunk in his chair, went chalk colored, eyes bulging out of his head with the purest raw terror that Sharon had ever seen.

"Mr. Goines, are you okay?" she gasped.

The old man recoiled in fear and put his hands against his ears, shaking his head, lips moving like a beached carp. "Get away from me!" he bawled. "Nurse! Nurse!"

The nurse was there in a shot, hustling Sharon and Rudy out of the recreation room with a steel grip. "You have to leave. I'm sorry. You can't upset our residents like that!"

Within moments, the agent and the trucker were escorted out in the hall, with the nurse guarding the closed door to the rec room like a Secret Service operative. Sharon looked at Rudy in dismay, and his expression was troubled and enthralled all at the same time. He gave her a look asking her what they were going to do. The SA thought for a few seconds, then smiled politely at the nurse, apologized, and led her companion away down the antiseptic smelling hallway.

Neither spoke as they stepped out of the Teamster retirement home into daylight, crossing the gravel driveway toward the parked eighteen-wheeler. Rudy broke the silence as they reached the cab. "You see how freaked out Goines was when you mentioned White Knuckle? If this ain't our guy, he's some kind of guy."

Sharon nodded. "That old man's terror was palatable. They have a history. He knows something. What I don't know this hot second is how we're going to get him to tell us."

"Well, he better start talking soon, because he's going to croak any day now."

"Agent Ormsby?" The Asian nurse was walking down the front steps onto the path toward them, gesturing with her hand.

Sharon turned.

"He wants to speak to you."

Bobby Ray Goines, what was left of him, regarded Sharon and Rudy sitting across from him. His lips were quivering, but he had settled down except for some old age palsy. "Sorry I flew off the handle back there. I'm past seventy and I'm falling apart and you surprised me that's all. Haven't heard the name White Knuckle for a long time. He put me in this wheelchair, but I guess you know that was why you come to see me."

An attentive nod from Sharon.

"I take it he's still on the road, you being here and all."

"Yes."

"I don't know his name, never saw his face that I can remember, so don't know what help I can be."

"If you can please tell us anything you know, any of your dealings with him."

The old man sighed, but his eyes were hard and tough, and the SA could see in his prime he was nobody to mess with. Goines continued. "White Knuckle was a handle of a trucker, long hauler I'm pretty sure, I used to hear on the CB back when I was driving in the 80's. The guy was an asshole. I mean, there's lots of a-holes on the citizen band, lots of drivers hide behind their handles, talking trash. But there was something about this boy I just didn't like. He was constantly bragging about what a King Stud he was, talking about all the pussy he picked up. But he also bragged about keeping his women in line by smacking 'em around and being violent to 'em and I was just sick of this son of a bitch's shit."

"But you say you never met him."

"No, ma'am, not as I can recall. So I was doing a three day run from Allentown to Spokane hauling refrigerators, and this one night White Knuckle comes on the CB and he's going on about some woman accountant he had in his truck that he picked up in Kentucky and how she was begging for it—"

A remembered detail jarred Sharon's brain and she interrupted. "Sir, do you remember what year that was?"

Goines didn't miss a beat. "1981. Right before I had to stop driving. What went down between White Knuckle and me happened during the next three months, so you bet I remember the year." He paused, eyes flinty.

Sharon was staring at Rudy. "Janet Majors was an accountant," she said tightly. "Abducted in Florida. I remember the file." She threw her attention back to the elderly paraplegic. "Please go on, sir."

"I mixed it up with him that night on the CB is what happened. White Knuckle was talking about this girl that was begging for it in his truck and I told him he was a lying bullshit artist and I didn't give a shit the FCC didn't like my language. Started making fun of him right on the air and before you know, a couple of the other truckers start getting in on the act and laughing at this White Knuckle jerk. Upshot was he got mad, crazy angry, and there was something weird and wrong in his voice, kind of tone makes you want to back down if you know what's good for you."

Goines looked down, sad.

"But I didn't back down, like I should have. I laid into him and when he said he'd tune me up I said you name the place and we'd meet up face to face, settle it like men. It was a truck stop outside of Casper, Wyoming. I delivered my load, drove right out there. Said we meet at dawn on Tuesday. Like two proper cowboys in a Western.

"He never showed. I got there, waited hours. White Knuckle was a no show. Or so I thought, which was what he wanted me think, so I'd drop my guard. I think he was there, I just didn't see him. Probably having a coffee in the truck stop, getting a good look at me. Two days later I had to pick up a load of machine parts outside of Tulsa so I got on the road. That whole drive I had the weirdest feeling that I was being followed, but it's hard to tell with all the rigs on the road; even to truckers they sometimes all look alike. But the hackles of my neck were up. I tried to raise White Knuckle on the CB, called him all kind of names when he didn't respond, told all the other truckers on the airwaves what a pussy this guy was and I felt like King Dick right up until I stopped at that truck stop in Flagstaff. It was night. I was tired. Wasn't paying attention.

"Don't remember much. I parked and got out of the truck and was walking across the asphalt and that sonofabitch came out of nowhere. Heard those terrible diesels screamin'. Saw those big headlights. It was a black Kenworth. Then POW! I bounced off the bumper and then I was under his truck and I felt those tires crushing my legs into the pavement and it was the worst pain...then everything went black. White Knuckle took my legs, took my life. Been in this chair ever since."

Chapter Seventeen

His gloved hands rested comfortably on the wheel. Through the windshield, inky night Interstate unrolled in an endless stretch of ribbon, bending and straightening, the lulling blacktop and broken white lines sharp and crystal clear, the tarmac a reassuring, luxurious blank void. His virile diesels rumbled powerfully. The warm, cozy confines of his cab were baleful with shadow in the lustrous underglow of dashboard lights. The trucker downshifted the thirteen gears and kept a comfortable cruising speed of 85 mph. It was one thousand, two hundred and seven miles to Portland. A twenty-ounce cup of piping hot black 7-11 coffee sat in the beverage holder beside him. There were no cars on the road at 3:00 AM and he relished the sense of peace and well-being on the deserted highway. He was King of the Road. He was an astronaut in his rocket blasting through outer space. He was the Grim Reaper, trolling for souls out on the open road.

But he wasn't alone. He had company.

The piercing female screams punched through the special speakers he had installed in the doors. The raw gut-wrenching sound of terror and hysteria and indescribable agony were music to his ears, and an appalling primal satisfaction and visceral release settled over the long hauler as he turned up the volume until the hideous shriekings were deafeningly amplified. It was better than Country & Western music. And there was none of those annoying commercial interruptions you got on FM radio.

Reaching over, the trucker switched on the portable television monitor rigged on the roof between the sun visors. Immediately, the infrared security camera image popped on of the nude woman shackled in the special soundproof compartment/torture chamber he had constructed under the trailer, near the back wheels. He had stripped her down after she pulled that stunt with the cell phone. Her body was lacerated with deep knife slashes and she was bleeding out slowly, her face and body covered with a paint job of her own blood pooling on the floor by her naked feet. The high definition picture and surround sound of his diabolical rolling home entertainment center gave him such joy. Based on extensive past experience, she would last for another six hours, passing out at increasingly frequent intervals. Then he would have to pull over to a quiet rest stop, climb in back and jump start his victim by injecting her with more saline drip he would intravenously feed into her arms to keep her conscious. He had a system, tried and true. She'd be dead by Portland, but the sweet music of her agony would keep him entertained all the way to Oregon.

The trucker picked up the CB radio mic and pressed it to his lips. His gravelly, affable voice had a sharp Tennessee twang. "This is White Knuckle. Got a copy, come back? I'm on Alligator Station, hammer down on the big slab from Big A to Derby City. Givin' all you Bean Boppers and Beaver Pleasers the "hi" sign on this dark night road." And he chatted on over the airwaves as the miles rolled away, a bucket-mouthed ratchet jaw, all mouth and no ears, a man who liked to talk just to hear himself.

His name was Roy Tremble and it was like his mudflap said.

Gas, Grass or Ass. Nobody rides for free.

Chapter Eighteen

This is how I die.

Carrie was so weak.

The pain was coming and going now, replaced by periods of euphoria—she knew it was the body's natural morphine and that she was going into shock.

The transom of the trailer—the part of the truck she'd guessed by now she was imprisoned in——rumbled and shook beneath her back. The piercing *clink* and *clank* of the jouncing vehicular construction wasn't hurting her ears as much now that she was used to it.

The nurse had no strength left. She just wanted it to be over.

SSSZZZZK-TZZZK. BZZZT.

Every now and then the static reverb of the closed circuit radio.

But the driver had been silent for a while now.

Thank God for that.

It was so dark.

Spots in her eyes.

The bite of the iron clamps on her wrists and ankles.

The raw dryness in her mouth.

So thirsty.

So hungry.

Breathe through your nose.

The truck decelerated.

The storage locker shimmied and shook as the big rig took a rough road.

Gradually it slowed and stopped, brakes *hissing.*

She heard the dull, muffled sounds of movement.

The trapdoor dropped with a *thunk.*

Fresh air and the smell of wet soil came rushing in, wiping away the stench of her own body odor and urine and sharpening her senses.

They had to be off the highway someplace.

A shaft of dim moonlight filtered in, barely bright enough to see by. It glowed faintly on the rise of her naked breasts and curve of her bare thighs.

The figure of a man wearing a denim jacket rose up through the hole in silhouette like a zombie from an open grave. She squinted to make him out but could discern nothing of his features or any identifying characteristics below the trucker's cap.

Her legs were spread by the shackles.

He was coming to rape her.

Moving with practiced skill, her captor grabbed on to two iron rungs welded to the roof of the compartment. He pulled with a grunt and hauled his upper body into the vault. Kneeling, he crawled forward over her nakedness, hand over hand. He wore heavy work gloves.

One fist touched her breast and played with it.

The other felt between her legs, pressing up inside her and moving around.

Ugggggh. Oh God.

His smell was thick, animal, aroused.

You'll get through this, she kept telling herself. *You can endure anything when your survival depends on it.*

"You thought I was gonna fuck you, didn't ya?"

She stared into the featureless gloom of his face only inches away, smelled his hot breath.

Could see his head shake slowly side to side in sadistic amusement.

"Don't worry bitch. I like my pussy cold. I ain't gonna *fuck ya* until *after* yer dead."

That was when she saw the blade.

Big, serrated, glinting.

On the move, slashing down in a sweeping metallic blur.

CRUNCH!

The pain was unendurable as was the horror as she saw the knife plunge through her flaccid tit into her chest cavity, driving into her heart and everything went black, but as it did and her time on earth came to an end, Carrie Brown's last thought was elegantly simple.

This is how I die.

Chapter Nineteen

From: Sharon.Ormsby@ic.fbi.gov

Subject: Rebecca Pratt/Megan O'Reilly

To: Frank.Campanella@ic.fbi.gov

We left Portsmouth, New Hampshire yesterday after reviewing the police files and interviewing the detectives on the case. Unfortunately, they provided no new information. Nobody saw anything unusual the day she vanished.

We are now on our way through Michigan to revisit the location where Megan O'Reilly's body was discovered and interview the police. From there, we will continue on to Eugene, Oregon to interview the police, reinterview eyewitnesses and try to turn up further clues to her abduction.

I believe there is sufficient justification to pursue an investigation of White Knuckle, the CB handle for a trucker who is a potential suspect in the serial killer slayings. He has committed at least one deadly vehicular assault, crippling a now-retired trucker named Bobby Ray Goines who we interviewed in Florida. The black Kenworth conventional model truck Goines said hit him matches the description the witnesses in the Tuttle and Pratt cases gave of a big rig seen in the area. I spoke to White Knuckle myself on the CB and he indicated first-hand knowledge of Carrie Brown's abduction, as well as aggressive misogynist tendencies. Rudy Dykstra and I continue to question truck drivers and truck stop staff along the routes between where the murder victims were abducted and their bodies later discovered.

SA Ormsby

Sharon walked back across the vast cement pavement of the Midland Truck Terminal in Michigan by the sweeping vista of the I-75 that stretched beyond the endless succession of big rigs rumbling in both directions to the snowcapped peaks of the distant Iron Mountains many miles off.

The wide-open spaces embraced her and she felt healthy and free for a few precious moments. The agent sipped the steaming coffee and it seared her mouth in a good way. The fresh air was crisp and clear, and the sky was slate blue above her with canyons of titanic clouds, as epic as a western movie. She huddled the down jacket around her shoulders.

Then she remembered there was a killer out there.

She had a job to do.

So the SA stopped dawdling, picked up the pace, and walked over to the cab of the Mack Cruiseliner. The door was already open and Rudy was sitting sideways on the driver's seat, cowboy boots dangling, giving her a big grin.

She smiled back, feeling like she was home.

"Let's get on the road," he said in his gravelly voice as she handed him up his coffee.

They pulled out.

She holds her mommy's hand all the way into the food mart that day they pull in for gas.

The air-conditioning feels nice when they push through the door and her mom lets go.

"I have to pay for the gas and fill up so you pick out some snacks and I'll be right back," her mother says. There is a man behind the cash register and a fat bald man by the drinks but nobody else is in the place.

The child's eyes instantly spot the colored packages in the racks of candy and she makes a beeline for it.

M&M's, Milk Duds, Milky Ways, Twizzlers.

All her favorites.

"Can I get three?" she asks her mom.

"Two or you'll get sick," comes the reply.

Two is good.

"Stay here, I'll be back in a minute, honey," she hears her mother say.

There is a movement by the door as she sees her mother head out again back to the car but the little girl isn't really paying attention because of the candy.

She has been told she can buy anything she wants.

So many choices.

She can pick two.

The child stands by the rows of candy bars and bags and runs her fingers over the packages, deliberating. Baby Ruth looks good. So does Milky Way and Three Musketeers.

It is a big decision.

She isn't sure how much time has passed by the time she grabs the Juicy Fruit and the Milky Way but her mother still hasn't returned. The child takes her stash up to the cashier and waits patiently.

It seems like a long time.

A few people come in and pay for gas or buy things and leave.

Looking through the window, their car is still parked at the pumps, the gas thingee still stuck in the side of it but her mother is not at the car.

Maybe she went to the bathroom.

More time passes and her mom doesn't come back in the food mart and doesn't go back to the car.

Other cars come and go.

The little girl is getting scared. She has a dark, bad feeling in her tummy that starts like a tiny pain and then gets bigger and bigger like a belly ache. There is a terrifying sense of being alone she is starting to feel. It feels like a trapdoor is opening under her feet and she is dropping out of the security she feels with her parent into a scary hole that has no bottom.

Mommy, where are you?

She is thinking maybe she should go looking for her.

But she has been told to stay in the store.

So she does.

For a while anyway.

The hands on the clock have moved all the way around and she knows from what she had learned in first grade that an hour has gone by and her mother hasn't come back and something is very wrong.

She leaves the candy on the counter because she knows you can't take it out of the store without paying for it and she doesn't have any money.

The little girl goes out the door into the parking lot and the hot air hits her and all the noise of the trucks pulling in and out and the air smells of gas fumes and the engines hurt her ears.

Mommy she calls.

Mommy she yells.

Mommy she screams.

A five-year-old little girl standing small and horribly alone on the pavement, sobbing for her mommy.

She never sees her mother again.

"Sharon?"

The Shell station passing by her passenger window had triggered the agent's reverie and Rudy's voice snapped her out of it. He sounded worried, so she looked at him and smiled, brushing a wisp of hair out of her eyes. "Sorry," she said, distracted. "I was just trying to remember something."

"Everything okay?"

"Yeah, fine. Keep your eyes on the road."

The trucker went back to driving and Sharon returned her gaze to the distant tower with the yellow shell receding in her side view mirror.

By the time it had vanished, so had the thoughts of her childhood.

Chapter Twenty

Richard Hanson had been on the road fourteen hours.

Everybody else in the car was passed out.

His wife Mary was asleep in the seat beside him and his five-year-old boy Tyler slumbered in the back of the 4-door Toyota Camry.

The thirty-three-year old accountant was seeing double—the white lines of the night Interstate crisscrossing. His drowsy eyes were unfocused, the lids heavy, and he was cranked from too much coffee. He wished it was still daytime. The night highway made him sleepy. They were trying to make his brother's place in Chicago by dawn, but he gave up when his vision went wonky and his head lolled and he nearly sideswiped a car in the passing lane after nodding off for a few seconds. Hanson realized he wasn't safe behind the wheel and needed to find a place to pull over for an hour to catch some shut eye. He was carrying precious cargo.

Like his wife had told him, driving tired was as dangerous as driving drunk.

Luckily, he had seen the sign that read, "Rest Stop 3 miles" two miles back.

All those trucks barreling past on the road were making him nervous anyway.

In the gloom up ahead, the man saw the turnoff for the rest area and it felt like it took his last few ounces of conscious willpower to decelerate onto the ramp and exit, then to pull into a space and shut the engine.

The car motor *ticked*, cooling.

He hit the seat back button and settled back, feeling exhaustion wash over him.

Remembering to lock the doors, Hanson laid his head against the headrest and gazed out the windshield at the rest area. It was mostly deserted. A single streetlamp shed a pool of yellowish illumination over the cement restrooms bunker and trees, before everything fell off into blackness. A few cars and trucks were sitting in the darkness, quiet and still, engines off. He distantly heard the *whoosh* of vehicles passing on the adjacent Interstate, and the steady drone was somehow comforting and sedating. Two or three big rigs loomed huge in the gloom. The husband and father took a last look at the peaceful faces of his slumbering spouse snoring away in the passenger seat and his little boy curled up in the back. Everybody was fine. He could let go and sleep now.

Hanson was thinking maybe he should text his brother to tell them they'd be a few hours late but just didn't have the energy.

That was all he registered as everything went dark. His eyes shut as heavy sleep knocked him into a drug-like slumber.

He dreamed of Thanksgiving turkey.

Daddy…

A voice.

"Daddy…"

His eyes blinked open.

He was still in the car; it was still night in the rest stop area. Disoriented, he got his bearings as he woke up blearily to his little boy tapping his shoulder.

"What's up, pal?" Hanson managed.

"Where's Mommy?"

The man looked over and saw her seat was empty.

The lock plunger on her door was up.

Odd.

He'd locked the doors.

She would have too, if she had left the car.

The keys were in the ignition.

"Mommy's probably in the little girl's room, Buddy."

"She's been gone a long time." The child's voice was tinged with worry.

Sitting up, Hanson wiped sleep crud from his eyes, suddenly fully awake. He looked around him at the single SUV and two tractor-trailers that remained in the parking lot—different vehicles than were there when he passed out.

Something wasn't right. The man felt it in his gut. Looking back at Tyler, he ruffled his son's hair and smiled, wondering why he felt like he was being brave. "I'm gonna go out and check the ladies' room, see if maybe she fell in."

He opened the driver's door and stepped out onto the concrete. The Indiana air was sweet and dry. Mosquitoes swirled around the overhead streetlamp that cast dim mercury vapor orange light around the pavement. Hanson looked both ways at the one passenger vehicle and two eighteen-wheelers slumbering in the long shadows of the silent and still rest stop. He felt very alone as he walked past the map of Indiana on the side of the bunker, following the arrows pointing to the opening of the bathroom with the female insignia.

It had no door, just an adjacent entryway behind a cement wall that blocked the view. Florescent light spilled out onto the ground.

"Honey?" he said loudly, standing by the door.

No answer.

A loud diesel roar made him jump; as he turned he saw the red taillights of one of the big rigs flare as it pulled out and got back on the highway.

"Honey, it's Richard."

He'd actually gone inside to check in case she'd passed out—"*baby, is something wrong?*"—or been attacked but there was nobody in the ladies' room, or the men's room either. He'd searched the surrounding area but it was just scattered brush and scrub. The sleeping drivers of the tractor-trailers and SUV were pretty unappreciative when the harried-looking stranger woke them up asking them if they'd seen his wife but both had been asleep and saw nothing.

By the time Richard Hanson sat in the Indiana Highway Patrol offices with his crying son filing out the Missing Persons report, his wife was two states away.

She'd be dead before Roy Tremble's rolling torture chamber on wheels crossed into Minnesota.

Chapter Twenty-One

Roy Tremble was sixty-one years old, in his twilight years, and was reflecting on his life.

Thinking he missed his dogs.

The beagle dangled on the rope, back legs kicking, eyes bulging. The high tree branch the rope was tied to creaked. The puppy mewled in terror, hung by the neck.

Tremble was six years old.

The little boy stood across the clearing, .22 Marlin Model 60 rifle to his shoulder, peering down the gun sight. He lined up the pooch's struggling head between the notches and squeezed the trigger.

There was a sharp crack and the dog's head flew apart in a chunky red spray and its lifeless trunk plopped in a pile of bloody meat on the grass.

Lowering the rifle, Roy smiled, feeling the charge of power even at that young age. The tang of gunpowder was agreeable. He'd begun killing squirrels and coons, but was moving up to dogs and the rush was indescribable. He was too young to know what sex was, but in time he would equate the two. All he knew right now was it was an appetite. He wanted more.

The boy strolled across the thick undergrowth and brush of Jupiter Hollow, where he lived. Beyond the ridge, the lyrical and untamed rural range of the Tennessee Smokey Mountains stretched as far as he could see. His bare feet stepped over the bones and rotting carcasses of a dozen dead animals he had executed on the tree.

His morning killing done, Roy was hungry for breakfast.

Maybe he'd shoot a cat after lunch.

The old man that was Roy Tremble came back to the present behind the wheel of his black Kenworth, realizing he had been drifting off into memory as he did more and more lately, and didn't even remember driving the last twenty miles.

He smiled nostalgically.

Ah, the good old days.

"Now turn."

His pappy had little Roy on his knee.

The boy had both hands gripped tight on the steering wheel of the old 1950 Chevy pickup. The tricked up Hemi engine sounded like a volcano. His old man had his boot pressing the accelerator to the floor and they barreled up the winding two-track into the wild mountains of Jupiter Hollow. The speedometer read 90 mph. Roy spun the steering wheel hand over hand, his adrenaline pumping as he guided the truck at breakneck speed around the curves by the edge of the steep mountain.

But he was totally secure.

Pappy had been schooling him on driving in his lap before he could walk it seemed. He never felt more at home than he did behind the wheel. In his father's lap, he felt safe. Vehicles would always be a comfortable place for him.

The road, or what there was of it, was getting real steep now. The little boy felt himself slamming back in Pappy's bony chest. Through the windshield there were thickets of briar and white birch branches that slapped and smacked against the glass. Nobody come back here.

Then the brambles parted and there it was.

The still.

Pappy lifted young Roy off his lap, plopped him in the seat beside him, grabbed the wheel and the stick shift, and parked the truck in the secret clearing.

The little boy got out of the truck and looked at the towering mechanical contraption, all bolted oil cans and coil wire that looked to him as if one of them UFOs in one of those black and white science fiction movies on the TV had landed in Jupiter Hollow. It sat there dripping white lightning into a big tank, steaming and smoking, rattling and shimmying.

But he knew the still was something his Grandpappy built for making moonshine and it was how they made money.

The air reeked of hops, corn mash and oil.

His Pappy gave him a wink and took a chaw off a plug of chewing tobacco he pulled from his suspendered denim overalls. His old man was long and lean, with a face like old leather and he didn't have all his teeth like Roy did. The man poured a spigot of the clear liquor into a tin cup and took a swig. He grinned in satisfaction.

Then gave Roy his own 'lil taste like he called it.

Passing the little boy a cup of 'shine, the kid bore up because he wanted to be a man and not a baby even though the rotgut stuff burned like liquid fire in his throat and hurt something fierce.

He drank the whole thing and the world went funny in a good way like it always did.

Father and son spent the next few hours pouring the moonshine in big glass mason jars and Roy was happy and drunk though he didn't know what drunk was. It was just he and Pappy working in the cool shade of the oak and birch trees. When they had three cases, his parent started to load them in the back of the pickup truck.

Suddenly his father froze.

His body turned to steel and his eyes became flint.

His hand went up and Roy didn't move.

Not a twitch.

Quick and quiet, Roy Sr. tugged a double-barrel Remington shotgun from the rack custom built under the transom of the pickup truck.

Roy didn't budge, he knew better, and he heard it too.

Footsteps crunching on leaves.

Heading toward them.

Pappy cocked the weapon.

Nobody come up here. Just the Revenue Men Daddy said was the Devil in Suits that was always snooping around but nobody knew about the still.

Yet somebody was coming.

Then just like that, it walked out of the bushes like nothing was the matter.

Six-year-old Roy had never seen a hippie before.

The young feller was younger than daddy and he had hair all over the place, on his face and head so that first the child mistook him for a girl. Had on a shirt was dirty and with all kinds of weird glowing colors and his blue jeans got all wide at the cuff by his feet. He was barefoot.

"Hey, peace, man," said the stranger. He had glasses that were made of round pink glass.

Pappy had the shotgun at ready, finger on the trigger. "What are you doing here, boy?" he asked, his voice like sandpaper.

"Hey man, no negativity. We just drove up here to commune with nature. We're all peace and love, brother." Or some shit like that.

"There's how many of you?"

"Four."

"That's it?"

"Just us, my brother. Come on and hang out with us. The more the merrier."

Roy had never met a person so friendly but Pink Glasses seemed very out of it. He had a smell about him that was like oregano. The little boy was still loopy from the 'shine himself.

He looked at Pappy.

Pappy nodded at him, then looked at the hippie. "Sure."

"Follow me," said the stranger.

They followed him through a few trees to a little farther up the two-track dirt road. Roy saw the bright, glowing colors of the weird van with the painted circle that he knew was a peace sign on the side.

It was the first naked woman he had ever seen.

She was all hairy between her legs and her big breasts had pink nipples and she was painting herself with flowers. Even at six he popped a boner. The girl smiled at them and waved and it was like she was in a trance. The air was thick with smoke. There were two more men, both as bearded as the first one and they were buck naked with their things hanging out and they weren't embarrassed at all.

Later, after they'd killed the hippies, Roy Sr. told his son they were called Acid Heads.

His father delivered the first blast to the stranger right in the back and the buckshot cut him in half, sending his arm and part of his shoulder bouncing off the side of the van, splattering it with blood but it looked like the same paint job the van already had.

The hippies just stared, too wasted and drugged out to register the surprise killing of one of their tribe with more than blank stares.

Pappy blew the tall one's head clean off with the second barrel before the screaming started and by then it was too late for them. The fat one tried to run away, dingus shrinking like an acorn, and Pappy flicked the shotgun open with a twist of his wrist, ejecting the smoking .12 gauge shells and popping in two new fresh, cracking it closed. He one-armed the hog leg and blew the fleeing hippie's legs off at the knees and he was crawling then with bleeding stumps but only got a few feet before shock kicked in and he twitched and died in a pile of gory leaves.

That left the girl.

Naked and screaming and crawling backwards on all fours away from the man with the smoking shotgun.

Roy had never been so excited or seen anything as wild or beautiful. All the blood and meat everywhere and he could see right between the girl's naked legs and the wet spot in all that bushy black hair. She was crying and screaming like a wet cat as Roy Sr. reloaded.

Pappy handed him the shotgun.

"Time to be a man, son."

Little Roy Tremble knew what to do.

Nobody had to tell him.

He saw the trepidation in his father's eyes, like he didn't know if he should be having his son do this. But his father didn't know his little boy was already an old pro at killing and had been dreaming of killing a real live person for a year now.

The child raised the shotgun to his eye and drew a bead on the heaving bare bosoms of the girl, whose eyes were insane with fear seeing a little boy pointing a shotgun at her. Despair and terror that it wasn't all Peace and Love but Blood and Hell twisted her features. "Please, God, no!"

The little finger pulled the trigger.

The girl lost both breasts with most of her ribcage.

And Roy lost his cherry.

Chapter Twenty-Two

He was twenty-one.

The year was 1975. Roy had been making moonshine runs for two years now, taking the back roads from Knoxville to Tulsa so he wouldn't get weighed. He and Pappy drove a Bergamot tractor-trailer truck, a Y-38 Red Belt Buckle.

They still operated out of Jupiter Hollow. The moonshine trade remained active, but grass was taking over with the seed come back from Southeast Asia after 'Nam. Roy wanted to start running it like some of their successful competitors did, but Pappy thought it was unAmerican—he was old school and it was white lightning and was gonna stay that way till they put him under the ground.

Roy hadn't killed anybody for four years.

The last had been a transient hobo walking the Tennessee highway near where they lived. He used a knife because he wanted to get his hands in it. Then he cut the bum to pieces and buried him in the woods.

Since he'd hit puberty, however, he preferred sticking his dick in girls rather than his knife in them. There was a couple of good whores out Pansy Road and he worked off his frustrations and urges in the backroom with that one had the tight shaved cooter, couldn't been more than fourteen. Still, every so often he'd drive past the glen where the tree still had the bloody rope where he'd hung and shot all those puppies, and he felt the tingle.

He'd been getting ready to do a run to Bakersfield, helping his Pappy load a few cases into the welded steel compartment they'd custom built in the trailer of the Bergamot. It was six feet long by four feet wide by three feet deep. Big enough for ten cases of shine. It was hidden in the trailer of the big rig down by the undercarriage. A trapdoor to the vault was latched and wired to a special switch on the cab dashboard. If the police was after the driver, he could press the switch and the trapdoor would drop, dumping the liquor on the highway. That way, if he was pulled over there'd be no evidence. It was standard moonshiner equipment since the blazing days of Prohibition in the 30's.

The stash hold was sweet.

In later years, he would find whole new evil uses for it.

Young Roy Tremble finished loading up the cases, tied them off with buckled leather straps, closing and sealing the rusty steel trapdoor. He got out from under the trailer, wiping his hands on his overalls. He was a gawky boy, all elbows and Adams apple, and his bristly hair was buzz cut to his bumpy skull. His Mom and Dad were first cousins. Grandpappy and Grandmomma were brother and sister. So it went in Jupiter Hollow.

Roy stood and looked at Roy Sr. The old man was only sixty but the lung cancer had got him and he had a hole in his neck with a speaking tube. His color was gray and folks was saying he wouldn't live out the summer. "Don't use too much gas," was all he said, and while Roy didn't know it then, those were the last words the mean old bastard would ever say to him because he'd be dead by the time his son returned from the liquor run.

Pappy was leaning hard on him now the old country rat was riddled with the Big C from the five packs of Luckys he smoked every day. Roy was having to make all the booze runs from the stills to the suppliers by himself and that was fine with the youth, because already he loved the freedom and pull of the open highway. It got him off the farm and the stench of death from his dying old man—the sooner the dirty, miserable, old fuck died the better it would be. In fact, the kid daily considered helping him along.

But when Roy was alone in his truck driving on hard concrete, the world opening up, seeing new places, the road cleared his mind and hardened his dick.

Roy swung into the tractor, threw the truck into gear and was on his way. Rolling onto the back road, he had his trip all mapped out. The young moonshiner meant to take the Tennessee and Kentucky back roads to Nashville where he'd get on the I-55 at Memphis and push on through the cornfields of Kansas on the I-70 for hundreds of miles until he'd see the sun set over snowcapped peaks of Colorado if he made good time. He planned to drive all night. The kid was in heaven. He was free. The engine between his legs, wheel in his hand, pushing all this power. He could go anyplace. Drive anywhere.

Tremble knew that road would one day be his.

Even at that age, Roy knew every weigh station in a thousand mile radius and every back road he could take to avoid them. The boy had a photographic memory for that.

He was lean and wiry, with a lot of acne and a feral stare, and he packed three knives on his person. The .45 he kept in the glove compartment. His hard-on was perpetual in his tight jeans.

It was the era of the CB radio heyday and CW McCall's "Convoy" was the number one song on the airwaves that year. It was what young Roy had playing as he barreled down a Tennessee back road near the Smokey Mountains and blasted past the squad car hidden in the bushes.

When he heard the wail of the siren and then saw the flashing red flares of the rooftop gum bubble he floored it and the speeding cop vehicle disappeared behind him in a cloud of country dust kicked up in his exhaust.

The turbocharged V-12 quickly outran the rural clunker police car, even with the trailer.

Inside, the ten cases of white lighting were strapped tight and Tremble was thinking they better be when he saw the second state PD car coming straight at him—its cherrytops strobed the air with flashing red flares.

There was a firecracker pop on the side of the car.

Sonsofbitches were trying to shoot out his tires.

No way even the ornery young Roy was going to shoot it out with no police so he started looking for a turn in a hurry and luck was with him.

The side road showed itself between his big rig and the police car rushing at him several hundred yards ahead on the right. Tremble's hands moved quick and competently—he braked his trailer, braked his tractor, and swung the steering wheel hard with both sinewy paws. The hairpin turn was tough and the cab lurched dangerously on its suspension, gravity gone wrong as the compartment was pulled sideways. Hearing the screeching tires of his trailer skidding in a fishtail, Roy saw in the side view mirror the trailer veering off the cab in skewed L position that revealed the tires twisted sideways and burning rubber. He compensated urgently with the wheel, steering hard left and swinging the trailer back into alignment with manly effort. His biceps bulged as he fought his way up the gears and double-clutched like a maniac. The whole fifth wheel and kingpin groaned with a tortured steel on steel scream—but his tires caught purchase on the side road and the truck didn't flip.

Shifting up eight forward gears with quick jerks of his wrist, Roy stared straight ahead through the windshield. Up ahead, the broken tarmac two-lane road led into untamed backwoods bottomlands. He put the hammer down, pedal to the metal, laying rubber.

In his side views, he saw both police cars in his wake on the main road slam on their brakes and swerve to avoid each other before colliding and spinning out in twin 360s that showered glass, the impacted cars shrinking behind him.

The kid let out a whoop and holler.

Damned if he wasn't Burt Reynolds today.

He better be, because the Bears were coming after him again.

Time to dump the load.

That's what Pappy built the trapdoor for.

The hydraulic hatch in the bottom of the trailer rigged to a cable that fed out the transom on eyebolts past the hitch through a hole drilled in the underside of the cab leading to a switch under the dashboard.

Pappy would be pissed at losing all that liquor, but Pappy wasn't here, so Roy flicked the switch.

In the back trailer, the trapdoor dropped open.

The ten cases of moonshine resting on top of the hatch in the trailer compartment fell through and got dumped on the road, wooden cases shattering to splinters and glass bottles exploding in galaxies of busted glass and clear white liquid that drenched the roadway behind the truck.

If pavement got drunk that roadway was going to have a hell of a hangover.

But there was no more illegal liquor in the truck and no way the law could say he had been moonrunning if they caught up.

Roy watched a week's worth of his still's finest brew disappear on the road in his mirrors, and flattened the pedal, steering through the back country. He could hear the police car sirens in the distance, but they wouldn't catch him. He'd blown their doors off.

That trapdoor was pure redneck engineering genius.

Roy embarked on his career as a serial killer for real on the drive back to Tennessee.

Wendy had been her name.

He'd forgotten or never known the names of hundreds of others since.

You always remember your first.

He picked her up fifty miles outside Mobile.

She was a pretty young hitchhiker in cut-off shorts and no bra under a sweaty T-shirt just thumbing a ride off the Interstate. The girl had a guitar on her back and a bright white smile to pass the time of day with.

Roy had been in a bad mood about dumping the shine and the money he lost, but the sight of those perky young teats just brightened his whole mood.

He braked.

She got in.

Said she was heading to Nashville.

He took her as far as Knoxville.

She was all sweaty and funky and she asked him how such a young kid like him could be driving this big 'ol truck.

The girl said his driving gave her white knuckles.

He thought that had a ring to it.

They'd laughed, sang along to the radio, and she strummed her guitar, making up a song about him.

Killing her was easier than anything he'd ever done—natural as breathing.

Chapter Twenty-Three

"Signal, honey."

Frank Campanella sat in the passenger seat beside his fifteen-year-old daughter Cindy as she hit the left turn signal and steered the car onto the busy Virginia street.

"At the next light, make a left turn."

His girl was doing well after a few weeks behind the wheel, driving defensively, and was well on her way to getting her learner's permit.

The thought terrified him.

It was irrational, Frank realized, but because of his job it was understandable—he knew the dangers out there on the road.

The pretty, freckled, blonde teenager accelerated up the street and eased in front of a Lexus, giving it plenty of room before settling behind the back bumper of a Subaru in the turn lane. A little close for her father's taste, and his stomach clenched although they were only going 25 mph. "One car length for every ten miles per hour of speed, please."

"I know, Dad."

"So do it."

She heaved an exaggerated adolescent sigh and braked an acceptable distance behind the other car as it made the left just as the light turned yellow. "See," Cindy grumbled. "I could have made that light."

"Drive defensively."

His own words stuck in his head as they waited at the intersection. Far up the avenue, Campanella saw the highway overpass and the freeway cars and trucks rushing past—somewhere in the US between Dayton and Albany, SA Ormsby was among them. Was she driving defensively on her fishing expedition to find a monster? The SSA felt a similar twinge of fear and dread for his agent that he felt for his own daughter now learning to drive—a feeling that what happened to her was out of his immediate control. That didn't make much sense, he knew. Sharon was a trained FBI Special Agent—not as much field experience as others but capable, resourceful and smart. And she was under the wing of a veteran trucker. Campanella didn't fret about the other agents under his command when sending them out on risky field assignments, because it was all part of their job, and his.

But he fretted over Sharon.

He felt like a protective father.

With agents under your command, you always had your favorites.

Something very, very bad was out there, and she was driving straight into it.

The SSA willed himself to stop thinking like that. It would compromise his objectivity and ultimate abilities to effectively supervise and protect her.

Let go.

Would he let go if it were Cindy, out there hunting a serial killer? No, he would never let her even join the FBI when she was old enough to. It was too dangerous.

Nothing would stop him worrying about SA Ormsby, who felt a little like a daughter to him, he knew that.

When Campanella snapped out of his brooding reverie, he didn't recognize the surroundings—they had left the intersection and were driving through the business district. Cindy beamed, keeping her eyes on the road.

"I guess I did good, Dad, you didn't say a thing for the last eight blocks."

"You're doing great, hon." Preoccupied, the SSA snapped open his Android smart phone and hit speed dial. It rang once and picked up.

"Hi, Ormsby," he said, relieved at the sound of her voice. "Just checking in."

"Why do you have two brakes?" Rudy asked.

"One for the cab, one for the trailer." Sharon indicated with her palm the top and then the bottom lever by the transmission. "You brake the trailer first, down here, and then and only then do you brake the cab," the agent said, behind the wheel of the Mack Cruiseliner as she drove it down the deserted stretch of country road. The long hauler had been giving her driving lessons, because if the SA was going to be credible undercover as a truck driver, she better know how to handle a rig.

"Tell me why that is, why you brake the trailer first."

"Because if you brake the cab first the trailer will run into it before you can brake it," she answered.

"Right. That would be bad, particularly at road speeds where the trailer would hit the tractor at over 65 mph and jackknife the rig."

"Got it." The SA had seen it happen, the tangle of twisted steel and tires on the highway after that kind of crash. There was nothing left of truck or driver.

Sharon had been schooled hour by hour as they crisscrossed the country. Her FBI training and skills made her a quick and enthusiastic study. Rudy's instructions were non-stop and thorough. Everything he told her stayed in her head.

"You're loaded with gauges. You got heater controls, air-conditioning controls, and fresh air controls. The driver constantly monitors heating, braking, cooling, electrical and powertrain systems."

She learned what the differential was, and what all the gauges and controls were used for.

"Night driving presents its own special problems. First, you need to see, and then you need to be seen. You very rarely see a rig at night without a lot of running lights, or gingerbread we call it. This truck has quartz fog and driving lights too. If you're driving in the dark all by yourself, you can't see much, but if you got traffic out there, you can see a long way by always keeping taillights out in front of you, so you got an idea where the road is and what's happening."

And so on.

The SA had learned plenty as the days passed and it filled the time as they laid rubber from coast to coast. In the last week, he was letting her get behind the wheel for an hour at a time on side roads free of traffic. While Sharon had been pestering Rudy for days to let her drive a big rig so she could pose more convincingly as a truck driver, the truth was she'd always privately dreamed of driving a great big badass tractor-trailer. Her partner understood this, so on the way to New Hampshire he gave in. It took all of the agent's self-control not to squeal like a delighted little kid.

The driving lessons continued throughout the week. An empty parking lot in Vermont, an abandoned fairgrounds in Pennsylvania—anywhere there was enough space to put the truck through maneuvers. The training sessions broke the tedium of the investigation and those long days on the road, and helped Sharon feel more knowledgeable and confident in her long hauler UC role.

Backing up took her some doing—easing the truck in reverse into a tight spot was tricky and nerve-wracking and she took a chunk out of the Mack's bumper, which Rudy was a good sport about because the FBI was going to pay to fix it.

He showed her how to disengage and reengage the trailer from the cab, and how to unhook and reconnect the brake lines.

Soon, she learned how to perform the spot checks on tire pressure, fuel leaks, and brake pressure the Federal Transportation Authority required of truck drivers every time they pulled in for gas or had to stop for any significant period.

Before long, Sharon was talking shop to the truck stop commandos they interviewed on the road, before she got to questioning them covertly about the serial killer.

Now in Wisconsin, Rudy nodded at her affably from the passenger seat. "You try it. Pull to a stop. Nice and easy. Brake the trailer."

There was no other traffic on the small service road to the I-94 under the blue and cloudy Wisconsin sky outside of Madison. She took her foot off the gas—they were doing about thirty—and closed her fingers around the back brake.

"Give 'er a pull," he encouraged.

She did and felt the huge force of the tug of the trailer pulling against the cab.

"Now the front brake."

Grabbing the cab lever, she adjusted it downward and the tractor also braked, in sync with the rear of the rig. Slowly, she eased the eighteen-wheeler to a stop at the side of the rural road and put it in park. The girlish grin just happened; nothing she could do about it.

"Girl, you just put paid to it." He patted her shoulder.

"You know," Sharon joked in a loose moment as they switched seats and Rudy took over the wheel again in Wisconsin, "it's good to learn how to be a truck driver and have something to fall back on if this Special Agent thing doesn't work out."

"Pays better," was all he said.

He was right, she thought wryly.

Chapter Twenty-Four

"We're bout two hours out of Minneapolis," Rudy said while the long strip of Minnesota strip malls and fast food emporiums of the 94 rumbled past the windshields in a mind-numbing blur. "Mind if we make a pit stop for a few hours?"

"What's up?" Sharon asked. The trucker had seemed a little preoccupied since they left Dirty Land, the trucker jargon for the east coast. After another dead end visiting the Michigan woods where the body of one of the victims had been discovered and learning nothing new, they were grinding their way west to Eugene, Oregon.

"My boy lives with his mother in St. Cloud. Haven't seen him in six months and I'd like to drop by."

The agent brightened. "Sure, of course."

"Cool." Rudy smiled and seemed happy. Signaling, he eased the truck into the Big Lake exit lane onto Route 25. "We'll just be a couple hours."

"I'd like the meet them."

"Just say you're a trainee trucker I'm breaking in. Not a complete fib, right?"

"Will do. How old is your boy?"

"Six."

"So you see him when you're in the area?"

"Every chance I get. Mostly." The truck driver had a distance in his eyes, and the agent observed him closely. "My job keeps me on the road most of the time. I call him a few times a week. Try to stay in his life. He has a good mama."

"Are you and his mother still married?" Sharon hoped she hadn't put her foot in it because she didn't know if they ever were man and wife.

He just shook his head.

"How long were you guys hitched?"

"Three years. Molly didn't understand the life. She always was on me why I couldn't work another job. Be home more. But this is all I know. Suppose I just can't stand still. Get impossible to be around if I'm stuck in the same place more than a few months. Get that itch. Need to get back on the road. I miss my boy, though." He exhaled. "It's no kind of life for a married man. I would say that most of all the long-distance drivers have had some kind of family problems and the rest, if they haven't, will. That's the way it is. You can't expect some gal to sit home and wait for you all the time." He reflected. "If a guy has been truckin' a long time and he gets diesel fuel in his blood and up his nostrils, it's sort of like bein' on drugs. It just sort of stays there. And if you quit, you quit and get right back in. That's one of the reasons I ain't married today. I'm gonna make a livin' in the way that I'm happy."

The SA just listened and began to understand what made this truck driver, and others like him, tick. They were not whole people until they climbed inside the cab, turned that engine over, heard the roar of the diesels and jammed that shift lever into the first of all those forward running gears. It was a way of life that was free and unhitched, yet lonely, dangerous and uncertain—but one that no truck driver would trade for the world. It seemed to Sharon they were like modern day cowboys and that the men behind the wheel had much in common with the men who rode the range.

Taking out his iPhone from his vest, the long hauler hit a number on the speed dial and Sharon noticed a picture of a grinning six-year-old boy appear with the caller ID "Tommy." After a few rings he got an answer. "Hey, Molly. I'm fine. Listen, I'm in Minnesota and wondering if I could swing by and see the big guy for a few. Thanks, babe. My 10-9 is about an hour." Rudy was smiling his big and wide cracked grin behind his beard as he hung up and pocketed the device.

They took some of the back routes and traveled past some industry into a nice neighborhood of middle-class homes and then he downshifted the amazing amount of times he needed to, bringing the truck to a halt at the curb. They were taking up the space between two driveways of two single story tract homes.

"This is us," he said.

"Want me to stay in the truck?" Sharon asked considerately.

"Hell no. Molly's a good gal. Come in and be friendly, meet the fam."

"Great," the agent said, and she and trucker unlatched and climbed out of the cab.

Sharon stretched as Rudy walked around the front of the truck and crossed a flagstone patio past an oak tree up the lawn of the house on the right. A Big Wheel and child's baseball equipment were scattered on the front lawn. The SA watched observantly as he straightened his hair and knocked on the door. Moments later, it opened. An attractive thirty-something woman in jeans and a pale blue blouse stood inside, her long brown hair pulled back in soccer mom style. She and Rudy exchanged curt pleasantries Sharon couldn't hear and gave each other a perfunctory kiss. The woman's eyes were hard, she saw.

The trucker reached into his pocket and took out the roll of hundreds she had seen him put together earlier. He gave Molly the money and she took it without looking at it or saying thank you. Sharon figured that was how they managed child support—him coming by, giving her cash when he could.

The ex-wife's face warmed just slightly when she had cash in hand, losing the initial caution and reserve, and she went back inside the house.

The SA leaned back against the passenger door of the Mack Cruiseliner, hands in her pockets, just hanging back and observing.

Moments later, there was a child's squeal in the house and a little boy with long hair burst through the front door and ran into Rudy's arms. It had to be Tommy.

Crouching down to meet him, the trucker scooped the kid up in his bearish arms, ruffling his hair. Rudy was grinning happily, bursting with love as he put his son down and talked to him.

Kid looks just like him, Sharon thought. Same broad, wide face and big brown eyes. Smokey and Boo Boo. The image of the cartoon characters brought a laugh up in her throat and she covered her mouth and coughed to hide it, her eyes watering with a mirth she was glad they couldn't see.

Rudy gestured her over with a friendly sweep of his arm. Overcoming her natural reserve, Sharon put on a nice smile and sauntered up the path to where the man stood with the boy. "Tommy, I want you to meet my new trainee, Sharon."

"Hi, Tommy," Sharon said affably, shaking hands with the little fellow, who watched her without blinking.

"You drive Daddy's truck?"

"When he lets me. I'm just learning."

"He's going to let me drive his truck when I get bigger."

"I bet he will. Your daddy's the best truck driver in the world."

"I know."

The agent stood there grinning for no good reason at all while the six-year-old studied her in the indecipherable way that children did. *Christ, he thinks I'm Rudy's girlfriend.* Sharon felt her grin get uncomfortably tight. Kids had always made her nervous because she didn't have any and didn't think she ever would in her job.

She glanced at Rudy for help but he just stood there watching them both, staying out of the way.

Tommy wiggled his forefinger for her to crouch down so he could whisper something.

"What's up?" she asked. *Oh no.*

"Can I tell you a secret?"

"Sure."

She put her ear by the boy's mouth and felt his sweet warm breath on the side of her face. "My daddy did let me drive his truck once. He let me steer the wheel while he did the pedals in a parking lot. So he let me drive his truck before you did."

Sharon laughed and stood, patting the boy on the head. "That's because you're his big man."

"I'm Molly."

Sharon looked up at the husky sound of the woman's voice in the doorway and saw the ex-wife giving her careful, wary study. As soon as they made eye contact, Molly put on a smile and extended her hand.

"How you take your coffee?"

"Black."

Molly stood at the counter, pouring two cups, kind of chatty with her back to Sharon who watched her as she sat at the kitchen table. "Me, I can't drink it black. I need lots of milk."

Presently, as if gathering herself together, the ex-wife carried the two mugs of coffee to the table, handed one to Sharon, and sat down. For several moments they sipped it in the air-conditioned cool of the small dining room. Both watched Rudy shooting hoops with Tommy at the basketball net mounted above the garage through the patio window.

Sharon could feel the weight of the other woman's gaze on the side of her face. "Looks like they're having fun," the SA offered cheerfully.

"My son likes seeing his father, even though it don't happen enough. Rudy just drops by when he feels like it, gives me money, spends an hour with his kid and he's in the wind again."

Oh shit, Sharon thought, *I have to sit and listen to a bitter ex gripe about her spouse.*

"So," Molly said. She came right out with it, casual as you please. "You Rudy's new girlfriend?"

Sharon had been expecting that curve ball. "No. I'm a trainee trucker."

The woman did not look convinced. "Where'd y'all meet?"

Sharon had been trained in and performed enough interrogations in the FBI to know when she was on the other side of one. She wasn't used to being on the receiving end except when she was being debriefed by her superiors, and then it was all about telling the truth.

Now she had to lie her ass off.

Luckily, SA remembered the story a truck driving husband and wife team had told them in Syracuse almost verbatim. The agent's photographic memory enabled her to repeat the woman driver's whole story of how she'd been a waitress who had met the long hauler in a truck depot in Arkansas, and how she'd kept asking questions about driving a rig because the money was better, and finally he'd talked her into going to that truck driving school in Texarkana before he took her out on the road to get her wheels under her. That woman she and Rudy met had liked to talk and tell every detail twice, so Sharon's story sounded convincing in its minutia. The straight arrow agent still felt guilty about the fabrication, and her ethics training stuck in her craw. It wasn't like lives depended on what Molly knew about her true identity, but then, given the monster they were after, maybe it did—Sharon didn't know if the ex-wife found out she was FBI, if she'd get on the phone with all the other truckers' wives and blow Sharon's cover, because truth was the agent didn't know anything about this woman except she was angry and that was justification enough to lie to her.

Don't get killed by being stupid.

When she had finished her tall tale about how she and Rudy met, Sharon still had half a cup of coffee left, Rudy was still out there playing B-Ball with his son, and Molly was giving her the hairy eyeball. The ex couldn't argue with the story, but wanted to argue anyway. "How you work the sleeping arrangements?"

"The Cruiseliner is a twin sleeper. I take the top, he takes the bottom." That at least wasn't a lie.

"Rudy always made me take the bottom."

"Did you drive with him?"

Molly shrugged, shook her head, lit another cigarette. "Nah, just did ridearounds while he took me on his runs sometimes, so's we could spend some time together." She sighed. "That there's the problem. Too much time apart. It's why most trucker marriages fall apart."

"I can see that."

"Listen, I don't know if you and Rudy are together or anything and it's really none of my business, but one thing you should know. Rudy loves one thing, that's his truck. He's in love with his truck. All truckers is. No woman can compete. Even Tommy out there, he can't compete. We're Rudy's family, but that truck is an extension of his body."

"I know he loves you both."

"Yeah, well, I got to get to making dinner. You're welcome to stay."

Sharon saw that outside Rudy was putting away the basketball and had crouched down by his son, looking him meaningfully in the face and speaking quietly. The boy nodded, smiling now and again. The trucker was taking his leave and his ex had sensed that like internal clockwork.

How the other half lived.

Getting to her feet, Sharon carried the empty coffee cup to the sink and started to wash it. "I think we're probably going to be on our way."

"I got that," Molly said, taking the cup.

The agent was politely escorted to the front door and when they got there Rudy was already out on the patio, his arm around Tommy, waiting. "Best be on our way. Got that load to deliver to Chi Town."

"Bye, daddy."

They said their farewells.

The long hauler gave his son a last bear hug. "When you coming back?" his boy asked, trying to be brave.

"Reckon next month. One way or the other. We'll go see that Twins game."

"Promise?"

"Promise."

"All right! I love you, Daddy."

"I love you too, big man. You take care of your mama and do what she says now, y'hear?"

"I will."

Sharon stood, observing everything, as Rudy stood up and nodded at Molly in the doorway, mouthing a tender kiss with lot of complicated things in his gaze. His ex gave him a little, affectionate wave with her fingers, looking at him steadily.

The trucker turned and walked with purpose back toward his rig and the agent started to follow.

"Sharon…"

The agent stopped and turned to face Molly standing in the doorway, a friendly look on her face—she was a decent person underneath it all. "It was nice to meet you."

"Nice to meet you, too. And Tommy."

The ex fixed him in a bittersweet gaze. "Don't break his heart."

Meaning Rudy's.

Sharon not knowing how to respond, thinking, *On a trip this dangerous, knowing what we're up against, I hope that's all he gets broken.*

Rudy and Sharon buckled up, and he fired up the tractor and geared down, pulling out. The diesels snorted as they rumbled off up the block. The roar of the engines now sent a regular thrill up the agent's spine—when this case was over, she was going to miss it.

The trucker waved to his son and tooted his steam horn at his little boy standing on the stoop, waving back like his father was off on another great adventure. Gradually the figure of the child shrank to a speck in the shimmering, tall, West Coast side view mirror, disappearing from sight as they turned the corner.

In minutes they were back out on the 94, back in the familiar chute of Interstate with the cars and always the trucks, like a corpuscles in a vehicular bloodstream.

The familiarity of the highway open road at 65 mph gave Sharon an unexpected flood of security and comfort. She looked over at Rudy, expecting that usual look of satisfaction that the trucker had when the rubber hit the road.

He didn't have it.

Damned if she didn't notice moisture in his eyes, a deep sadness just below the surface.

It hit her just then—the loneliness of the lifestyle of the gypsy on eighteen wheels. He didn't talk for a while—didn't need to. In the last few hours she had peered through a window into the long hauler's life and soul that she knew was the same for countless other truckers—the families visited for a few moments, the disconnection, the separation from anything but the embrace of the highways. The road was their home. They were essentially loners, by themselves in the world.

It wasn't just the job.

They had no choice.

It was in their DNA.

Sharon just rode in silence, sensing Rudy's discomfort at exposing his melancholy side to a basic stranger, being used to experiencing it alone in his truck. So she gave him his space.

By Sioux Falls, South Dakota, when they had put a hundred miles behind them and St. Cloud, Rudy leaned over and switched on the radio, speaking for the first time since he'd left his boy. "What you want to listen to?"

He was all right again.

Chapter Twenty-Five

The Burger King was still open in a little town called Evanston, Wyoming off the I-80 about forty miles from the I-84 that led into Park City then Salt Lake, Utah.

It was nearly midnight as White Knuckle rumbled through the empty streets of the town and saw it. He had been driving nowhere in particular, just scoping out the neighborhood and casing all the houses.

Window shopping.

Tremble was hungry, so he pulled his rig into the mostly empty parking lot and went inside to order a double cheeseburger, fries and a shake. He took his food outside and had dinner in his cab. As he gnawed a French fry, he stared out the windshield at the rows of tract homes.

He had the *urge*.

He had the urge all the time these days.

The truck was turned off, its enormous black shape a hulking shadow in the darkness with its headlights dead. He knew nobody paid attention to just another parked tractor-trailer in these little towns—just another redneck trucker sleeping it off to them. Even the cops didn't hassle you, because better you rested at the curb than driving tired and causing a wreck in their jurisdiction, creating all that paperwork. In the cold moonlight, his reflection in the windshield glowed like a gaunt ghost and hovered over him in the glass like a spooky angel as he ate and watched one house in particular.

The one with the light on.

A middle-aged woman in a bathrobe and curlers was taking the trash out back. There was just one car in the driveway.

The serial killer knew right away she lived alone.

The woman went back inside and closed the door, unaware. In a moment, all the lights went out.

Ten minutes later, the Burger King closed and the neon lights and signs went dark.

Tremble watched from the gloom of his cab as the two teenaged figures, employees back in street clothes, left through the back door, climbed into a run-down used Toyota and took off.

His rig was alone in the parking lot while the town slept.

Presently, he got out of his cab and stepped onto the asphalt, pulling on a pair of work gloves. Looking both ways to see he was not being watched and that nobody was on the street, White Knuckle tugged a black ski mask down over his face. He ducked under the chassis of his trailer back by the rear eight wheels, and unlatched the trapdoor into the storage compartment, leaving the lid hanging open.

Ready to be loaded.

Moving with assurance, power and precision, all but invisible in his dark gloves, dark ski mask, and jacket, he crossed the street in the shadow pools of the streetlights.

Staying low, he trespassed onto the lawn of the single story tract house with the floral awning. She had no dogs—that was good.

Just then a dog barked up the street, but it was several doors away and would not give him any trouble.

Taking his lock pick from his jacket pocket, he sidled up beside the back door. A hose and some gardening tools lay beside the wooden fence that shielded him from view of the other houses.

Tremble looked through the windows but the house was pitch dark past the curtains. He listened alertly but there was no sound.

Then he worked quickly, with practiced ease and efficiency. Using the tool to unlock the latch, the home invader carefully opened the back door. The smell of linoleum and macaroni and cheese from the kitchen filled his nostrils. The killer loved the charge of danger and penetration he got from breaking into people's houses—it was one of his big thrills and it never got old.

Closing the door carefully behind him, he was inside. His old cowboy boots were silent on the carpeted floor. Looking around, he saw he was in a short hallway. It broke off to the right to a laundry room with a washer and dryer. A load quietly tumbled and he felt the cozy heat, its activation lights green in the darkness. To the left the house opened up into a living room with an old TV and doilies on a coffee table. Everything was tidy and neat. Ahead, the hallway led past a small door he assumed was the bathroom to the open door of what he knew was the bedroom because it was the last room in the house.

There was no security system. People in these towns never thought they needed them because they figured nobody would rob them. White Knuckle's only worry was she might have a gun by the bed and be a light sleeper.

Tremble crept down the hall to the bedroom door, and when he heard her snoring he knew he was in the clear and it would be a cakewalk. Leaning up against the side of the door, the monster sniffed the air and smelled the woman's sweet funk in the next room. He stepped through the doorway, coiled and ready to pounce, prepared to jump on her and break her neck if he had to do.

The woman was slumbering soundly in a blue sleeping gown, her covers ruffled. She had no bosom to speak off, but a nice big hind section and her gown was up by her hips, so he could see some of her smooth naked buttocks.

She was all his.

Tremble couldn't wait to get her into his truck.

So he moved fast. Stepping over to the bed, he clapped one gloved hand over her mouth, her wakened eyes bulging wide in horror, and punched her face, closed-fisted, hard as he could, knocking her out cold.

Draping her limp body over his shoulder, he hurried back down the hallway to the back door and stole into the night.

As soon as he stepped out of the house, the loud dog in the nearby yard went crazy, barking and howling, but no lights came on.

Tremble carried his captive across the street, staying in the shadows of the elm trees. Nobody was around. He hauled the woman into the parking lot and dropped her with a grunt on the darkened asphalt below the open lid of the stash hold in the underside of his trailer by the back tires.

Then he froze, hackles on the back of his neck rising.

Her heard the engine and the *squawk* of a radio.

A police car was coming.

The monster didn't move a muscle, huddling in the pitch blackness under the truck with the supine body of the abducted woman.

Headlights passed slowly across the side of the truck as the police car pulled into the parking lot.

Tremble reached into the holster behind his belt and closed his gloved fist around the Smith and Wesson .44 Magnum with an eight inch barrel. He braced, stone still, ready to fire at the slightest provocation.

False alarm. The police car did a 360 in the parking lot and made a full turn back out onto the small side street and was gone.

Heart pounding in his chest, adrenaline surging reliably through his system, White Knuckle holstered his weapon.

Holding the woman under her limp shoulders, he heaved her up into the traveling coffin of the locker. Grabbing the iron manacles welded to eyebolts on the inside of the chamber, he shacked her wrists and ankles, noting to his pleasure that she was beginning to stir. He climbed out of the compartment, swung up the lid and latched it. The trapdoor was invisible among the struts and drive shafts of the undercarriage of the trailer.

Feeling sharp as a tack, the trucker climbed into the cab and sparked the engine. He threw the eighteen-wheeler into gear and drove out of the parking lot, not kicking on his headlights until he was a half block away.

The rolling monster left town and hit the highway, fresh meat in its belly.

His victim was a shopkeeper named Norma Wallace and nobody noticed anything amiss at her house until nearly a month later when all the plants had died, the mail was piling up and there were shut off notices from the utility companies on her door. By then it was too late. The neighbors of Norma Wallace never saw her again. They all figured she'd gone to Florida to visit her son.

Chapter Twenty-Six

The day was rainy and a cold sweeping spray played across the asphalt and sides of the trucks moving in and out of the Oregon Truck Plaza.

It was gray and overcast and Sharon was soaked in her raincoat as she walked to the pay phone against the wall. The thunder of diesel engines and hiss of brakes was grating her nerves, and the piercing headlights of the big rigs stung her eyes. She couldn't shake a nagging, constant paranoia and unease that any one of those truckers could be their serial killer.

What the hell did Campanella want that was so fucking important it couldn't wait?

And why didn't her cell phone work? The agent had no network the last fifty miles, which was why she had to resort to a landline.

Disgruntled and wet as a drowning rat, she picked up the receiver and punched some change into the slot. She stood under the eerie green and red glow of the huge truck stop illuminated sign, a blurry smear of neon colors in the smattering rain.

Sharon dialed Washington.

"Come home."

Not hi. Not how are you. Just get your ass back.

She felt her heart sink. "Sir, I don't understand."

"I wasn't looking forward to this call, so I'm just going to say it. The Bureau feels this undercover operation is wasting valuable money and manpower. You're my best analyst and I need you back at the office. You're not getting anywhere being on the road. It was an idea worth trying, you've gotten some good leads, but from this point forward there's nothing you can't do with our resources here."

Sharon felt like she'd been kicked in the stomach. This was so sudden. She reeled. "Sir, please. Just give me a few more days."

"What do you have for me right now?"

"Nothing more yet. But it's only been a few weeks and—"

"Come home. Thank Rudy. But tell him to turn that big rig around and drop you off at the nearest airport."

"What about Carrie Brown?" A desperate last plea.

"She's dead, Ormsby. I know it. You know it. We both know it."

Sharon Ormsby stood small and alone, a little figure by the pay phone in the isolated depot, the gloomy serpentine shapes of the eighteen-wheelers trundling slowly past on and off the highway. The rain came down relentlessly, like it would never stop.

That was good.

Nobody would see she was crying.

"Yes, sir."

She hung up.

Back in the truck, Rudy took the news in stride. He knew how disappointed she was but the supportive man had her back. "Listen," he offered helpfully. "I'm here if you need me. Just call."

"I know, thank you."

"Well, how about I buy you a drink?"

"How about you buy me two? I guess I'm off duty now."

"I know a good trucker bar about thirty miles from here. I'm the designated driver, but feel free to go on a tear."

The SA smiled in spite of herself.

Chapter Twenty-Seven

Sharon shouldered after Rudy into the raucous trucker bar off the I-5 in Medford.

Warmth and noise washed agreeably over her as they entered the roadhouse, stepping into an amiable roughneck atmosphere crammed with truckers wearing denim jackets, caps, sporting beards and leathery faces. It was noisy, with the *clinks* of glasses and *smack* of billiard balls punctuating the laughter and loud voices and the electronic *pings* and *buzzes* of arcade games and a pinball machine sounding against the wall. There were several tables with seated drinkers in the room, and the air hung with the smell of beer and sweat.

Sharon knew that this was an oasis of camaraderie in the occupational loneliness of the long hauler. She felt suddenly blue collar, unkempt, and pleasantly shabby.

"What are you drinking?" Rudy asked with a bearish, affable grin.

"Whatever you're not having," she replied.

They bellied up to the bar, Dykstra squeezing between a fat driver in a T-shirt and studded cut-off denim vest and two Latino truckers. "A Heineken and an O'Doul's." He signaled to the female bartender, who brought the bottles over and took his cash.

Handing the beer to Sharon, they sipped the cold froth. The SA leaned against the Formica bar and eyed the stacked shoulder-to-shoulder crowd of truckers, studying them. There were a few women too, she observed.

Sharon irrationally hoped Tremble was one of the faces. *You in here, freakshow? Come on. Show yourself.*

"Want to give it one last college try?" Rudy asked.

The agent took another sip. *Next trick question.* "Let's show Carrie Brown's picture around," she answered.

"Where you hauling your load to?" Sharon turned to a high-pitched friendly voice with a southern twang beside her. The fat trucker with the ZZ Top beard had turned to face she and Rudy, his eyes glittering with boozy friendliness. The SA was at a loss for words, suddenly, overcome with defeat.

Dykstra picked up the slack and leaned in, shaking hands with the other man. "Flagtown. Got us a load of air circulation equipment. Rudy Dykstra. This is Sharon, she's my trainee."

"Fresh meat." The man laughed.

Fuck you, fatass, Sharon thought. "Can I ask you a question" she interjected. "This girl in the picture was a friend of my sister and she went missing two years ago. Would you take a look and tell me if you've seen her?

Sharon showed a photograph of Carrie Brown to the man, who studied it and shook his head. "Never seen her."

"Can I ask you a straight question?"

"Shoot."

"You ever meet up with a trucker who was just wrong?"

ZZ Top looked at her for a moment, confused. "You mean like crazy?"

"Yes."

"You a cop?"

"No."

"Well, you get the odd lone wolf who been on the road too long and gone rabid, but most truckers I don't mind."

An hour and a few beers later, they were still questioning long haulers. Stubborn to the end, Sharon was displaying Carrie's photograph to an elderly truck driver who squinted and put on his reading glasses, rubbing his drawn and skeletal face. The man was as taut as a length of beef jerky, and his pale gray eyes looked up to regard Ormsby for a long beat, considering her. Then he returned his gaze to the picture. Sharon pressed, hopeful. "Do you remember her?"

"I never forget a face."

"You've seen her."

"Yeah, I seen her."

"You sure?"

"Said I never forget a face. Was maybe two weeks ago outside Selma. She was in the truck of this big black fellah. Truck was green. A Peterbilt, no, wait. It was a Jimmy. They was filling up at a Texaco depot and they was in a big argument I remember." The old driver's voice was soft and low, and she had to strain to hear him.

"Can you describe the driver, the man she was with?"

"Big ass ape nigger. Had a scar down the side of his cheek. Wore a windbreaker. I think he'd been knocking her around."

"Did you report it?"

"Lady, I mind my own business."

"Selma. You mean Alabama, not Louisiana?"

"That's the place."

"Anything else?"

"Nope, I went in to pay for my gas and when I came out the truck was gone. Didn't think much of it."

"Thanks."

"Friend of your sister, you said, eh?" He drained his glass.

"Yeah."

"Well, I hope you find her. Best be on my way."

The lean, wiry trucker left the bar.

In the next hour, the agent polished off another beer and showed the photo around to another ten truckers, none of whom recognized Carrie. Nobody could think of any strange truck drivers, although some bad mouthed fellow long haulers they had axes to grind with. Sharon began to notice Rudy was getting restless, eager to get back in his cab and on the road, his sanctuary. So they paid their tab and left.

It hadn't been a total loss.

They had a lead.

Ormsby was talking on her cell as she and Rudy walked back across the tarmac toward the parked eighteen-wheeler. "No, I didn't get the trucker's name. But he said he recognized Brown being with a large African American trucker with a big scar on his face… No, he didn't give me height or any more description than that, just that he was wearing a windbreaker. It was outside of Selma, Alabama… I know it's not much but we can call around and find out about any black truckers with scars on their face and where they work… Okay, sir… Thanks."

Chapter Twenty-Eight

The night highway unfurled, the broken white lines against sheeny blacktop like a zipper pulled down on a black rubber body bag, opening, opening…

White Knuckle drove with a troubled mind.

He figured the piece of meat in the storage chamber of his truck had been dead for a few hours and rigor and stench was kicking in. Once he crossed the Oregon state line, he'd head out into the big pine forests past Eugene and dump the remains. It was an old drill. He could do it in his sleep.

He needed coffee.

He had a bad feeling.

An itch he couldn't scratch.

Like he was being tailed. It had happened before, over the years, law enforcement getting wind and tracking him for a few months until he shook them off.

Back in '77 they'd been on his ass for a whole year and the Bears had nearly caught him outside of Nebraska. He'd had to torch the whole truck, buy a new rig, and a damn new trailer. White Knuckle was the name of the old truck, with letters stenciled big and beautiful on the side, and he still missed her. His Pappy had driven her. Named the truck after what that pretty hitchhiker who had been his first kill had said. But here he was, with that same old queasy feeling of somebody breathing down his neck.

Suddenly The King of the Road didn't feel safe.

He'd heard that bitch on the CB, and she wasn't making idle chatter—she was like a fisherman throwing out a line, trying to land a catch.

Asking questions about locations, where he was driving, talking about those places he'd dumped the bodies.

Hot Patootie was her handle. Real cute.

At first he thought the bitch was an undercover cop, but then he realized if she were the heat she had to be a Federal agent because they were traveling interstate. He'd spoken to her in Georgia, then heard her on the CB in New Hampshire and North Dakota. Hell, Tremble had to admit he was probably on the Feds radar by now with all that newfangled internet hardware.

He told himself he was getting too old for this shit.

That he just needed a cup of hundred mile coffee.

But he was lying to himself, he knew.

White Knuckle had to admit he'd been getting bored.

The routine was getting stale.

Everything was old.

Killing just didn't pack the satisfaction it used to.

Knowing the G-Men was onto him was a cattle prod up his ass.

This chase was putting some lead in his pencil.

Keeping him on his toes.

It was new and interesting prey.

What was funny was that they probably thought they were hunting *him*.

This is my road, motherfucker.

Yeah, it was.

I'll see you soon, he kept thinking, *I'll see you soon.*

Roy Tremble had been finishing his fourth cup of coffee at the counter of the Truck Terminal off the I-5 in Santa Rosa, California, when he overheard the two truckers in the booth next to him.

White Knuckle had been studying the busty, thick-hipped waitress and admiring how her jeans molded the crack of her ass and cleave of her crotch, and had been thinking of his knife and the way he wanted to use it to add a nice addition to his collection.

That's when he picked up on the conversation a few feet away. Tremble recognized his handle, not being used to hearing it in polite conversation.

The burly, bald-headed long hauler was dropping the name White Knuckle. The black thin driver he was eating with in the "Truckers Only" section was talking about him, too. Both of them jawing about these two other truck drivers who had been asking them if they knew White Knuckle.

Tremble sipped his coffee, his ears and antennae radar suddenly alert.

He eavesdropped.

Both of the men were obviously co-drivers, who shared the same rig. They were joking how the woman driver had been really pushy, asking all these questions a few hours ago. The gab shifted to her tits, and whether she had B or C bra size fun bags.

A slow grin split like a cut throat across Tremble's face. The woman trucker had to be the uppity bitch who had been baiting him on the CB the other day. And her going around questioning truckers proved she was some kind of cop. Probably a Fed, likely FBI, because his victims were transported interstate. He known right away talking to her on the citizen band she'd been wrong. And she'd been here not long ago. The cunt was in a big rig posing as a trucker, going up and down the highway questioning long haulers along the way if they knew White Knuckle, since she would only know him by his handle, not his actual name.

So far, the bitch was on a fishing expedition.

Right then, one of the truckers started talking about the black Kenworth conventional the woman asking questions said White Knuckle drove. The men were discussing the good and bad points of the model.

Shit, Tremble thought.

The Feds had his truck, at least the make.

But they didn't have his plates.

If they did, he'd have been busted by now.

But he better shut this G-bitch down.

Tremble didn't like the feeling of being hunted, especially by a gash.

His mind turning over like a lethal machine, Tremble sipped his coffee, trying to think like this cunt lawdog would. If she had stopped here, she must be visiting the major truck stops along the I-5, questioning drivers and staff—it was what he'd do in her position if he was trying to find one specific long hauler. She had only left the truck terminal he was in a few hours ago, so Tremble might catch up to her if he got a move on.

Problem was he didn't know what kind of truck the bitch was driving.

Or whether she had headed north or south on the I-5.

Figuring he better pump these two good 'ol boys for information, Tremble got off the stool crotch first and casually ambled over to the booth. The bald and black truckers looked up at him from their meal as the monster gave them his friendliest grin. "So that lady was asking you about this White Knuckle fellah too?" he said.

"Yeah, she talk your ear off too?" The bald one chuckled.

Tremble nodded, rolling his eyes. "She was a regular ratchet jaw about him."

"Nice tits," the black driver observed.

"Perky." Tremble smiled—he had every intention of getting up close and personal with those boobies before he cut them off and hung them on his wall. "You boys didn't happen to see the truck she was driving, didja? Dumb broad left her jacket on the table and I want to give it back to her."

"Yeah, she and the other guy were in that big white Mack Cruiseliner cabover."

"Right." So the bitch had a partner. "The thin fellah."

"No, he was a big guy, with a beard. STP cap."

"Oh yeah, right. You happen to see which way they went?"

The truckers shook their heads. Didn't know.

That was okay, Tremble figured, odds were the bitch was going to be on the I-5 checking the truck stops and there were only two directions that she and her partner could go—north or south.

The serial killer nodded thanks as he paid his check, left a few bucks on the counter, gave a last look at the waitress's denim clad snatch and pushed out the swinging door into the night air and headed to his waiting truck.

It wasn't south.

Tremble had checked in at two Truck Plazas in the Sacramento area and the gas jockey in the one said the woman and the man in the white Mack Cruiseliner who asked after White Knuckle had left hours ago.

Turning his truck around, the monster got a full head of steam on pushing his semi north past Santa Rosa and across the Oregon border. The next truck stop in that direction was the Oregon Truck Plaza outside of Medford, he knew.

It was starting to rain, the day gloomy and dark as he barreled up the highway, wipers slashing spray. Finally the big neon letters of the terminal appeared, ballooning in the blurry wet glass and immediately he saw the white whale of the big Mack Cruiseliner cabover parked at the pumps and his dick got wood.

Tremble turned off the highway and pulled his Kenworth in the back of the truck terminal, beside a few other conventionals parked nose to nose. He sat in the tractor and watched the white cabover a few hundred yards off past the swishing wash of his windshield wipers.

And he saw her in the phone booth.

Blonde, cute, wearing denims and a cap, telephone pressed to her face. So this was the cunt that was giving him trouble. She didn't look like much, but even at this distance he could make out the bulge of the pistol on her belt under her jacket.

White Knuckle felt the black Smith & Wesson .44 Magnum with the eight inch barrel bump against his ribcage in its leather shoulder holster.

He always packed.

Always.

One powerful round from the cannon would break the engine block of a car and stop it dead in its tracks or take a man's head off at the shoulders. He used .44 grain hollow point ammo and the kick of the mighty gun was fierce but it killed what it hit. It was a revolver so it held only six rounds but he had four speedloads in his jean jacket pocket and could reload in seconds, faster than a fly could fuck.

Ready for anything.

On the road, you best be.

A minute later, the blonde woman hung up the phone and ducked through the rain over to the open passenger door of the white Cruiseliner. She got in and they pulled out.

Giving them a three-count head start, Tremble shifted up the forward gears and pulled out after them.

White Knuckle had pulled his rig off the Oregon I-5 and downshifted into the roadhouse parking lot, right where the Mack Cruiseliner had pulled in ten minutes ago. He had been tailing it four truck lengths behind but hadn't pulled in after the white truck when it parked at the roadside bar, because that would have attracted attention. Instead, he drove past the bar and got off at the next exit, turned around, came back the other way, took the other exit, and was back at the roadhouse ten minutes later. The white Mack cabover was still there, like he knew it would be.

Tremble parked his truck and walked toward the bar, his cowboy boots crunching gravel. He always liked these places and had been to this joint many times. He remembered the bartender's name used to be Fred. Man, he could use a drink.

The sound of the bassy jukebox playing Travis Tritt fought to be heard over the Packers game on the big screen TV. The air was dense with body heat and the burble of conversation. Pulling off his work gloves, Tremble shouldered his way through the crowd to the end of the bar. He leaned against the rail, with his shoulders up around his ears and dipping his cowboy hat, keeping to himself.

The bartender tonight was a big-tittied middle-aged broad with a friendly smile and mouth built for blowjobs whose face didn't ring a bell. He lifted two gnarled fingers. "Bud and whisky straight up," he half spoke and half mouthed and she heard him and set it right up and he paid her just as quick.

The shot and the beer went down sweet.

He ordered another.

The warmth spread through his throat and gullet and he relaxed, feeling better. His eyeball rolled sideways like a lizard and took in the bar, though it looked to anybody he was facing forward. Truckers and bikers with beards and caps, cut-off denims and rodeo brass belts and cowboy boots everywhere you looked.

Him with a corpse in the compartment of his truck, none of them the wiser death was here in the bar with them. He'd always liked that.

Eyeing the bartender, Tremble saw her twin ass cheeks were busting out her jeans. He liked 'em chubby. The monster imagined strapping her naked and spread eagled to the compartment of the truck and whipping it out and shoving it in and pounding her senseless and he got wood thinking about her wet spot and the number he'd do on it. Then caving her skull in and getting covered with her hot blood. He could come back after he'd dumped the body he had now, be back after closing, follow her home, run her off the road, have his way, and nobody'd do jack shit.

These cunts were all his for the taking, they just didn't know it.

Mister, that was power.

But Tremble was here for one cunt in particular.

He had to meet her face to face, for shits and giggles.

The second round came and he was putting that away when he noticed the chatty blonde in the unwashed denim with the obviously seasoned trucker at her side like they were an item and he knew right away she was out of place. A fool could see that gash didn't have no road miles on her.

He felt the charge when he saw her.

The connection.

Tremble sipped his drink, and tried to listen in over the din of conversation, hearing snippets.

"Did you ever meet—?" The blonde leaning in close to a big, fat, beefy-faced long hauler.

Him shaking his head. "—seen her."

Her showing him a photograph.

Asking questions.

White Knuckle recognized her voice on the CB.

Tremble didn't move and didn't need to because she was coming his way. Giving a smile and a pat on the arm to the big honcho, she and her man moved down the bar.

Next thing he knew her face was in his, all teeth and big warm but probing brown eyes. "Hi."

Now he had a face to the voice. His heart thundered in his chest.

"I'm Sharon. This is my husband Rudy. We're running a load of lumber to Spokane."

He shook her hand. "Howdy."

"Didn't get your name?"

That's cause I didn't give it, bitch. "Joe," he mumbled. Something about this FBI cunt's whole forward manner, something about her in general, made him want to knock her teeth down the back of her fucking throat. He restrained himself, nodding at the big man beside her. He looked harmless enough—built but with a hesitance in his gaze that the natural predator and people reader Roy Tremble made for ex-con right away. He had that look.

"Have you seen my sister's friend?" The blonde displayed the photograph of the girl and right then he knew.

This was the nurse he killed in Omaha and dumped in North Dakota.

No doubt about it. These two were the ones who were hunting him. The ones on the CB who went by the handle American Iron and Hot Patootie.

Feds. Least she was.

And here in the cozy bar they didn't have the faintest hair on a fly's ass idea who he was.

It was beautiful.

They were dead meat.

Tremble put on his reading glasses, rubbing his chin. He eyeballed the G-bitch for a long beat, considering her. Then he returned his gaze to the picture. The woman pressed him. "Do you remember her?"

"I never forget a face." Aware she might make his voice from their conversations on the citizen band, Tremble lowered his voice a few octaves and spoke softly, losing his accent.

"You've seen her."

"Yeah, I seen her."

"You sure?"

He knew that with her agent training she would read his truthfulness about knowing the dead girl, and he had to act sincere about the rest. So he lied like a pro, put on his best folksy hillbilly drawl. "Said I never forget a face. Was maybe two weeks ago outside Selma. She was in the truck of this big black fellah. Truck was green…" He cooked up and fed her a whole cock and bull story about seeing a nigger with the girl at Texaco to throw her off the track and when he saw it worked, he said his goodbyes.

White Knuckle left the bar with purpose.

Chapter Twenty-Nine

It took him less than a minute to reach their truck, with the big "*AMERICAN IRON*" letters on the side. Tremble identified the year as a '96 Mack Cruiseliner cabover. Nice rig. He was familiar with the model and knew it had the brake lines near the wheel wells. So, pulling on his gloves to not to leave any prints, he looked both ways to check that nobody was watching him. In the pools of shadow and fluorescent lights that danced off the glossy paint jobs of the sleeping dinosaurs parked at the stop, there was no movement.

White Knuckle pulled a big hunting knife out of the back of his belt sheath under his jacket and swung like a monkey beneath the undercarriage of the eighteen-wheeler.

Within thirty seconds he had located the brake lines and punctured, not severed them, using a precision with the knife he had gained from cutting off heads.

The brake fluid started leaking, draining in a slow drip.

White Knuckle swung out from under the truck onto his cowboy boots with the silver razor tips.

A small pool of brake fluid began gathering on the darkened asphalt beneath the cab, but nothing anybody would notice for another two hours. They'd be back on the road in less time than that.

He figured they'd get about fifteen miles before the brakes quit.

Right smack dab around the long ten-mile fifty-degree highway downgrade leading to Eugene—a treacherous stretch of steep winding road with dense traffic going both directions on the edge of steep ravines plunging off the switchback.

Not the place you wanted to lose your brakes.

It wouldn't matter whether the brakes quit on the upgrade or the downgrade—one way they'd slide back and the other way slide forward, but either way there would be a massive wreck neither would survive.

The blonde Fed said they were going to Eugene.

They weren't going to get there.

Roy Tremble got back in his truck and hit the road again. This was going to work great. Eugene cops would be so busy with the big truck wreck an hour from now on the major artery to the city nobody was going to be paying attention to him while he drove into the woods outside town and buried the body. He figured he'd do a big sixty mile circle of the I-5 and then come up around the switchback in an hour just in time to savor the wreckage.

Good times.

Chapter Thirty

Sharon watched Rudy gear down as the mighty Mack Cruiseliner topped the steep grade of the I-5 just past Creswell. She noticed his furrowed brow as the big rig lumbered over the night highway rise. "What's up?" she asked.

"Truck needs a tune up," he grunted.

They left the roadhouse about a half hour ago, and Sharon had too much to drink. She felt woozy in the passenger seat.

Her window was rolled down and the rugged smell of timber, soil and cut lumber swept into the cab, a refreshing, invigorating scent carried with the cold wet air. Droplets of rain pelted her face, but it felt good and sobered her up.

They had scaled a mountainous switchback of the 5, Rudy giving her a lift to the Eugene Airport where the SA was booked on a red eye back to DC. Sharon felt a leaden sense of failure and disappointment. While the case was far from over, her field work was done for the foreseeable future and Sharon knew she would be back on desk duty the next day. It could be a long time before she left that desk again. What did she think would happen, the agent asked herself? Her UC operation had turned up squat and the Bureau's other Special Agents needed to be assigned to cast a wider net to actually apprehend White Knuckle, if that even was the guy, or dead him in a righteous kill.

Still, it irked her because she had yearned to distinguish herself on this case.

And now, some other SA would get the collar.

Some other SA would get to blow his head off.

Thank you, analyst.

We couldn't have done it without you.

There is no "I" in "Team."

Sharon snapped out of her self-pitying funk and studied the gloomy mountain woods passing by. *Suck it up. Those trees don't whine, lady. They endure, like you will.* During the day, she figured the big forest they drove by would be a spectacular view.

Through the windshield, the sea of red taillights of the passenger cars below and other tractor-trailers spangled the luxurious night blacktop and broken white lines. As the roadway evened out she saw the sprawling city lights of Eugene, Oregon peak over the crest of the highway.

Then the eighteen-wheeler was taking the downgrade. The twisting and turning mountain highway spread out before them for miles down into the city. Rows of forest pine trees rushed past on either side.

When she glanced over at Rudy, he was frowning again, regarding his dashboard, puzzled.

The truck was picking up speed.

Right away, Sharon knew they were going too fast. "What's up?" she asked.

When the trucker started stamping on the brake and uselessly yanking the trailer brake lever, she knew they were in trouble.

"I got no brakes," her partner gasped.

Make that deep shit.

The agent sat bolt upright in her seat, the blood rushing from her face as she stared at him surgically spinning the steering wheel.

"You sure?"

"Yeah, no brakes."

He stomped on the pedal again, but the big rig kept speeding up, its tonnage and velocity accelerating it through traffic on the downgrade. Past the windows, the brightly illuminated tailgate of the tractor-trailer ahead was rushing up at them—five truck lengths, two truck lengths, one—and now they were about to impact. Rudy punched the horn and she heard the deafening klaxon blast over the revving roar of the diesels. He was staring out his driver's window until he was just ahead of two passenger cars beside him, then fiercely steered his eighteen-wheeler out of the truck lane just in time to narrowly avoid the transom of the rig ahead.

"Do something!" She choked, hands clutching the armrest.

Jumping out of the truck was not an option. Reflexively, Sharon cast a glance out her passenger window and saw the road rushing past in a dark blur, knowing that a leap from the cab at this speed would be fatal. She wasn't a coward and wouldn't have dived out and left Rudy to his fate, but her survival instinct was on autopilot and the option had to be consciously considered and rejected.

"Don't panic," he growled. The trucker's jaw was set and his eyes unblinkingly fixed out the windshield as he kept his cool.

"What are we going to do?" Sharon was disgusted by high-pitched edge of hysteria in her voice.

"There's a runaway truck ramp about five miles down the road. We're gonna make it there and I'll steer the rig off the highway and the incline of the ramp will stop us."

"Five miles?"

They'd be lucky to get one mile.

His hands clenched against the steering wheel and his teeth gritted, Rudy was steel. Ahead, through the windshield where his eyes were riveted, there was a lot of four-wheeler traffic—a sea of red taillights in a long twisty line down the distant descending black ribbon of highway. Those lights were coming at them like a meteor shower of rubies as they gained on the cars ahead.

He sat on the horn.

Cars and smaller trucks peeled out of the way to let him pass and the forty-ton battering ram of iron and steel and rubber carrying a loaded 150-pound bomb of diesel fuel plunged safely through them.

Sharon held on to her seat.

The four lanes of traffic came rushing at her, endless and seemingly unavoidable. She threw a desperate glance at the dashboard.

The speedometer needle was up to 90 mph.

95 mph.

100 mph.

The back-to-back lines of long haulers in the right lane washed past in a blinding sequence of running lights. Looking over, she caught the startled and alarmed faces of the truck drivers staring at them as the Mack Cruiseliner thundered past.

And the highway was getting steeper and steeper, a twisting and turning switchback through the mountain range ever downward.

"Hang on!" Rudy roared. She was. Tight. "This happened to me before, twenty years ago. It's gonna be all right. Trust me."

"What choice do I have?" she screamed.

"Thanks for your support," he quipped. Cracking a joke even in this situation—Sharon gained sudden total respect for the trucker and his operating skills as she watched the power and command of how calmly handled his machine under pressure.

The cabover headlights washed explosively across a passing road sign that read,

"Runaway Truck Ramp 3 miles."

It might as well have been fifty.

Horn blaring, the big rig plowed mere inches safely past the fleeing tailgates of the scrambling cars in front that peeled out of the way in the nick of time to either side, but new blockades of vehicles appeared in their place—a phalanx that never ended, resurrecting their peril.

A row of swivel-jockeys were bumper to bumper across three lanes ahead, leaving them nowhere to go and no way to get around them. The headlights of the truck brightened on the rear bumpers as the titanic shadow of the Mack Cruiseliner loomed over them.

They were going to crash.

Sharon covered her head.

Suddenly wheeling his big rig across the fast lane, Rudy swerved his tractor and trailer into opposing traffic in the oncoming lanes, the eighteen-wheeler coming off its right tires and tipping. He worked the trailer brake desperately and the back half of the truck rammed into the cab, threatening to jackknife the rig. Squealing tires and the rank stench of burning rubber filled the cab. Sharon's and Rudy's faces were blinded by brilliant head-on car headlights in a swirling blur, and the highway was a cacophonic symphony of urgent horns sounding like an amusement park ride from hell.

Visions of herself in little pieces on the road swam in front of Sharon's eyes.

Then the big rig was off the road!

It slammed and shook and quaked on its suspension as the eighteen steel-belted radial tires hammered onto the dirt of the runaway truck ramp.

Slamming back in her seat, Sharon felt the whole truck hit a steep upgrade, the chassis sledgehammered by the resistance the cab met from densely packed piles of dirt and sand that it bobsledded up through like a humongous toboggan.

Slowing.

Slowing.

Intertia and piles of dirt doing their work to bring the rampaging juggernaut of a semi to a halt.

And then the Mack Cruiseliner was at a standstill.

Just like that.

Rudy cut the engine and rested his head on the steering wheel.

Sharon took inventory. *Arm. Arm. Leg. Leg. Hand. Hand. Fingers. Move them. Good, they move. Have all my pieces. Everything works. I'm alive.* She gasped in relief.

And threw up all over the cab.

Tremble drove past the sea of swarming red lights created by the clustered police cars.

He could see right away that the truck hadn't crashed.

Hell, he'd expected it to be scattered all over the highway, maybe in a big beautiful ball of flame, but he'd had a bad feeling when traffic hadn't been stopped, just routed through.

There the cabover and trailer sat, stationary and intact if plenty dirty at a ninety-degree angle, at the end of the runaway truck ramp. Haze from the displaced dirt kicked up from the stopped rig's tires still hung in the air, haloing all the cherrytops and illuminating the whole area with pulsing red light.

And there *she* was.

Still breathing.

Motherfucker. The woman, standing in one piece talking to a group of police officers and gesturing with her hands. Lucky fucking cunt survived.

Tremble saw his own rangy glowering face in his tall West Coast Side Mirror, demonically flashing with the police beacons.

The slowing traffic of rubberneckers gave the monster time to get a good look at her face and commit it to memory as he idled and inched forward with the rest of the slowing traffic past the ramp and truck and cop cars. The bitch didn't look like much.

He'd get her next time.

But the searing coil of red-hot frustrated rage burned like a fire in his belly until he crossed the Washington state line.

Chapter Thirty-One

Johnson's Truck Parts & Service was a sprawling mechanic's yard thirty miles northeast of Eugene, and Rudy's tractor-trailer was over there by noon the following day. The shop specialized in eighteen-wheeler repair. Behind the barbed-wire fence, the place was stockpiled with salvaged and dismantled big rigs—cabs and trailers, engines and chassis of all makes and models in stacks or up on cinderblocks—some new, some old and rusting like an automotive graveyard of dismembered dinosaur bones in the sun.

The wrecker drove the Mack Cruiseliner in on two flatbeds.

The tractor was up on a hydraulic lift and Rudy stood by watching with a furrowed brow as three mechanics examined the brake lines and drums.

Sharon observed from where she sat across the yard the grim, frightened expression on her trucker-partner's face as he examined the undercarriage of the cab. Rudy was rubbing his eyes.

The loss of brakes had been no accident.

Even though she couldn't hear the conversation, Rudy's body language confirmed it.

Frank Campanella had gotten there fifteen minutes ago. She had been on the cell with her SSA for the last five hours as he'd traversed the airports. His Bureau car was parked nearby in the yard. Grave concern etched his features as he stood beside her, shifting from foot to foot in his rumpled suit. The SA could have sworn the gray hair at his temples had just gotten grayer.

"It could have been mechanical failure," she offered with little conviction.

Her superior didn't respond.

They were about to find out.

Rudy was coming over.

Running his hand through his long lanky hair, the trucker exhaled. "Brakes were cut. By somebody knew what they were doing."

Sharon shot an urgent glance to Campanella. "It was him, sir. White Knuckle knows we're onto him."

The SSA nodded, lips pursed. "Hard to argue with that." He hunkered down and eyeballed both of them. "That means you probably saw the subject or met him face to face over the last few days. Either of you two think you can ID him? Maybe one of the truckers you talked to?"

Sharon and Rudy exchanged glances—a blur of trucker faces ran through her head like sped up movie film. "We talked to a lot of truck drivers, questioned a lot of people. Hundreds. Hard to say."

"Anything suspicious about any of them you can recall?"

"A few."

"You believe you heard his voice on the CB. Anybody you talked to sound the same?"

Sharon tried to think. "Nobody comes to mind."

Rudy interjected. "Whoever cut the brakes had to have done it less than fifty miles before we lost them on the downgrade. It wasn't a clean cut in the lines—it was a partial slice so that the brake fluid would leak. I'm thinking it must have been somebody we met last night."

Sharon shook her head. "Let's assume he cut the brakes while we were in the bar. He could have been following us for days, made us two weeks ago for all we know, tailing us and waiting for his chance. There's so many black Kenworth conventionals on the road we've probably seen hundreds in the last few weeks. I didn't notice any in the parking lot last night, did you?"

Rudy shook his head.

The agent went on. "Who knows how long he could have been tailing us, waiting for his chance to strike? His pattern shows he's careful, methodical and cunning. He doesn't make mistakes. It's how he survived this long."

"He made one mistake," Rudy growled.

"What's that?" Sharon asked.

"He didn't kill us."

"This time."

They all fell silent, a chill in the air.

Sharon felt her stomach curdle.

She knew the men were thinking the same thing she was.

White Knuckle knew who she was, but she didn't know who he was.

That gave him a fearsome advantage.

And put her at a terrifying disadvantage.

Everywhere she went, every mile she rolled, he could be there, watching and waiting to strike. Maybe he was in a truck, maybe in a car, any one of millions of people on the highway. Sharon would be constantly looking over her shoulder now. Her mind flip-flopped from relief to anxiety. The uncertainty at least was gone—the needle in the haystack had been found and everything had escalated. The serial killer knew she was on his trail and it was mano a mano now. It was on.

Too bad she had been taken off the case.

Or had she?

The agent studied her SSA, whose mind was working behind his eyes—she knew that look he had when making the tough decisions. Finally, he looked at the trucker and spoke quietly and firmly. "Give us a minute."

The long hauler nodded and ambled back to his tractor up on the lift and exchanged a few words to the mechanic.

The FBI agents were alone now.

"You're operational again," Campanella stated flatly.

Sharon felt a surge of excitement as she looked up at her superior's decisive expression. He nodded down at her. "Your instincts have been right about this case all along. You're going back on the road."

"Thank you, sir." She meant it.

The SSA began to pace, thinking out loud. "That may flush him out. White Knuckle knows who you are and we can expect him to try to kill you again. You can't do this alone. I'm putting backup on with you. I'll assign four SAs to travel with you, escorting your truck."

"Won't that alert White Knuckle?"

"They'll work UC in two plainclothes cars and we'll rotate them every thirty miles. They'll tag team. Two armed agents will be no more than a few car lengths behind you at all times."

She wouldn't be alone on the road anymore.

Why didn't that reassure her?

"You've baited the fish." Campanella patted her shoulder and went over to his rental car, already on his cell snapping orders and mobilizing the operation.

Sharon got up, walked over to Rudy and took a look at the mechanic in dirty overalls working on the brakes. The trucker smiled at her. "The good news is the repair will take about three hours, then we're back on eighteen wheels."

She gave him the thumbs up.

"He put you back on the case again, didn't he?" Rudy's eyes were twinkling at her.

The SA smiled.

Sort of.

The trucker nodded back, his gaze acknowledging her mixed feelings. "Let's nail this desperado."

With that, he accompanied the mechanic back into the office, embroiled in gearjammer shop talk Sharon didn't understand.

She waited by the truck.

The CB crackled.

Without knowing what spooky intuition compelled her, Sharon Ormsby climbed up into the cab and picked up the hand mic. She held it by her lips. It was as if he knew she was there on the frequency by some monstrous telepathy, even though she hadn't uttered a word.

The gravelly twang came over the citizen band speaker.

White Knuckle's voice.

"I'll see you soon."

Her whispered reply owned a deadly tone she had never heard pass her own lips before as she spoke two words.

"Ten-four."

There was a chuckle, and the line went dead.

Chapter Thirty-Two

The Pittsfield Inspection Station in Illinois located off the exit of the eastbound westbound US 35/54 between Old Martinsburg Road and Shetland Drive was quiet at three in the morning.

Only two Illinois HP officers were on duty since the weigh station was supposed to be closed at this hour. Officer James Stamper stood outside in his hat and uniform, checking his watch. He had an hour left on the graveyard detail before the shift change and he'd be relieved by the new rookie, Kincaid.

The officer was in a foul mood because he wasn't supposed to working a double shift and the Commercial Vehicle Enforcement Facility, as it was officially known, wasn't supposed to be open around the clock. The FBI had issued a temporary directive keeping selected weigh stations around the country open at night because of a nationwide search underway for a truck driving serial killer. The idea was they might net the killer who wasn't expecting to encounter a chicken coop open at night. The stations being kept open were chosen by some random selection in a rotation that the feds in their infinite wisdom came up with. Tonight, his Illinois outpost had pulled the short straw—at least Stamper would pick up some overtime, he thought.

The highway he was sick of looking at loomed dark and still under the mercury-vapor lamps with just the occasional passing car. Far in the distance, he could see the intermittent lights of traffic on the Interstate. Otherwise, it was deserted.

The officer stood by the loudspeakers near the rows of metal scales plates on the ramp beside the weigh station bunker. One story up, the lights of the office glowed and he could see Officer Phil Buckman manning the computer console. From the way his fellow officer was rubbing his eyes, Stamper saw he was still hung over from his birthday party they'd had with the wives yesterday.

It was boring as hell out here in the lonely outpost. Just a lot of waiting around at this hour.

Come six, there would begin a steady traffic of the morning truckers coming through getting their loads checked, but for right now it was, literally, crickets.

They droned in a steady *buzz* in the trees on the warm night.

Pinprick headlights.

Stamper saw them up the road, probably coming off the 35. From their height, he made them right away for a big rig.

He stood and watched as the eighteen-wheeler slowed and signaled and eased off the road onto the entrance ramp to the weight station. It approached—big, shadowy and dirty.

A black Kenworth conventional.

Tennessee plates.

The officer immediately noticed it matched the general description of the rig the Feds wanted them to keep an eyeball out for, but that was a common make and color, so he didn't break a sweat.

A loud voice boomed electronically over the loudspeaker. "Hold it there, Driver." Buckman was on the mic.

The tractor-trailer eased obediently to a halt, engine idling, smokestacks coughing fumes. The highway patrolman smelled the hot tires. The windshield was dark and reflective of the fluorescents on the front of the building structure. Stamper made a rolling motion with his hand for the man behind the wheel to lower the driver's window.

"Next queue, Driver. Pull forward," the loudspeaker chirped.

The diesels snorted and the eighteen-wheeler lurched into motion, nosing forward slowly, wheels rotating onto the plates of the scales in front of the weigh station with a metallic clank.

"Hold it." At the behest of voice on the loudspeaker, the truck came to a standstill again in the dock.

The driver's window was still up.

The officer rapped on it with his knuckles.

The glass lowered.

Inside, behind the wheel, the silhouette of an old skeletal man wearing a trucker's cap grinned with yellowed teeth in the dashboard light.

"Evenin'," he said in a raspy drawl.

Squinting to make out the trucker's face in the shadows, Stamper didn't recognize him, which didn't mean much since he only knew his regulars by sight. Loads of truckers came through here, sometimes a thousand a week. "How are you tonight, Sir? Can I see your paperwork, please?" Stamper said with professional courteousness.

The driver just looked at him. Shook his head. "No paperwork. Just dropped off my load in Chicago. I'm empty, heading over to Wisconsin to pick up some freight."

"Kind of a waste of gas, ain't it?" Stamper asked, a little suspicious. This old guy had to be a private owner/operator because no freight company would pay for the empty mileage without some cargo being shipped—most private truckers wouldn't either in this lousy economy.

The man in the cab didn't answer, just watched.

Stamper threw a glance up at the second story offices and saw Buckman's face watching the screen of the computer connected to the scales.

He'd know soon enough if the truck was empty or not.

Upstairs, HP officer Phil Buckman looked down from the big office windows at the top of the big rig parked on the scales, watching Stamper talk to the driver, whom he couldn't see. Then he returned his gaze to the large bright computer monitor next to his coffee thermos.

The screen displayed a digital graph for five axles each that had columns with two categories for Axle Weight and Overweight. Then below that, a column for Accumulated Weight and boxes for Accept and New.

Axle weight could be up to 13,460 Lbs or 16,920 Lbs with the fifth axle. Maximum legal weight limit for trucks was 80,000 pounds. The weigh station's job was to check for overweight trucks.

The scales were showing the first through fourth axles at 7,405, 7,960, and so forth.

The truck was empty.

At that weight, there was nothing in it.

But wait a second.

The fifth axle was 11,419 pounds.

Totaled up, even with a full tank of fuel, that was about 400 pounds heavier than the maximum weight of an empty tractor with trailer.

He ran the numbers again.

"Can I see your license, permits and registration, please?"

Stamper pulled the flashlight out of his belt. It was situated beside the Ruger .357 Magnum with black rubber grip holstered there. He switched on the torch and shone it through the open driver's window at the darkened figure of the trucker inside. The beam showed a gaunt, unshaven man with sunken cheeks wearing a red checkerboard shirt blinking like a mole in the beam.

"There a problem, officer?" The man squinted.

"License, permit and registration *please*, Sir." The wary officer repeated the command. The driver shrugged and leaned down to open the glove compartment, out of sight of the highway patrolman from his lower position below the cab. Reflexively, Stamper's hand dropped to hover over the pistol in his belt. An instant later, the trucker sat back up into the flashlight beam, blinked again, and handed over the heavy bound binder that every trucker carried containing their personal identification and that of the rig.

Stamper took it, keeping his eyes on the driver's skeletal face.

The fellow matched the general age description all right.

The FBI had distributed a physical and vehicle description of a serial killer trucker who went by the handle White Knuckle to every weigh station in the continental United States. The Bureau had issued the Highway Patrol a BOLO—Be On The Lookout—for the serial killer, to report in immediately if he was spotted. White Knuckle had just been added to FBI's Ten Most Wanted List and was classified as Armed and Extremely Dangerous. However the conventional wisdom among the HP was that having the weigh stations involved was a mere formality, because a tough customer like this veteran highway killer would know which roads to take to avoid inspection.

The cop's stomach clenched because this grubby driver matched the age and regional accent of the suspect—but then so did several hundred long haulers he knew. The FBI description applied to any number of the old timers.

But his truck matched the description, too.

Keeping a poker face, the officer dropped his gaze to the binder and leafed through the paperwork. It was all in order. The truck was a registered to a private owner operator in Memphis, Tennessee named Lewis Crabtree.

And that wasn't the name on the Kentucky driver's license with the photo of the man in the truck.

It could be a counterfeit ID. Stamper had seen his share. But the papers looked to be in order so he handed them back.

Inside the cab, in the underglow of the dashboard lights, the skeletal trucker lit an unfiltered cigarette and exhaled smoke. He seemed in a hurry to get out of there from the way he was fidgeting.

The walkie-talkie on Stamper's belt gave two bursts of static. "Jim, a minute." Putting the radio to his face, the HP officer stepped out of earshot of the trucker, keeping the rig in his field of vision the whole time, and got on the walkie with his partner. "The truck is a few hundred pounds over for a rig with no load. We better check it out."

"Copy. Listen. I got a good look at the driver and his age matches the general description of the serial killer composite the Feds circulated."

"Holy shit."

"Think we oughta call it in?"

"It'll take fifteen minutes for backup to get here. What do you think?"

"I think if we cry wolf once and this is not the guy, it's going to be damn sight harder to get them to take a backup call from us seriously if we ever do get the guy."

"Sounds about right, but what if it is the guy?"

"You want to come down here? We may have a situation, maybe not." Stamper looked away from the rig for only a moment to watch the office window upstairs as Buckman got out of his seat and put his pistol in his holster, moving away from the window.

"On my way."

"Over and out."

The eighteen-wheeler sat on the scales, engine running, exhaust drifting upwards from the smokestacks on the side of the cab like gray fog against the black canopy of the starless night sky. The road running past the weigh station was devoid of traffic. The isolation of just being one of two guys with a possible serial-killer truck driver in the middle of nowhere tightened Stamper's sphincter.

The door opened and Buckman came out into the scales area, screwing on his hat. His gun was in his holster.

The HP walked up to the side of the rig.

"Sir, will you please step out of the—"

The cab was empty.

Nothing but darkness and vacant seats visible inside the open driver's window.

Both cops drew their guns immediately and braced for action, looking left and right along the cement paveway of the lot and inspection station perimeter. There was nothing—no moving shadows, no dark figures fleeing. "Show yourself, driver."

Stamper nudged his jaw and Buckman nodded, leaping out in front of the cab with his pistol out and up in a two-hand grip, seeing the ramp was deserted.

Buckman ducked around the back of the truck, covering the area. Nothing. They regrouped on the far side of the rig.

The driver was gone.

"We better call this in," Buckman said as they lowered their guard and walked to the front of the building.

A metal *creak* and the sound of hinges opening made them both anxiously raise their pistols, cocking back the hammers and yelling "Freeze!" in unison as the restroom door cracked wide open!

The lean wiry trucker on his way out was looking at them like they were nuts as he froze in place like a deer caught in the headlights. "Had to drain the snake, officers. There a problem?"

Lowering but not holstering their guns, Stamper and Buckman approached the trucker one on either side—the old man appeared genuinely shaken. "Sir, your truck is a few hundred pounds heavy even though you're saying you're empty. We're going to need to have a look inside."

Stamper thinking *and underneath,* knowing from the FBI release about the stash hold the serial killer's rig was outfitted with. A glance at his fellow officer indicated Buckman was thinking the same thing.

The grizzled, gaunt trucker nodded and shrugged a few times too many for Stamper's liking. "Do you have any weapons in your truck or on your person?" the HP asked.

"No, officer," replied the driver in a hard-to-place drawl. His eyes were shifty now, sizing up the men. "Frisk me if ya like."

"Open the back, please."

It seemed like a long walk twenty yards to the rear of the trailer with the old timer trudging slow, each move carefully considered, as he took out his keys and undid the heavy industrial padlock sealing the rear doors. "I didn't break no law," he grumbled.

Clicking on his flashlight in the hand that wasn't holding his pistol, Stamper lifted the torch as the trucker hauled open the rear doors with a rusty *creak.* The beam shone into dusty darkness, revealing fifty feet of empty steel walls and flooring in the gloom. He didn't need to go inside, because there was nothing there.

What gives, Stamper thought. "Sir, can you explain the extra weight on this truck?

Did you make any modifications to the vehicle?"

"Nope," came the flat reply.

Taking a step back, the officer peered around the side of the truck and saw the streaks of Buckman's flashlight beam shining though the dirty windows from inside the cab. Stamper kept an eye on the driver, who just stood with his shoulders slumped and head hung. Stamper recognized that body language from when he once worked as a prison guard and knew this driver had done time at some point—truck driving being one of the few jobs ex-cons could get. There was a shadow movement by the driver's door of the cab and the other HP dropped to the ground, shaking his head—nothing in the tractor.

Buckman took a few steps past the kingpin hitch on the fifth wheel and crouched down with his flashlight, shining it along the undercarriage of the trailer. The huge rubber tires and dirty mud flaps were emblazoned in the passing torch beam that sent threateningly exaggerated silhouettes of the axles, driveshaft and brake fixtures along the pavement.

The old man flinched out the corner of Stamper's eye and the cop took a step around him, lifting his gun. The smell of fear was palatable in the air now.

"Jim, we got something."

Crawling under the truck, Buckman's torch was fixed on something in the undercarriage.

"What you got?" Stamper asked.

"You better take a look at this."

Clicking the handcuff closed around the dodgy trucker's bony wrist, Stamper locked the other end of the cuff on the back bumper of the trailer. "Officer, I swear I don't know nothin' about nothin'," the old man mewled dismally. "I'm just driving my friend's truck for him. He don't tell me nothin'."

"You stay put," the HP said. Then he walked around the side of the trailer, ducked under the chassis strut between the front and back tires and crouched down next to Buckman, looking where the man was pointing his flashlight.

A narrow welded steel chamber was installed underneath the trailer, about six feet by three feet.

It might pass casual inspection, but the weigh station cops had been alerted to be on the lookout for one of these.

"Let's call it in," Buckman said.

"We better open it first. Might be somebody inside."

Stamper got the crowbar.

The lock on the trapdoor was a simple soldered metal bolt and came loose easily, the lid dropping away.

Black beckoned inside the hole.

A strong smell of plastic drifted out.

Buckman got to a crouch and stuck his head through the opening, just wide enough to fit his shoulders. He shone his flashlight down the six-foot metal enclosure.

In the beam, the stash hold was piled with stacks of what looked like bricks wrapped tightly in plastic. The HP immediately recognized another smell in the compartment.

"Marijuana. Looks like over a hundred kilos."

Buckman lowered himself out of the stash hold and looked at Stamper, and they both looked at the denim-clad legs of the truck driver, visible past the rear axles, bathed in red taillight glow.

"He ain't the guy."

Chapter Thirty-Three

Tremble turned off the rural back road where the tarmac was broken and cracked, steering the Kenworth up a gravel two-track that cut through the Smokey Mountains.

Untamed branches, twigs and thickets *thwacked* against his windshield and hood. Nobody ever came back here.

It was slow going and unsteady progress. A few hundred yards up, a barbed wire gate appeared with a sign that read, "No Trespassing." It was rusted and peppered with shotgun pellet holes.

He put the tractor in park.

Clambering out of the cab with a grunt, the wiry trucker opened the padlock on the gate and swung it wide. The familiar, rich, leafy smells of forest and damp earth filled his nostrils and gave him the sense of well-being that came from being home. After he'd driven the semi through the gate, he got out again and closed and locked it behind the trailer. Such precautions were probably not necessary, he knew—nobody came back here—but he was a careful man.

It was how he'd kept on killing these forty years.

The road narrowed and White Knuckle switched on the headlights as gathering darkness closed through the trees. The dashboard lights illuminated his face in undershadow. The big rig lumbered through the trees, knocking aside branches as it negotiated the narrow road. Up a grade. Down an incline. Nearly tipping sideways as it veered slowly around a sharp curve.

Then he was at the house.

Home sweet home.

Road weary and stiff, White Knuckle sat back in the big bucket seat for a few moments, staring through the windshield at the ramshackle front porch of the rickety farmhouse, windows black as skull sockets in the encroaching gloom of the failing light. The place went to seed years ago. Tremble had not been back for three months, and he could see the sad shape it was in.

It has been his Grandpappy's, who had built it after the Civil War.

Then it had been his Pappy's.

Now it was his.

White Knuckle had made a few home improvements to suit him he figured the prior owners wouldn't have approved of. Didn't matter, they were dead now.

It was just him.

An overpowering wave of mind-bending loneliness and dislocation engulfed him, and he had to get out of the truck.

Leaving it in the driveway, the trucker crossed the ankle deep piles of dried dead leaves piled around the side of the looming, murky, old house. All the power was off.

An antique electrical generator stood on a cinderblock, trailing cables in a nest of cords to a dynamo on the side of the place. He threw the lever and heard the machine hum on.

A huge barn was in back of the house and that was the first place White Knuckle went. Two big combination padlocks were on the steel bars securing the doors and he undid them. With a grunt, Tremble heaved open the fifteen-foot doors.

His other truck was inside.

Fifty-five feet of Peterbilt eighteen-wheeler tractor and trailer loomed in the shadows. The cab had a 600 horsepower turbo engine under the shiny black hood. The big rig was gassed up and ready to roll.

The trailer had a matching stash hold to the truck he now drove.

White Knuckle got wood just looking at his big, beautiful, second truck—always have a backup, that was his motto.

Returning to the decrepit porch, his cowboy boots creaked on the moldy boards as he went to the doorstep.

Before he did anything else, Tremble went to the pile of wood and felt behind it for the small switch he installed.

Flicked it.

Taking out his keys, he opened the two locks on the front door.

As he entered, Tremble took care to step over the trip wire that strung from the door to the trigger of the double-barrel .12 gauge, sawed-off shotgun rigged by metal braces at head level across the room. The switch he had thrown outside had already disengaged the booby trap, but there was no reason to risk an unhappy accident.

The inside of the house was dark and the air stank of death—a lingering atmosphere of bone and bad meat mixed in with the scents of old wood, dust, mold and mildew.

Blind in the near total darkness, White Knuckle nonetheless moved with a precise and unerring knowledge of his surroundings as he went about the house, disabling the other booby traps.

The unsprung bear trap in the parlor.

The bungi stakes below the trapdoor in the living room floor.

In the hall, the huge twenty-pound rock with the sharpened spikes mounted on it attached to the rope set to swing down against the face of anybody who stepped on the hidden lever.

One by one, in the close and comforting darkness, Tremble disarmed the dozen jury-rigged house protection devices he had sinisterly engineered by hand.

Only then, did he turn the light switch.

After a flicker, the bulb glowed on. It cast a warm and welcoming golden glow through the lampshade made of stretched, dried human flesh.

The illumination emblazoned the couch built out of bleached human femur and arm bones. The cushions were big and plush, straw-filled stitched balloons constructed of tanned female torso skin, breasts and beaver bush. He was looking forward to stretching out on it and watching TV in a few minutes.

Tremble went to the fridge and took a warm beer out of the six-pack inside, already feeling the cool air beginning to circulate in the unit.

He selected his favorite cup from the rack and washed out the dust in the sink. Then he poured it full of fresh brewski.

Sitting down on the couch, a dried nipple nudged his elbow as he lifted the television remote and switched on some sports. He rested his head against the stitched thigh of the couch covering where he had taken the leg off.

He took a deep, satisfying sip of beer.

Served up just as he liked it—in the hollowed-out lower half of a human skull he was using as a cup.

Home sweet home.

Chapter Thirty-Four

"I was seven," Sharon was saying.

"I remember it like it was yesterday. My mother and I were driving up to my grandmother's in Pennsylvania. Don't where my dad was, but it was just me and my mom having an outing that day and I remember how exciting it was being just me and her on the highway. The day was sunny and clear. We were laughing and playing Punch Buggy, socking each other in the arm when Volkswagen Bugs passed and all the colors of the cars seemed so pretty that day."

Rudy looked over at her with a smile as he drove the big rig. The chassis rumbling comfortingly beneath them in the traffic stream on the morning Interstate.

The agent sipped her 7-11 coffee. "Mom saw we needed gas and pulled off into the Shell gas station and convenience store. I remember the big yellow seashell. I play it over and over in my head and try to remember, but I'm pretty sure in the lot there were four passenger cars, a blue Ford and a yellow Toyota. Three big rigs were there, a red one, and two black ones. And a motorcycle. Two of the four pumps were occupied. So Mom pulled up, got out, opened the tank and started fueling. I was hungry so she took me by the hand and we walked out of the car across the parking lot into the store. I was so happy. It was so sunny. She looked down at me and smiled. It was just me and her."

Feeling the tears well up as Rudy downshifted, Sharon put her hand to her face to pretend to scratch her head so he wouldn't see she was tearing up. "She let me wander down the aisles to get a snack while she paid for the gas at the counter. There was nobody but us in the convenience store. I dawdled, deciding on which candy to get and I guess I was thinking about it for a while because when I got the candy and went up to the counter, Mom was gone."

Rudy was staring at her now, keeping one eye on the road. "What happened?" he asked.

"I never saw her again."

"You're kidding me."

Sharon gave up, wiped a tear. "The car was still at the pumps. I thought she was in the bathroom. So I stayed holding my candy by the counter. It was taking too long. One by one all the cars and trucks in the gas station pulled out onto the highway and new ones came in. Maybe an hour passed before I went out and checked the ladies room, and it was open and empty, and then all I remember was this bad feeling in my chest and crying for my mother. First, the convenience store guy came out and asked what was wrong, then the drivers of a few of the cars did, and I was crying and saying I wanted my mom but nobody had seen where she went. Finally, this Highway Patrol car pulled in and the party lights were flashing, and these nice policemen came over, and I just knew somehow that my mother was gone for good. I was inconsolable. I felt that *thing*, that darkness like a bad cloud, and it was the first time I ever felt that things were not going to be okay. I probably never got over it."

"What happened to her?" Rudy asked gently.

"Never found out. Not to this day. The cops couldn't find her. Mom just vanished from that gas station that morning and fell off the grid. The HP took me to the station, impounded the car and got the contact info for my father from the registration. He came to pick me up a few hours later. It was the first time I'd ever seen my dad cry."

"Did you ever find out—?"

"The police determined she'd been abducted. My family didn't tell me for another ten years. My dad knew the police decided Mom had been kidnapped a few years later, but until I was in college, he always told me that the cops were still looking for her, trying to give me hope, but I wished he'd told me the truth earlier. For all those years, I held out hope I'd find her, save her, every time we drove on the highway. I looked and checked, trying to pick her face out in every passing car and gas station, thinking she was out there somewhere. Guess I saw the sad look in my dad's eyes and should have known he was just trying to protect me from the truth. But he was so kind, always coming up with stories about where mom really was with me, a game we played for years, where she was always in a nice place. One day, dad was picking me up at college during spring break, we sat down in my dorm room, and he finally told me the truth."

Sharon sipped her coffee thoughtfully. Cars and trucks whizzed passed on the other side of the median out the wraparound windshield. In the high cab of the tractor, it was like they were floating over the other traffic, above it all, omnipotent.

"I remember that day she disappeared at the gas station from every angle, think about it every day, imagining that day when indescribable terror entered my mother's life. Maybe she was watching as they took her away, watching me shrink away, out of her grasp as they took her probably in one of those cars and trucks I saw there. Too bad I didn't get the license plates because from that day on, from when I was five, I memorize the license plates of every vehicle I can every place I go. Anyway..." She trailed off. Blew on her coffee. Sipped.

"The beautiful face of the mother I loved became a random faceless victim for a highway nutjob."

"Is that why you do this job?"

"No, the Bureau just assigned me to HSK. And here we are. Guess it's the age old question about whether you choose the job or the job chooses you."

Food for thought.

They drove the next hundred miles in silence and it was fifteen minutes before Sharon turned on the radio and dialed in a country station.

It was the same dream, but she is remembering new details.

The yellow seashell gas station—eggshell-blue sky through the window of the convenience store—rows of beef jerky and candy and chips and pretzels passing by her in slow motion as she walks down the aisle—the empty place by the counter where her mother should be but isn't—the little girl looking out the window—

The big truck pulling out—

Past the other cars driving in.

Big and black and covered with soot and she barely notices it or the truck driver looking out the driver's window at her and catching her eye, his face thin, wrinkled like beef jerky, with those gray eyes—and he smiles at her, right at her, which the child thinks is strange because he doesn't even know her and his teeth are black with that stuff those truckers chew, which she thinks is yucky and he tips his hat and then he is gone up the road—and she has never forgotten this, it is just she hadn't remembered it for some reason.

But she has seen that trucker's face again recently—older yet familiar.

And what she remembers next rips her straight of the dream, sledgehammering her wide awake into present day reality.

Letters on the side of the truck.

She hadn't seen all of the letters, just one word...

"WHITE—"

The double sleeper of the Mack Cruiseliner cab was air-conditioned and cool, but Sharon was bathed in perspiration as she sat gasping on the upper bunk in the darkness. The rig was parked for the night at a rest stop. The dream had wakened her violently.

"Sharon, you okay?" Rudy stirred in the lower bunk.

"I think he killed my mother. I think it was him."

Rudy's voice was groggy with sleep. "You think this why?"

"I just know."

"You know this how?"

Sharon was still shaking in the close confines of the truck cab bunk, hugging herself. The face of Rudy's watch glowed on his wrist in darkness below, illuminating the worry on the trucker's face as he watched her. She took a deep breath. "I just remembered when I was kid I saw his truck. I saw the words 'White Knuckle' on the side. Or the letters that spelled 'White,' I saw that at least."

"A memory from when you were five. That's thin. And how does it make a difference? You know who we're after. How does it change anything?"

"It changes everything."

The agent picked up the CB microphone and lifted it to her lips. "Breaker breaker, this here is Hot Patootie putting the hammer down."

It took less than an hour for the monster to modulate.

"This is White Knuckle. You got a copy on me, Hot Patootie? Come back."

The disembodied actual voice of the mass murderer on the airwaves sent a shock wave through the agent's system. She pressed the mic to her lips. "Copy. This is Hot Patootie. For sure, for sure."

A twangy chuckle. "Hi, Darlin'. Knew I'd catch you on the flip flop."

"Copy that. Get your ears on me, suicide jockey. I'm gonna put you in a ditch, White Knuckle."

"Not if I blow your doors off first. This here's my road."

"And my ass is on it." Sharon popped bubble gum.

"Mine too. Fact is, might be I'm those headlights you see in your rearviews right now. Every truck you see out there, just this very minute, you're thinkin' that might be the Knuckle. I got your front door and back door. The road is dangerous, girl; ain't no place for no rookie. You got your ears on me good?"

"Negatory, White Knuckle. It's you who's running out of road. I'm dying for your company. Whadya say let's us meet up and have us a cup of hundred mile coffee, White Knuckle. Come back."

"Copy that, Hot Patootie. I'm around. I might be in Michigan. Might be on a stretch just outside of Savannah. Might be I'm up in Alaska. And I might be right behind you."

With Rudy double-clutching and fighting the gears, Sharon dropped the question, abandoning the CB lingo. "How many?"

"How many what?"

"I said, how many?"

There was a burst of static crackle on the radio while, in his warped head, Tremble figured out the actual number of his victims. "I lost count. Upwards of five hundred by now, I reckon." He sounded very pleased with himself.

"You're a monster."

"I am King of the Road."

"I want to ask you a question. Come back."

"Shoot."

"Why did you come after us, let us get on your tail? You know who we are and that it's just a matter of time before we put you in a ditch. Thirty years you've kept below radar."

"Forty," he corrected her edgily.

"Okay, forty, then you got stupid. So why now?"

"Why, why, why...why what?"

"Why did you mix it up with me?"

There was a long pause on the CB.

Then a sigh.

White Knuckle's voice became subdued and thoughtful. "Well, y'know, I like the sport. Was planning on retiring, but you being out there, this thing we have, it put some lead in my pencil. It's been boring and kind of lonely the last few years, even though I like my job. Been in a rut. You've been fresh blood. Given me a second wind."

"You should have stayed lost."

His response was a feral snarl. "Speed on, sister. Hell ain't half full."

She hung up the mic.

Chapter Thirty-Five

PARTIAL TRANSCRIPT OF JUPITER HOLLOW POLICE DEPARTMENT INTERROGATION OF BURGLARY SUSPECT LUCAS BROWN:

DETECTIVES: STATE YOUR NAME FOR THE RECORD.

BROWN: LUCAS BROWN.

DETECTIVES: YOUR AGE IS SEVENTEEN, IS THAT CORRECT?

BROWN: YES SIR.

DETECTIVES: TELL US WHAT HAPPENED THIS MORNING.

BROWN: (SOBS).

DETECTIVES: TAKE YOUR TIME.

BROWN: MY FRIEND FREDDY—HE—FREDDY AND ME, WE KNEW ABOUT THE HOUSE. WE GREW UP—(SOBS)—I'M OKAY. WE GREW UP NEAR JUPITER HOLLOW OVER IN GREEN WATER AND THAT PLACE EVERYBODY KNOWS USED TO BE MOONSHINER'S TERRITORY BACK IN THE DAY. IT'S ALL RUNDOWN AND NOBODY GOES THERE. WHY WOULD THEY? IT'S A DUMP. THERE'S NOTHING TO STEAL.

DETECTIVES: YOU WERE ARRESTED TODAY FOR BREAKING AND ENTERING ON THE PROPERTY.

BROWN: I KNOW. THAT'S WHY I TURNED MYSELF IN. I CAME TO GET

HELP FOR FREDDY—BUT—IT GOT TO BE TOO LATE.

DETECTIVES: WHEN DID YOU FIRST SEE THE TRUCK?

BROWN: IT WAS PARKED OUT BACK OF THE HOUSE. BUT IT DIDN'T LOOK LIKE ANYBODY WAS HOME. I TOLD FREDDY IT WASN'T A GOOD IDEA. BEING THERE LIKE—IN CASE, I MEAN—THE GUY WAS THERE, Y'KNOW. THAT'S WHEN FREDDY BROKE THE BACK WINDOW AND WENT IN. I TRIED TO STOP HIM.

DETECTIVES: WHAT HAPPENED THEN?

BROWN: AS SOON AS HE WAS INSIDE I HEARD THIS LOUD SOUND LIKE BREAKING BONES AND THEN FREDDY WAS SCREAMING AND HE DIDN'T STOP SCREAMING. IT WAS SOME KIND OF BOOBY TRAP. IT WAS SO HORRIBLE. WHAT HAPPENED TO HIM HAD TO BE, LIKE, REALLY BAD. I NEVER HEARD NOBODY EVER SCREAM LIKE THAT BEFORE.

DETECTIVE: DID YOU TRY TO HELP HIM?

BROWN: I RAN—(SOBS)-I FUCKING RAN, MAN. AND I CAME HERE TO REPORT IT TO THE COPS.

Chapter Thirty-Six

Sharon Ormsby hunkered in the bushes in her Kevlar bulletproof vest, holding her M5 submachine gun close to her face. She looked around at the team of ten FBI SWAT officers wearing gray fatigue jumpsuits under black body armor vests in their helmets and goggles, clenching M5 submachine guns behind the trees and foliage surrounding the house. It was an army, but they weren't taking any chances with this particular suspect.

White Knuckle's house was quiet, too quiet. The ramshackle hillbilly hovel sat still in the shade of the afternoon-dappled oaks and pines.

The call from the Jupiter Hollow Police Department to HSK had come in three hours ago. A big rig with a stash hold matching the description on VICAP of the one belonging to White Knuckle was found on the property, although it was a Peterbilt not a Kenworth. The vehicle had been discovered by local police responding to a report of a burglary related fatality on the property. Campanella had immediately used his federal authority to order the local cops to stand down until he had deployed an FBI SWAT team from the Knoxville field office. It took an hour to chopper the unit to Jupiter Hollow and during that time, Campanella had Sharon picked up by helicopter near Atlanta to join the strike team—her knowledge of White Knuckle's background was considered indispensable. She climbed into the siege armor in the bay of the chopper as it lifted off, watching Rudy Dykstra waving to her in front of his tractor-trailer pulled in the supermarket parking lot.

It was almost over—maybe.

They were minutes away from taking down White Knuckle—if he was home.

Her orders were to let the first team move in and keep to their flank.

The Peterbilt sat in the barn. All indications were that White Knuckle would be inside the house. If he was, the tactical unit would neutralize him.

Right now, it was preternaturally quiet as the SWAT team moved into position, glints of black armor and plastic reflections advancing through the bushes.

She saw the hand signal.

The three tactical officers came in on good lines of approach to the door, submachine guns shouldered. They took positions on the porch on either side of the doorway.

The first SWAT commando kicked the door in with a splintering crash, raising his M5.

The sudden blast was frighteningly loud, shattering the silence and scattering birds from the overhead branches. The officer took twin barrels of shotgun pellets in the chest and goggles, whiplashing his helmeted head back and catapulting him off the porch, where he lay on the ground, writhing. His helmet was scarred and cracked and it was hard to tell if the pellets had reached his face, but he was hurting.

The second tactical officer lobbed a tear gas canister through the open doorway as the third one leaped around the edge of the black opening and fired a string of twenty rounds inside in rapid-fire succession.

No shots were returned, and Sharon held her breath.

Maybe they got him.

Tear gas haze curled like dragon mist through the doorway. Three SWAT members rushed to the fallen officer and dragged him out of harm's way.

"GO, GO!"

Nine heavily armed and armored cops trundled onto the porch and shouldered through the front door into the fog.

Sharon waited until they were all inside. Adjusting her helmet and goggles, she sprinted through the open door and entered an eerily surreal environment. Tear gas spritzing from a can on the floor filled the place with gray-white mist. Out of the haze, she saw the hulking silhouettes of the tactical squad and their weapons. Strange objects half seen loomed out of the miasma, but they weren't right.

"CLEAR!" Came a gruff voice somewhere nearby.

She saw then why the furniture wasn't right.

It was made from people.

Human remains.

Ed Gein post-modern style.

Oh my God. The words swam around her head. *Oh my God. OhmiGod.* She was dizzy with horror.

There was something tall and narrow right beside the SA and what it was made of looked weird and grotesquely familiar. The object beside her was a coat rack constructed of a human spinal cord and hip sockets. A trucker's cap rested on the grinning skull at its apex. Sharon recoiled in repulsion, knocking it over, and the spinal cord shattered and exploded like flying poker chips as it struck the carpet.

The noxious tear gas fog was thick and vaporous, reducing visibility to nil. It stung her eyes, even behind the goggles. She swept her gun back and forth, the room a clamor of heavy boots trampling old floorboards while the tactical unit invaded the mysterious recesses of the house. Flashlight beams carved through the soup like crisscrossing lasers, fixed beside machine gun barrels held in gloved hands.

"KITCHEN CLEAR!"

Then came a *snap.*

A *swish.*

A *wet thud.*

And then the awful screaming.

Swallowing her fear, Sharon rushed with her gun out after the black Kevlar reinforced bodies toward the source of the terrible noise. She felt her heart pounding out of her chest.

"THIS WHOLE PLACE IS BOOBY TRAPPED! EXERCISE EXTREME CAUTION! LOOK FOR TRIP WIRES!" The commander was barking orders, his voice sounding strained, behind her.

She approached a figure writhing on the ground, a hideous jury-rigged device with sharp spikes on a sprung platform jammed in his legs. He didn't stop screaming as some of his fellow offers tried to pry the bungi stakes out of the meat and bone that was horribly visible. Blood was everywhere.

The whole FBI SWAT unit had stopped dead in their tracks.

They stood like statues in the fog, scared to move.

"THIS WHOLE PLACE IS A DEATH TRAP!" the commander roared. "EVERYONE, WATCH WHERE YOU STEP! WE DON'T KNOW WHAT ELSE HE'S GOT RIGGED HERE."

So they all remained frozen—Sharon with them—realizing that they were trapped in a place filled with insane devices of death and that the tables had been fearsomely turned.

"GET SOME LIGHT IN HERE!" There was the sound of shattering glass from several places at once and then daylight streamed in through the broken windows showing the tactical officers using the butts of their weapons in their gloved hands to break them.

The tear gas was already starting to dissipate, and the recesses of the house and what it contained were becoming visible.

By now, the paralyzed SWAT team could see the furniture constructed of human bones and dried flesh and were petrified by the dreadful décor.

"Found one!" shouted a commando in a side room. Sharon turned to see him throw a chair into a huge, rusted bear trap. The jaws of the device sprang and slammed shut, shattering the legs of the chair.

Thereafter, the tactical unit moved through the house with great care, step by step, inch by inch.

And they found the traps that Roy Tremble had set.

Tripwires were located.

The ball with the spikes on the rope in the hallway was disabled.

The crossbow aimed at the bedroom door was dismantled. Inside, Sharon discovered that the mattress of human skin was covered with stitched female breasts and the frame built of yellowed skeletons—thinking she would never be able to sleep in a bed again.

By now the SA could hear ambulance sirens approaching outside. They were followed by the *whop whop* of rotor blades outside that announced the Medivac helicopters flying in to transport the wounded FBI SWAT members to the hospital. Sharon looked around and saw the commander on the walkie-talkie barking instructions.

A half hour later, the door was found that led to the cellar.

Four tactical offers went first, standing in front of a gathered throng of other SWAT team commandos in body armor. Sharon squeezed in between them, ignoring her directive to hang back. She felt a lurching sense in her gut that something important was down in the basement—it was like a rat running around a wheel in her stomach.

"On three. One, two, three."

The basement door was kicked in.

A forest of gun barrels pointed into the dank darkness.

There was silence. This doorway wasn't booby trapped, at least.

Flashlights shone down into the gloomy recesses of the cellar, beams crisscrossing. She craned her neck to see better, keeping her M5 submachine gun at the ready. The light illuminated a creaky wooden staircase of about twenty-five steps leading down to a dirt floor at the base. There was a glint of metallic reflection on a water boiler they could just see the edge of, from where they stood.

"FBI! COME OUT WITH YOUR HANDS UP!"

No response.

"Single file formation. Nice and slow. Watch for trip wires."

The first tactical officer began his cautious and deliberate descent—Sharon could smell his fear and see the sweat gleaming on the other faces behind the black helmets and goggles around her. It was so quiet she could hear every creak of the point man's boots on the old wooden steps as he moved a fraction of an inch down the stairs, taking them one at a time, his automatic weapon at his shoulder.

The commando reached the basement floor, making a quick sweep with his M5 and the flashlight fixed to the barrel. They all held their breath.

"CLEAR!" he yelled.

Sharon wasn't so sure about that.

The SWAT unit descended the steps to the basement, close behind one another. Sharon went last.

When she entered the cellar, the agent knew right away something was wrong.

The four tactical officers split off in different directions, ducking under the low, old ceiling beams, decrepit roof boards, and torn asbestos insulation. Rats scuttled out of their path, red eyes gleaming. There was a workbench and tools in one corner. The SA adjusted her flashlight as she approached a dark and disjointed corner of the deep cellar. Another wall was laden with taxidermist tanning equipment and supplies she knew were used to skin human beings.

When the agent saw the empty meat hooks and manacles hung from a bolted steel rack on the roof, her bowels began to clench.

Something was beyond there—another corner of the basement at the far edge of the cellar. And something was in it.

Sharon lifted her flashlight to reveal what was on the wall.

The unspeakable horror of what the SA beheld was so incapacitating that sobs and sickness burst from her throat, and as Sharon dropped to her knees gagging and puking into the inside of her vomit-splattered helmet, she just managed to choke out the words. "OVER HERE!"

There was a thumping of boots on the earthen floor as the four SWAT tactical officers rushed over. The air went bright as explosions of flashlight beams ignited the darkness and emblazoned the corner with light.

"Jesus wept." A man's voice behind her, cracked with emotion.

There must have been over two hundred of the bushy pelts mounted on the wall like scalps.

The female human flesh, now dried, were patches carved from below the navel, around the inside the inner thigh to the apex between the legs under the buttocks and below the anus. Some of the genitalia were thick as a garden with pubic hair, some neatly trimmed, some shaved. The vulvas of all shapes and varieties were stretched open with pins like screaming lips.

White Knuckle kept his victims' private parts as trophies.

Sharon staggered to her feet, legs unsteady, and forced herself to open her eyes, to somehow compartmentalize.

It was lucky she did.

Because she was the first to spot the stacks of clay-like bricks with wires trailing out rigged to a Claymore landmine.

Enough C4 explosive to blow the place higher into the sky than Dorothy's house in *The Wizard of Oz.*

"*Bomb,*" she said, voice taut with fear as she pointed to the charges.

Now everyone saw it.

The commander spoke with a firm even tone. "Everyone freeze. Do not move. The house is heavily wired with explosive and we don't know where the detonators are. I want everyone in this basement to retrace their steps, slowly, directly to the staircase and get out of the house. On my go. Nice and easy. Go."

And so the FBI SWAT team began their careful retreat, one foot in front of the other, flashlights sweeping the darkness for trip wires or other types of triggers. Sharon felt surprisingly safe in the company of these tough and capable agents. God, she wanted out of this house, this hell.

She took a last look at the horrific trophies on the wall.

They were reclaimed by darkness as she moved away.

It was a snapshot she would keep with her all her days.

It was the image she would hold in her skull when she blew White Knuckle's head clean off.

As the small army backed out of the cellar, The commander got on the walkie-talkie. "Code red. All personnel are to get out of the house now. The place is wired with explosive. It's a trap. I repeat, all personnel out of the house now."

The SA could hear the running footsteps above her and shouting voices outside.

They were at the stairs.

The commander stayed below as he watched his team hurry up the steps and into the hallway corridor.

When she was on the ground floor, Sharon started to feel a little safer. She was right behind the quick stepping body armor of the other members of the tactical unit as they approached the daylight streaming through the doorway and then she was outside in the open air, the trees high above her, the vomit stench inside her nose replaced by fresh oxygen, running now as fast as her feet would carry her away from the house.

Then she heard the commander's voice back in the house on the walkie-talkie. Two words, short and sweet.

"Aw, nuts."

The *click* was audible.

The gigantic explosion erased most of the yard and what was in it.

The house blew sky-high into smithereens of flying debris in fulgurations of fire clouds, flattening tall trees and turning the blast radius into scorched earth as a towering plume of ugly black smoke pillared into the atmosphere.

When Sharon came to on her back in the bushes, the house was gone, a huge smoking crater in the ground like a meteor hit, flames were everywhere and FBI tactical unit members were urgently running to and fro, but it was so quiet it struck her as odd— peaceful, even.

It wasn't until she saw the alarmed face of the SWAT sergeant behind his goggles screaming into her own with no sound coming out of his mouth that she realized she was deaf.

Chapter Thirty-Seven

From: Frank.Campanella@ic.fbi.gov
Re: White Knuckle investigation.
To: Michael.Robertson@ic.fbi.gov

Agent Ormsby suffered a complete hearing loss due to her close proximity to the explosion. Doctors say there is no permanent damage to her eardrums and that she should recover some of her faculties in several days and the rest in a few weeks. Because she incurred no other injuries, she remains in the field traveling with truck driver Rudy Dykstra on reduced duties. We are in steady contact with Dykstra who reports her condition is satisfactory.

Chapter Thirty-Eight

Sharon felt the tap on her shoulder and turned to see Rudy's mouth moving silently. He was asking if she was hungry. She nodded despondently.

She sat limply in the comfortable bucket seat of the cab in a soundless bubble.

Visual stimuli unanchored by sound passed by the familiar wraparound windshield of the big truck as it slid down the Interstate—gas stations, tailgates, exit off-ramps.

A tractor-trailer hurtled past on her right and she jumped, the sheer steel wall surprising her because she couldn't hear it right next to her.

When she reflexively looked over to Rudy sitting behind the wheel he was looking at her, concerned. He mouthed it was OK.

No, it definitely wasn't.

It was so strange and unnerving not hearing anything.

The agent felt so helpless and the fear was palatable.

She needed all her senses if she was going to be able to do her job again.

It wasn't going to last, the temporary deafness. That's what the doctors said.

But it had been a week now. Nothing had improved.

The blast had blown out her eardrums, she knew it.

There was blood on her pillow last night, leaking from her eardrum.

Rudy was taking care of her. Trying to anyway. She knew she was a pill.

He was very gentle and patient. Sharon was relying on him, against her better judgment, because she had always been self-sufficient and now she wasn't.

It will come back—I will hear again.

A mantra repeated over and over to herself.

Everything hurt.

Her brain hurt.

Another titanic behemoth of an eighteen-wheeler unannounced by the unheard sound of its diesels rushed past her passenger window and overtook them and her stomach tightened again, jumpy.

What if that big rig was *him?*

She couldn't hear it if White Knuckle came up behind her now.

This was so bad.

She shouldn't be on the road.

The Mack Cruiseliner eased into the 76 Truck Stop off I-10 in an oasis of silence for Sharon. She felt the familiar vibrations of the suspension as the rig pulled to a stop after backing in between several other parked rigs. Her ass felt like they were driving by Braille.

It had started to rain and the windshield wipers were on, blades slashing splashes of water outside the glass that refracted moving jewels of red taillights and white headlights in the parking lot into blurry smears of moist light that had a lulling effect on her.

She was tired.

Looking over at Rudy, Sharon saw the bear of a man switching off the engine. Then he turned the key to keep the power on in the cab, so the heater and wipers stayed on. Grinning warmly at her and showing those cracked teeth of his, he gestured with his hands that he was going to grab some snacks for the road from the food mart. She nodded and smiled.

The trucker tugged on his cap, opened the driver-side door and slipped out into the wet darkness, closing the door after him.

The agent was alone in the cozy cab of the tractor filled with body warmth. Weary from worrying, she snuggled back in the seat, enjoying the comfort of the cockpit. Her muscles were stiff. Laying her head back, Sharon rested her eyes on the steady metronome beat of the windshield wipers.

Back and forth, back and forth.

Minutes passed.

The blooming pools of headlights and taillights filling the rainy wiper-swept windshield were hypnotizing, tranquil and soothing—a sedative. Beyond the rainy glass, the night sky was black as velvet and it made her sleepy.

It felt like she had been on this road forever.

There was no sound, none at all.

Her eyes grew heavy, spellbound by the action of the windshield wipers, and her eyelids closed. The occasional headlights passed across her lids, and then it was dark again.

Then her eyes sensed something had changed.

There were blinking red lights in her field of vision.

Everywhere.

Flashing pulsing red flares, rushing past.

She blinked groggily, still half awake, to see the windshield was a blazing wet galaxy of emergency lights from police and paramedic vehicles.

It was like a movie where the sound is off and there should be sirens but there weren't—she was deaf.

Blurry silhouettes of people were milling past the cab, half-glimpsed through dripping windows in a chaos of frantic activity.

Immediately, Sharon knew something was very wrong.

Snapping awake, she shouldered open her passenger door and felt the cold rain and night air punch her in the face. Not bothering to pull on her jacket, she clambered down the ladder onto the asphalt, looking around in growing alarm at the six highway patrol cars with cherrytops pulsing against the rain slick tarmac in a reflection of shiny red flares. An ambulance was parked fifteen feet from the truck. The cops had their guns drawn, holding back a gathering crowd of truck drivers staring in horror at something on the other side of the cab.

Terror choking in her throat, Sharon pushed through the people, whipping out her wallet and badging the policemen who tried to hold her back as she shoved through them. She saw the unrecognizable pile of squashed meat on the pavement with the two huge truck tire tread marks indented in the gory mess of crushed bones and guts and the STP cap she recognized as Rudy's lying in a vast lake of blood mixing with water.

And then Sharon felt but couldn't hear herself screaming, felt her vocal cords tearing from the exertion but no sound coming out and the world was swimming sickeningly as the police rushed toward her and everything went black as she staggered away before she fainted.

Her vision swam. Her stomach lurched. She lost track of direction as she stumbled between the rows of parked eighteen-wheelers until she fell against one tractor, buckled over, and puked her guts onto the asphalt.

After Sharon had vomited everything, she stood up and was facing a highly reflective chromium smokestack on the side of a semi. Her own traumatized, bloodless image stared back at her, distorted as a funhouse mirror in the curvature of the mirrored pipe.

The SA caught a glimpse of eyes in the chrome 'stack but remembered her eyes were brown and the eyes looking at her were gray.

Roy Tremble leapt forward in the skewed mirror reflection. His twisted, triumphant face lunged out of the darkness in the chromium smokestack of his black Kenworth truck as the soaking rag stinking of chloroform was smeared with fearsome strength over Sharon's mouth and she grabbed those big hands but it was over very quickly.

Chapter Thirty-Nine

The blast site was crawling with ERTs.

In the crisp pre-dawn air, Frank Campanella wandered through the wreckage of White Knuckle's house—piles of rubble scattered five hundred feet in every direction. Charred and blackened remains of the basement foundation lay in a ragged crater in the woods. His shoes crunched on burnt wood and incinerated debris as he wandered the site.

The SSA looked around him at the thirty diligent FBI Emergency Response Team Special Agents and other personnel sifting through the wreckage, diligently and meticulously combing the area for any physical evidence that could later be analyzed for clues.

Just because the place had been blown to smithereens did not mean that crucial tiny or even microscopic evidence could not be extracted from the debris.

Bone, hair and teeth fragments could be used to identify victims through Mitichondrial DNA.

Household items often yielded latent fingerprints—possibly the suspect's—by fuming with Cyanoacrylate.

Truck parts might be located with the confidential vehicle identification number, or CVIN, that was known only to the manufacturer and the FBI and was generally stamped on the vehicle's chassis in an obscure place—that was how the Oklahoma City and 1993 World Trade Center bombers had been tracked down and ultimately apprehended.

This was already a major evidence recovery operation underway. The ERTs swarmed like ants on a mound in a sea of white jumpsuits with the black stenciled letters "FBI" on the back, wearing yellow rubber boots and blue caps.

They were all volunteers whose job it was to collect, identify, manage and preserve the evidence at the crime scene. They were a diverse group who came from field offices for white collar and government fraud squads, foreign counterintelligence squads, drug squads, violent crimes squads and other squads. Each had been specially trained as ERTs in an intensive 80-hour program in addition to their regular duties.

The team was assigned with support personnel that included the division's photographer and evidence control technicians.

Several photographers snapped digital photos of every square inch of the blast site.

Other ERTs were packaging evidence in plastic bags.

Campanella watched two middle-aged SA forensic anthropologists kneeling on a black rubber tarp over some blackened skeletal remains, in deep discussion with an evidence collection specialist the SSA did not know.

The bones would be taken back to the new crime lab in Quantico for analysis, the mtDNA recovered, and the bodies hopefully identified. Despite the chaos in the wake of the explosion, the ERTs proceeded with the recovery as if they were at an archeological dig to ensure no evidence was further disturbed before it was documented and photographed.

A few local Jupiter Hollow PD hung back by the yellow crime scene tape strung around the perimeter, looking confused and letting the ERTs do their work.

Campanella knew people would be here awhile—more than a week. The evidence recovery at the literal mountains of Twin Tower rubble at Ground Zero after 9/11 made this scene look like a cakewalk. He remembered because he was there.

Stretching his neck, Campanella looked up at the trees—blackened, leafless, burned husks for hundreds of feet in all directions. Some were still wet from the fire department hoses that put out the fires when some of the birches were set ablaze by the explosion. Right now, it looked to the SSA like an evil fairy tale forest of charred skeletons and bones, but that wasn't what made him uneasy.

He knew what was wrong.

The silence. It was absolute.

There were no birds, no insects, nothing.

They were staying away, as if all the wildlife knew this was a bad place and evil was present.

It was.

Campanella tried to focus but was distracted.

That's when his cell phone rang.

Right after he hung up after being briefed on Sharon, the SSA wept for the first time in twenty years.

Chapter Forty

Everything hurt.

Sharon Ormsby didn't want to open her eyes.

Better it was all just black, better she didn't see it.

The pain was awful.

Her body was trammeled by metal manacles on her wrists and ankles that amplified the shock and vibration.

Her hearing had partially returned.

It was a mixed blessing.

Keeping her eyes clenched shut, the agent spared herself the view for the moment and processed the ultimate nightmare of her situation in increments by using her ears—the only way she could deal. Her arms and legs were tightly shackled and she knew she was trapped. So she listened. The rumbling surges of the diesel engines were close by, smothered behind thick metal and echoing very loudly around the enclosure she was in. Her cuffs jerked and heaved as the suspension shook and she knew she was in a truck.

His truck.

Her arms and legs were wet, warm.

Her own blood she knew.

The SA felt the gashes on her face and body—from the coming and going of the pain, she knew she was losing a lot of blood and going into shock. The needle prick in her arm must be saline, keeping her conscious.

Use your senses, your nose, she commanded herself. The place reeked of dried, rotten blood under a gorge-rising stench of industrial bleach.

Open your eyes.

Not yet.

Man up, bitch.

And she opened her eyes, bracing for the horror show of what she beheld.

But all Sharon saw was black.

The agent knew she was held captive in a stash hold under his big rig, probably in the trailer, since the roar of the engines was behind her head. This was where countless other victims died. The belly of the beast. As she hung manacled in the torture chamber, the SA heard the abrasive grind of shifting gears, then the blast of a horn, all muffled by the heavy steel walls between her and the tractor.

A static squawk.

"Howdy, Ma'am."

Her eyes spotted the source of the sound, a tinny speaker above her head, concealed in the blackness.

"Y'all can start screaming any old time now."

The cocksucker had a two-way radio to the cab.

"Fuck you," Sharon whispered.

"Now that ain't very nice, lady."

Her blood pressure spiked as she spoke into the stygian gloom. "You can hear me?"

"'Course I can hear ya. Can see ya too. Got me a fancy old night vision camera rig mounted yonder wall feeds right into muh cab. You bleed real good, but don't y'worry none, you ain't gonna die anytime soon, though you'll wish you done by the time we cross the Dakotas."

"I'm an FBI Special Agent, asshole." Lips dry.

"Know that. Found your badge. Nice tits for an G-gal."

"The Bureau is tracking me. They're closing in on you right now. Best thing you can do for yourself is pull over, give yourself up, and come quietly."

A cackle of laughter over the speaker in the dark.

"You hear me?" Sharon hissed. "Turn yourself in."

"Now let me ask ya. What you figure the chance of that is?"

"You're going to die, you lousy fuck!" She screamed. Falling apart. *Pull it together.*

"I reckon. Every man has his time. But not today."

"I know who you are. We know who you are. We have your truck CVIN. We have your plates."

"Darlin', I know that. My name is Roy Tremble. I know who you are, too, Hot Patootie, aka Sharon Ormsby. I've enjoyed our game, but the thing is, Sweet Ass, this IS MY ROAD!"

White Knuckle's voice became hideously vicious over the speaker, breaking apart in a feedback distortion that reverbed off the metal walls of Sharon's rolling coffin and made her wince in fright. She had lost a lot of blood and her nerves were in tatters. *Be strong. Hold tight.*

"THIS IS MY FUCKING ROAD, YOU FUCKING CUNT, AND IT'S BEEN MY ROAD FOR FORTY YEARS AND NOTHING AND NOBODY GETS IN MY WAY, LEAST WAYS SOME BADGED GASH! I AM WHITE KNUCKLE AND I AM GOING TO LEAVE LITTLE BITTY PIECES OF YOU IN FIFTY STATES!"

She heard lickspittle. He caught his breath. "Just so you and me got that straight."

The truck suddenly veered, and she heard the clanking of the kingpin on the trailer hitch and then the blasting horn as the eighteen-wheeler swerved into position.

Make your mind work.

He's tired.

Driving all over the road.

He's old.

He hasn't slept.

And that's his weak spot.

Sharon's brain became a machine as she fixed on her captor, figuring him out, collating what she heard, felt. Detecting the speed freak babble in his voice, she knew he was flying on pharmaceuticals. He had a bad case of White Line Fever. It might make him careless.

Think, girl.

The stash hold he had her captive in must have a hatch. He had to have some way to put her in there. If he could put her in, she could get out. But it must be locked, probably from the outside. Yet she didn't know that. Had to get loose of these bonds.

It took Sharon a few moments to work up a mouthful of saliva what with her parched dry palate and tongue. Turning her head to the left, she tugged on that wrist and targeted the position of the manacle in the gloom. It was tight, too tight to tug her hand out without some lubricant.

She spat.

Splattered her wrist with a wet glob of saliva.

Rotating her forearm back and forth, the agent worked the saliva under the manacle over her wrist.

Then she pulled. Very hard.

The sharp edge of the metal cuff sheared off a layer of skin and blood began to flow.

Combined with the spit, the blood greased her hand sufficiently so that with another savage, flesh-scraping pull, Sharon yanked her hand out of the manacle.

Bringing her left hand to her mouth, the SA spat again and again into her palm. When it had enough saliva in it, she swung her left arm over her right shoulder and smeared the spit on her right wrist around the other manacle.

That hand came out easier, with less blood spilt.

Her arms were free.

Reaching behind her, the agent's fingers touched the small camera fixed on the wall and located the optic cable feeding out of it. A quick, hard pull and the cable was disconnected—White Knuckle's TV monitor was now blind and he couldn't see her.

"What the fuck's goin' on back there?" The monster's gravelly voice snarled over the speakers. "Goddamn camera. Cheap Chinese piece of shit. Gotta spring for a new one."

Sharon could hear him in the cab banging in frustration on his TV monitor over the two-way. A string of filthy expletives followed.

Good, dumb fuck figures it's a camera malfunction and doesn't know what I'm doing.

Her legs were harder to free because she couldn't sit up and was having a tough time producing any more spit. By the time she had squirmed and squeezed and stretched her arms out of their shoulder sockets, reaching down far enough to lubricate her ankles with saliva and rip a few ounces of skin off her bare feet, pulling them loose of the metal cuffs, her muscles were absolutely screaming.

But her arms and legs were unshackled.

Sharon felt her way around the sides and roof of the cage.

It was about four feet wide by four feet high by seven feet long, little more spacious than a coffin. From the moist, drying meat her fingers and palms touched in the utter blackness, the agent knew this had served as a rolling steel crypt for many before her.

Under her legs, she felt the trapdoor.

It rattled on its hinges.

Her calves felt the plate shift under her pants, and she guessed it wasn't padlocked, just held closed by a latch.

That was good.

A latch she could break.

And she started kicking, hard as she could.

The trapdoor didn't give, not an inch.

White Knuckle's sick laughter echoed through the stash hold, taunting her.

Kicking again and again, Sharon drove her already bloody heels against the hinged steel plate on the floor, hammering her bones.

Come on, give you mother, you hear me, give!

The hatch fell, swung away.

Chapter Forty-One

A view of the hard blacktop tarmac hurtling past a few feet below was revealed in the daylight bursting into the torture chamber. The open lid struck the asphalt and dragged, the thick hinged steel shooting up cascades of sparks. The sound of screeching metal hurt her ears over the deafening cacophony of diesel engines and surging wind from the Interstate outside. Sharon felt her stomach heave and she threw up a little in her mouth. The ground was rushing by at 85 mph.

It was her only way out.

And she had to go now, before he heard her escape on the two-way radio of the cab.

No time to think.

Sharon crawled on her hands and knees, bending toward the opening, sucking the asphalt and grass-scented fresh air deep into her lungs, gathering her strength. Out of the corner of her eye, she caught a glimpse of the hideous rotted blood-and-meat-splattered inside of the unspeakable chamber in the daylight.

She poked her head out through the hatch.

Facing forward, the agent was instantly sledgehammered by surging wind, flattening the skin of her face back on her skull like the G-force of a centrifuge. Forcing herself to blink her eyes open, she squinted at an upside-down view of the trailer undercarriage, highway rushing above it in a blurred ribbon of hard blacktop and broken white lines, a foot from the top of her head.

Her hair bounced off the tarmac. Below the road in her upended field of view, she stared down the long, caliginous steel fortress of the trailer chassis, shimmying and shaking, past the spinning axles, gear shaft and huge eighteen wheels.

Far off, at the vanishing point, was the cab, where *he* was. The torture chamber was at the rear of the truck, all the way back.

Hot, stinging sparks lanced the back of her head from the open metal lid glancing and *clanging* off the speeding asphalt.

The agent knew for certain she would never survive a leap off the tractor-trailer. Impact on the highway would mean instant death at this speed, and her best hope was she would be extinct before experiencing the two double sets of big wheels crushing her to a pulp of human road kill.

But Sharon wasn't planning to flee anyway.

She was going to kill the motherfucker.

This was what her whole life had led up to—*just get across the truck somehow, bust into the cab, surprise the shit out of the monster, then murder him with the gun she knew he probably had up there, or with her bare hands if necessary.*

Whatever it took.

She better hurry. Any minute he was going to listen on his live feed and hear she was missing, then there would be the scream of brakes and shuddering lurch of the truck as it pulled suddenly over on the shoulder, the underside of the truck view showing his feet leaping out of the cab and the barrel of the gun pointed at her face and it would all be over and for nothing.

The vast, trembling bottom chassis of the truck beckoned to her—a bridge she had to cross.

She had to scale it, climbing hand over hand, foot over foot across the entire bottom of the trailer all the way to the tractor if she was going to kill him and survive. One false move and she'd drop off onto the road and be swept under the tires and crushed under seventy tons of semi.

Scanning the metal framework of the belly of the trailer, Sharon searched the shadowy metal framework latticing the vehicular structure. There were rods and bars.

She could use those to climb.

Time to find out if they would hold her weight.

Retracting through the opening, the agent caught her breath and counted in her brain.

One.

Two.

Three.

Go.

Pressing her stomach against the floor of the chamber, Sharon scooted around in the cramped few feet of space and rolled onto her back. Slowly, carefully, she reached her hands behind her head down and out through the open lid and felt around for purchase.

Her fingers on either side closed on three-inch-thick steel rods, and she gripped them tightly, pulling hard to ensure they wouldn't break off. So far, the rods held fast, and with a careful, steady pull, the SA eased her head and shoulders out through the hatch.

The 85 mph gust punched her in the face again.

She held tight.

The rods supported her upper body weight.

Highway hurtled below, mere inches from her shoulders.

The thunder of the engines and wheels was ear-splitting and terrifying. Left and right past the underside of the trailer, she saw cars and trucks on the busy Interstate flanking the big rig. *Don't think of them. Focus on the cab. Focus on the trailer. Hand over hand. Now for the legs.* Sharon held on to the rods like a chin-up exercise, most of her weight resting on her hips on the floor of the stash hold, and eased her ass out the hole into the open air.

With a piercing *KR-RANK* the hatch lid tore loose of its hinges from the constant pressure of being dragged on the pavement—it went bouncing free end over end, throwing fireworks of sparks and clanging metal. Sharon sucked wind, eyes wide, watching the trapdoor being swept under the back wheels—the horrifyingly huge twin sets of spinning tires a few yards behind her. If the agent fell, she was going under them. The spinning, bouncing hatch lid flew into the front bumper of another tractor-trailer a truck-length behind and left a big dent. The other big rig swerved a little, blasting its horn in anger. Sharon's brain swam.

Does that trucker see me?

Or is he calling the police to report the driver of the rig whose falling debris just hit his truck?

Maybe the cops will come in time.

Can't count on it.

Don't wait.

You're on your own.

The cab. Get to the cab.

Put one hand in front of the other.

So she pulled, and her buttocks slid free of the hatch opening.

Immediately she felt the strain on her arms, and understood how weakened she was from loss of blood. Adrenaline surged and her fists clenched around the rods. Now, her calves pressed like an isometric exercise against the hatch, the last thing holding her in. *Get your fucking feet on the transom. C'mon, move it!* Gritting her teeth, she pulled one bare foot free of the opening and jammed it in the undercarriage beam. *Now the other. Do it!* Using all her strength, she yanked her ankle out from the sharp edge of the open hatch that had been cutting her heel and shoved it against the opposite horizontal structural support.

Now Sharon was hanging completely outside and underneath the big rig trailer as it barreled along the freeway. Her body was a few feet above the rushing blacktop and staccato white lines. The road noise was punishing, petrifying. Wind surged against her body and clothes in a relentless onslaught, threatening to smash her off her precarious perch.

She began to climb hand over hand, foot over foot toward the cab an impossible, unreachable distance ahead. The agent was facing the filthy, mud-and-oil splattered chassis of the trailer.

Her foot slipped.

Legs dropped.

Sharon's bare feet fell against the asphalt speeding past at terminal velocity and suddenly she was being dragged, her feet and ankles turned to bloody cottage cheese as they scraped along the tarmac. The pain was unbearable, shooting like an acetylene torch up her calves. She fought with every ounce of will to stop from screaming her lungs out.

Arms now fully outstretched and clinging with both hands, joints getting jerked out of their sockets, the SA held on for dear life as she was dragged against the road under the trailer. The force with which she was being pulled was prying her off the truck. Desperately, she kicked one foot up and tried to sling it over a carabiner, but her bare toes slipped out and struck the speeding freeway with greater force than before and she felt the flesh peel off. Her fingers were slipping on their purchase on the shaft. The agent kicked her left leg up and this time her foot caught in a wheel well. With her last strength, her right foot kicked up and planted securely in the transom of the underside of the trailer, and once again she hung from the truck. Blood was pouring down her ankles and her feet were raw meat, smeared with dirt, crud, and oil. Infection was inevitable.

She would get to a hospital if she made it through this alive.

First things first.

Wind and noise brutally pummeled her. The vibration of the transom threatened to tear Sharon's grip loose, but she reached out a hand, feeling her weight and gravity haul her downward as she stretched out her arm to grab further purchase down the shaft. A foot came loose so she jammed it under the ridge of the metal beam, using her knee to propel herself forward. *Don't look down. Whatever you do, don't look down.* So she averted her gaze from the road rip-roaring below in a dizzying blur of black and white staccato. But the agent had to see where she was going, so she craned her neck back and looked upside down ahead of her at the long, intimidating bulk of the trailer. It was at the bottom of her skewed field of vision. A new section of shaft was only a few inches away and she grabbed it.

Sharon clung to the bottom of the truck.

The forward wheels were now just a few feet away—massive thick tires two deep spinning madly on their axles. A rock spat out from the hot rubber and hit her with slingshot force on her side, breaking the skin, making her cry out, but the sound was drowned out in the ear-piercing thunder of the engines.

She had made it halfway across the truck Sharon realized when she lifted her head, looking down the length of her body between her legs and saw the open hatch twenty yards to her rear. The agent had lost much blood already—while she willed her muscles to work, white spots appeared in front of her eyes and she was numb all over, losing motor control, extremities not responding to the commands of her brain. And right then she froze, paralyzed in terror, afraid if she moved she would fall off. Those terrible spinning truck tires behind her yawned like crushers of some nightmarish grinder machine—if she slipped she was going right under. Her eyes bulged.

Look down, you stupid bitch!

Glancing at the rushing highway below, terror kicked like a horse. *Suck it up!* The agent dug deep. Found the mettle to keep climbing, hand over hand, foot by foot, along the underside of the transom. The next set of gigantic tires were right next to her face, furiously spinning, as she ducked under the axles and driveshaft, and clambered like a monkey toward the fifth wheel and kingpin hitch.

And then she was there.

Her fingers touched the back bumper of the tractor.

Hand closing around the coiled brake lines.

Looking up through the gap between the trailer and the tractor, Sharon saw the roof and rear headache rack of the cab looming above her. The hammering impact of the two sections of truck on the coupling felt like a diabolical amusement park bumper car ride. Keeping her feet squarely braced in the opposing wheel wells, the agent reached one arm up into the edge of the hitch for the kingpin. Wincing, she felt the tree stump-thick-pole rotate menacingly beside her fingertips—if she caught her grip wrong it would crush her hand to jelly—but she held fast and got solid purchase.

With a deep breath, the SA let go of the trailer with her right hand, grabbing on to the bracket containing the coiled brake lines on the tractor.

Her grip held.

She was on the cab.

Chapter Forty-Two

A few feet from her, the ladder to the roof of the tractor beckoned. Carefully rising to stand on her butchered bare feet on the back of the cab, the agent grabbed on to the rungs to support herself because of the pain. Every atom of her body hurt—she was covered in grime and blood and the pallid color of the skin on her arms alarmed her. Sharon knew she was running on pure adrenaline.

Almost there, almost there…

Her fingers clamped shut on the cold metal bottom rung of the ladder. *Hold on!*

She held fast, with everything she had.

The big rig was downshifting and the tractor jackhammered against its load. The trailer rammed forward against the back of the tractor. Jarred, Sharon lost her balance and nearly suffered a deadly fall—*He knows I'm here oh my God he's braking and going to crush me*—but then the tractor accelerated again, and the agent heaved herself against the ladder with the muscles of both arms, but the swaying rig swung her sideways out past the edge of the cab.

Her legs were rubber and she again she almost tumbled off the truck. Hanging over the side of the cab, the SA suddenly noticed she was visible in the West Coast Side Mirror on the passenger side of the tractor—*White Knuckle might see her*—so she quickly ducked out of sight.

The truck kept going.

He hasn't seen me, the motherfucker hasn't see me yet!

Work legs, work!

Gotta get to the cab door.

Get in there and kill his ass!

Only then did the agent become aware of her surroundings and realize why the gears kept craunching in a grinding friction—the eighteen-wheeler was climbing a winding mountain road. Hidden behind the rear of the tractor, hanging on to the ladder for dear life, she peered out over the side. The highway was still four lanes and sped by in a blur beside a guardrail traversing a gorge plunging down a vast granite precipice ridged by verdant green forests of pine trees. The road was at an eight-thousand-foot elevation. A titanic mountain range formed a spectacular tableau of snowcapped peaks miles across the divide.

She recognized where she was.

The Teton Pass in Wyoming.

She and Rudy had driven it.

No time to admire the view.

Sharon was a mess, and forced herself not to look at her gory bare feet, resembling two hamburgers with extra ketchup attached to her ankles, leaving bloody footprints on the bolted steel of the transom.

In the next lane, a blue Ford pickup overtook White Knuckle's big rig. Some long-haired cowboy in the passenger seat locked eyes with Sharon through the open window, regarding the beat-up woman huddling on the back of the tractor with dull disdain like she was some dodgy hitchhiker. The SA wanted to cry out to the other driver for help, to tell the him to call the police, even considered leaping onto the back of the pickup to escape, but knew she couldn't risk White Knuckle seeing her and before she could rethink her decision, the other vehicle had shot on ahead in front of the eighteen-wheeler and was gone.

The tractor downshifted again and veered as it swung around a dangerous curve, climbing ever higher into the towering mountains. Sharon was losing steam as loss of blood and the relative temporary safety drained her resolve. She hurt so bad—now the adrenaline was wearing off, her pain threshold was breached by intolerable agony. Paralysis was setting in.

Time to kill him.

Now or never.

And Sharon let go of the ladder and clambered on her hands and knees like a spastic marionette of a meat puppet. *Get up, sister!* Grabbing the side of the huge chromium smokestack, she got a good grip. *Come around on the driver's side. Stay low. Below the window. Smash the glass and break his face then pull open the door and shove him out from behind the wheel and—*

The driver side view mirror.

He would see her approach.

Same with the passenger side mirror. The glass on the West Coast mirrors were as big as IMAX, showing the entire side of the truck.

The roof. Climb up, crawl over, and come through the windshield.

Move your ass, girl.

The ladder attached to the rear of the tractor led to the roof. Her feet were too damaged to climb so the agent used her arms to hoist herself hand over hand up the rungs, scaling the back of the tractor out of sight of the front mirrors as the big rig curved this way and that, climbing the mountain highway. The truck movement swung her side to side on the ladder and she had to bicycle her legs to stay put, like an acrobat.

This sure as shit wasn't in the FBI handbook.

Two rungs left, then only one remained. Sharon hauled herself up by her hands over the edge of the roof of the cab, peering over the dirty, black sheet of steel. Wind punched her face, whipping her hair into her eyes. Shutting them, she shimmied her stomach and hips onto the top of the tractor. From her lofty perch, the gut-wrenching view of the Teton Pass made her want to puke—it was a perilous drop down a vertiginous gorge past sloping forests to granite boulders hundreds of feet below at the base of the chasm.

There was not much to hang on to once she got past the ladder. She had to make it fifteen feet to the front windshield. Choking exhaust from the chromium smokestacks billowing in noxious clouds around her face made it hard to see. A large steel horn was fixed on the roof a few feet away—something to hold on to. *We'll take what we can get.* Ahead, a colossal granite cliff face blanketed with big pines walled the inside of the wending three-lane road opposite the guardrail. As the huge cliff drew aside like a parting curtain when the big rig rounded the curve, Sharon saw the road was straightening out, and they had reached the summit of the pass. Past the guardrail she could see, but wished she couldn't, that the drop was hundreds of feet straight into oblivion.

At least White Knuckle couldn't see her up here.

She better to make sure he didn't hear her either.

Crawl.

Flattening her palms against the slippery smooth rooftop surface, she pulled herself along away from the ladder, spread eagle like a spider, dragging her mangled feet. She felt the slick wet snail trail blood on the metal below her toes. The tractor lurched as it entered the bend. The big horn unit was a few inches away now and she grabbed hold of it with both hands like a mountain climber gripping a pike in the rocks and finally found stable purchase.

That's when the other truck came barreling around the turn. It was straddling the lanes and Tremble hadn't seen it because the cliff wall was blocking the view of the road ahead, and now the blue Freightliner was quickly swerving back into the opposing lane and blowing its horn in warning.

White Knuckle blew his.

And blew out Sharon's eardrums.

The blaring horn her fingers clung to vibrated and the piercing high-pitched detonation of the blast was indescribably loud. The sound felt like nails hammered into her eardrums and then she heard nothing at all. White noise filled her skull. There was no horn or truck engine or any sound at all as the Freightliner hurtled past on the left dangerously close to the tractor-trailer. The wind flapped her clothes like a flag as the big rig charged away behind her.

She was deaf again.

For now.

But she could see. And she could move.

Creeping on her belly, the agent slithered like a slug on her stomach the last few feet and then she was at the edge of the windshield. A small rain gutter between the glass and frame met her raw fingertips. The glass was thick, tempered.

It would be hard to break.

Her hands were bleeding.

Roy Tremble downshifted two gears.

Through the windshield, he saw the road was dipping downward as his truck descended the far side of the mountain.

He hated the Teton Pass.

He'd been driving forty years and never got used to the treacherous mountain roads in this part of the state. Breathing a sigh, he rolled down his driver's side window and let some of the good fresh air from the higher elevations blast into the cab. White Knuckle had been on the road way too long—driver fatigue, too much coffee and too many pills turning him into a zombie.

That's when his eyes returned to the windshield.

And he saw the single trickle of bright red oxygenated blood dropping down the glass from the roof.

At first it didn't register. Why would blood be coming from the roof?

It was at that moment he decided to check on his captive and turned up the two-way radio to the stash hold on his dashboard.

The blood trickled in a slow, spreading branch of dripping red wetness past the wipers.

Something didn't sound right.

There was the sound of the road rushing through the open trapdoor on the closed circuit radio when it should just be whimpers or screams of his victim in the muffled silence of the torture chamber.

Tremble knew right then the FBI agent had escaped.

The blood.

The roof.

"NOOOOOOOOOOOOO!"

By the time he grabbed the .44 Magnum sitting on the seat beside him, the shadow had already fallen over him as the two bare, bloody feet swung down to sledgehammer the windshield into combustive cubes of gory tempered glass breaking away in thick sheets, and she was inside.

Chapter Forty-Three

Sharon hit the back of her skull hard against the shattered window frame and the sharp crinkly patches of glass ripped into her skin but her left foot connected very hard with something soft and she knew she hurt Tremble.

The big rig immediately veered.

Her hearing was coming back.

Somewhere close behind her she heard the blare of a horn and screeching tires of an oncoming car, feeling the breeze of near impact as the vehicle swerved unseen around the truck hood while she rolled sideways into the cab, and her head and shoulders dropped into the glass-strewn passenger seat.

She was inside the cab with White Knuckle.

Her sideways view of Tremble showed him glancing at her and back at the road and back to her then the road again as he swung the steering wheel hand over hand, a metallic object glinting in his lap as he struggled to regain control of the truck.

Running on sheer adrenalin, Sharon kicked at his head and shoulders again and again with both bloody, ragged, bare feet. Pain shot up her legs as she pummeled his upper body—he struggled to drive and beat away her thrashing legs at the same time.

The gun, where's the fucking gun!

Feeling the foot well and the seat and opening of the glove compartment to locate the weapon while she kicked.

Then seeing the black .44 Mag revolver in his lap get swept up in his fist as he drove one-handed, his eyes wild and bloodshot and insane, looking down the barrel, muzzle pointing straight at her a foot away, she kicked blindly and knocked his gun hand up and in a deafening *KA-BOOOOM* the round *WHIZZZZZZZED* past her ear and exploded the passenger-side windshield. Glass rained.

Get the gun away from him! Her brain was on autopilot as she sat up and grabbed Tremble's gun wrist with both hands, twisting violently, bending back his tendon joints.

The two people struggled violently for the pistol in the cab of the eighteen-wheeler barreling out of control.

KA-BOOOOOM! PTANK! A round ventilated the ceiling.

The whole thing felt like hours but must have been seconds. And in those moments Sharon was so close to him, after all this time, all the hunting, now face to face. His contorted, pallid, leathery features like wrinkled beef jerky inches away, her gaze locked with his near colorless pale gray eyes. His lips were pulled back over his yellowed, tobacco-stained teeth in a hideous rictal grin, like an ancient skull. But he couldn't hold her gaze—he kept glancing back at the road, using his shoulder to try to steer the tractor-trailer. His hands were off the wheel.

Had Sharon time to think, she'd have realized the grand folly of distracting the driver of a hurtling seventy-ton piece of heavy machinery given their physical location, and in the back of her mind that probably occurred to her while struggling for the gun to kill him, because when she felt and heard the loud impact of the guardrail on the nose of the tractor cab it didn't surprise her.

Looking through the broken windshield she caught a hair-raising glimpse of the corkscrewing road of the switchback spur the semi rampaged along. Oncoming cars and trucks swerved out the cab's path, horns honking, tires screeching. The tarmac was straightening out into a two-hundred-yard line before the next sheer curve.

There was a bone-cracking impact on her skull and searing pain on her scalp as White Knuckle pistol-whipped her hard, and the agent fell back.

There was blood in her eyes, vision awash with red blur.

She saw two things.

Tremble steering with one hand and looking down the barrel of the Magnum in her face, his swollen skeletal features smeared with his blood and the gore from her feet, grinning hideously as his finger closed on the trigger to blow her head clean off.

And she saw the twin brake levers under the dashboard.

Remembered the first one is for the cab.

The second for the trailer.

Sharon Ormsby seized the first brake with her right hand and yanked it with all her strength.

Hearing Tremble scream, "NOOOOOOOOOOOOOOOOOOO!"

Too late.

The tractor shuddering and bumping as it slammed to a sudden halt at 60 mph, tires shrieking in protest as her nostrils filled with the acrid stench of burning rubber.

The impact of the abrupt stop was stunningly violent and the force of it lifted her whole body out of the seat as she felt herself catapulted through the shattered windshield in a topsy-turvy blur of movement. She floated for a moment in space, ears filled with screeching tires, until she hit the ground hard and was rolling over and over to lie on her stomach in a heap of broken bones.

She lay there on her belly on the shoulder of the road and saw it all happen as if in slow motion.

Through the windshield of the stopped tractor, Roy Tremble was desperately jerking at his seat belt that had jammed, wearing an expression of pure terror.

The unbraked trailer of the big rig rammed forward into the back of the stalled cab, plowing into it at 60 mph.

Jackknifing the truck!

The kingpin bent and snapped in the hitch as the cab flipped forward onto its hood and crumpled like a tin can, the trailer climbing over it like a bulldozer angling at ninety degrees and turning sideways and tearing free of the cab to go skidding ahead of it, down the road in fireworks of sparks and screams of tortured steel, wheels spinning, tires shredding.

The cab with White Knuckle trapped within flipped end over end across the Teton Pass, crumpling into a crushed ball of metal, windows and headlights exploding, bumpers shearing loose, smokestacks corkscrewing, and tires popping like balloons, to end right side up on busted wheels, completely decimated.

Sharon blinked.

Roy Tremble was still inside, his body broken in a dozen places and drenched in blood, the dislodged steering wheel crushing against his chest cavity and pinning him to the seat. The serial killer gasped grotesquely for air from his collapsed lungs, mouth puckering like a beached fish, arms squirming in insectile movement like a bug pinned to the wall.

Thirty yards away, Sharon Ormsby struggled to stand on one leg, the other dangling uselessly, to face the dying monster in the truck.

His eyes met hers and his gaze was filled with the rawest fear imaginable.

She didn't blink.

The gas fumes were making her woozy as the agent looked down to see the widening lake of gasoline draining from the punctured tanks of the tractor onto the tarmac surrounding the wreck.

Sparks and flickers of flame came from inside the destroyed engine through the rent open hood.

White Knuckle saw the pooling gas and dangerous sparks too—she saw he did, and he looked back at her in fresh panic.

The gas caught fire in a huge *WHOOOOOOOSH*.

An ocean of flame spread like wildfire up the sides of the diesel-soaked cab and Tremble's eyes were bugging out of his skull as he helplessly saw the flames reach in like blazing tendrils through the broken windshield.

White Knuckle went up in flames. His trapped body turned into a fiery torch that roasted the hair off his head and bubbled the flesh off his face.

The wounded Sharon gazed on with grim satisfaction.

Trapped in the blazing inferno of his own truck, Tremble's hideous high-pitched screams of agony rang out horribly over the pass. He swatted at the flames that engulfed him. His facial skin blackened and burned off the skull in bloody char as his locked gaze with Sharon was broken when the searing heat exploded his eyeballs like a pair of bloody grapes. It took forever for Tremble to die in huge suffering. The monster writhed in unspeakable agony, slowly burning alive in the fires of Hell right before the agent's eyes—she smiled in savage gratification because this was justice and just what the creature deserved. Sharon was glad to be present for his execution.

The tanks caught.

The cab blew.

Sharon was blown clean off her feet by the shock wave of the blast—boiling hot fulgurations of orange fireclouds and billowing black smoke rolled turbulently upwards, consuming the tractor and scattering fiery debris—a burning tire flew past her head and she was slammed back against the granite wall of the highway. The air filled with thick, acrid smoke as she dropped limply to the ground.

When Sharon looked up blearily, the burning, blackened skeleton of a demolished truck was all that remained of White Knuckle.

It was over.

She got him.

"Ten-four," the agent whispered.

Chapter Forty-Four

From: Frank.Campanella@ic.fbi.gov
Re: Operation White Knuckle.
To: Michael.Robertson@ic.fbi.gov

I am happy to report that the case is closed. The serial killer truck driver Roy Tremble was killed two days ago in a fight with SA Sharon Ormsby on the Teton Pass in Wyoming and White Knuckle died from injuries and burns sustained in the wreck of his truck and the subsequent explosion.

SA Ormsby survived with multiple injuries primarily received in captivity in the stash hold of the truck. She is currently under hospital care and on administrative leave. Her doctors expect a full recovery and it is anticipated she will return to work in the next three months. SA Ormsby showed remarkable courage, resilience and resourcefulness in the apprehension of Roy Tremble performing her assigned duties during her probationary period and I am recommending the review board make her a full Special Agent. As you know, sir, I assigned her an unorthodox UC operation and she took risks above and beyond the call of duty to stop this menace who has preyed on people in forty-eight states for forty years.

We may never know just how many people Tremble killed, but a conservative estimate based on his victim count over the last year stands at over 500. DNA tests on recovered bodies along the highway corridors of the United States are ongoing. I anticipate many more of these deaths will be ultimately attributed to this man. Roy Tremble appears to have been an anomaly, a unique psychopath like Henry Lee Lucas and Jeffrey Dahmer. All evidence leads us to believe this cunning and resourceful serial killer worked alone.

I eagerly await SA Ormsby's return to active duty at HSK or whatever divisions the

Eric Red

Bureau assigns her in the future of what will be a bright career.

> *Yours very truly,*
> *SSA Frank Campanella*

Chapter Forty-Five

The dream had changed lately.

Sharon Ormsby was a child again, back at the truck stop, watching her mother leave after giving her a kiss on the head before stepping out into the bright sunshine outside the convenience store. There were tears in her mom's eyes she hadn't remembered in other dreams. The little girl who Sharon was back then returned to sorting through the candies on the shelf with her small hands, looking now and then past the racks to her mother crossing toward the gas pumps. Then a moment later, she was gone.

White Knuckle's truck was not in the dream this time.

Tremble's face did not leer at her in the side view mirror as it had lately in the dream—pulling out onto the highway, she somehow knew, with her mother in the truck.

The monster was not there, anywhere.

It was just the nearly empty parking lot and a few cars pulling up to the pumps.

When, as if in slow motion, she remembered walking up to the glass doors of the store and looking out, and her mother was nowhere to be seen.

Just gone.

Sharon woke up now, recalling the tears in her mother's eyes when she kissed her on the head.

As the SA lay in the bed of the darkened hospital room, lit by the glow of the heart monitor, she held on to the dream before it evaporated into evanescence.

That's what had happened, she suddenly realized with stunning certainty after all these years—her mom had just taken off and walked out never to return.

Tremble was never there.

Lying in the comforting darkness, her body aching in a thousand spots, she knew that White Knuckle taking her mother had all been in her head.

The mind plays tricks.

Had it been wish fulfillment, she wondered? Had she wanted on so many levels to find and stop White Knuckle that her subconscious had cast him in her dream as her mother's killer to fully motivate her? Had to be. Ambition, vengeance, sheer drive to distinguish herself in the case of a lifetime had made every molecule in her being focus with a single-minded sense of purpose—an obsessive myopia that was what it required to face a serial killer beyond comprehension and get the job done.

She had gotten the job done.

Had gotten her man.

Inarguably distinguished herself in the line of duty.

The proof sat on her bed stand in the dim green glow of the hospital vitals monitors—cards of commendation from Campanella and Bureau senior staff for her outstanding performance in the field were clustered around vases of flowers.

Sharon rested her head on the pillow and tried to get her mind off the pain of her skinned feet and broken bones. Staring down her body under the sheets, the agent registered the bandages wrapping her arms and legs like a mummy and the IV needles and tubes leading out of them. *The car is in the shop*, meaning her, she smiled to herself.

Again, her mind traveled back to the dream, and the memory, of that fateful day at the truck stop in her distant past where she last saw her mother—with a truthful clarity like a lens focusing, the agent knew that her mother had simply left her that day.

Sharon had been abandoned.

Probably her mom was not ready to have kids or take care of her—still young and wanting to live and play. She had loved Sharon, there was no doubt—the kiss and the tears in her eyes demonstrated that—but her mother couldn't be her parent.

There in the quiet gentle gloom of the hospital, Sharon finally faced the reality she had always wanted to block out—the pain of abandonment. She wept a little, but the sting eased.

Her biggest terror seemed not so scary now after all she had been through and the other inconceivable horrors she had faced over the last few weeks.

The emotional dislocation that stemmed from parental desertion had shaped and molded her entire life, she understood—right up to working at a division of the FBI where she discharged her duties chasing highway disappearances. She saw that now.

Thanks were owed White Knuckle—the monster had given her profound direction and purpose where she was no longer tentative about herself, destroying that demon had exorcised her own, casting off her burdens of insecurity and dislocation, and banishing them forever. That's why she had invoked him in her dream about her mother.

Deserted she had undeniably been, but Sharon was not an abandoned little girl anymore. She was an adult now—a full FBI Special Agent, a blooded warrior. This case had been her trial by fire, her rite of passage. Now she was somebody. Nobody could ever take away her accomplishment and pride.

Sharon Ormsby had herself back, the part that was lost at the gas station when she was a child. About her mother she would always be uncertain, but she could live with that now.

Get over it and get on with it.

Epilogue

The stretch of Interstate 66 rolled away through the windshield.

Sharon sat staring out at it, lost in thought. An Arby's, a Wendy's and a Chevron station passed by the car, then it was just the endless road wending through the boring, nondescript Virginia landscape. She found herself wondering how many times he had driven this very same road, perhaps pulling into that gas station to refuel or stop at one of the fast food restaurants to grab a burger, before hitting the road again. He must have traveled every single highway in these United States a thousand times. It was the life of the long distance trucker.

She fingered the smooth, solid object in her hands. Cool to the touch, it somehow warmed and reassured her.

The agent was trying to find the right spot to do what she had come here to do, knowing it is what he would have wanted. So she rode patiently, watching the landscape. Her pants and jacket were freshly pressed, as was her jacket. The SA was professionally dressed except for the loose fitting slippers on her feet, which, five months later, were almost finished healing.

Campanella glanced over at her from behind the wheel of the unmarked Crown Victoria. It was Saturday and their day off, but he had agreed to drive her on this task. It seemed only fitting. The SSA didn't say anything, knowing she had a lot on her mind, but she caught him give a thoughtful glance to the urn she was holding, before returning his eyes to the road.

The drive was a last testament to Rudy. Sharon owed him this moment of mourning and contemplation. He had been a lonely soul, one who had made mistakes, who had accepted his separation from loved ones that his job required. But he was a good man who had put his life on the line to help her. It was his attempt to try and make a difference, and not fade away as one of the anonymous gearjammers on the road. In the end, he just wanted somebody to remember him. In this, Rudy Dykstra had succeeded, because

Sharon Ormsby would never forget him.

Keep it out of the ditches, good buddy.

She heaved a huge sigh.

This place was as good as any.

He had driven here like he had driven everywhere else.

It was all his road.

Rolling down her passenger window, she felt the wind in her face. Lifting the silver urn, she unscrewed the cap to solemnly dump Rudy Dykstra's ashes out of the car onto the highway, where they were whisked away.

Saying a little prayer to herself, Sharon Ormsby looked over her shoulder out the back windshield at the dust cloud of the trucker's cremated remains dispersing on the highway behind her into the vanishing point.

About the Author

Eric Red is a motion picture screenwriter, director and author. His original scripts include *The Hitcher* for Tri Star, *Near Dark* for DeLaurentiis Entertainment Group, *Blue Steel* for MGM and the western *The Last Outlaw* for HBO. He directed and wrote *Cohen and Tate* for Hemdale, *Body Parts* for Paramount, *Undertow* for Showtime, *Bad Moon* for Warner Bros. and *100 Feet* for Grand Illusions Entertainment.

His first novel, *Don't Stand So Close*, is available from SST Publications. His other novels, *The Guns of Santa Sangre*, *It Waits Below*, and *White Knuckle*, are available from Samhain Publishing.

Mr. Red's short stories have been published in *Cemetery Dance*, *Weird Tales*, *Dark Discoveries*, *Shroud*, and *Beware The Dark* magazines, as well as the *Dark Delicacies III: Haunted* anthology and Mulholland Books' *Popcorn Fiction*.

He created and wrote the sci-fi/horror comic series and graphic novel *Containment* for IDW Publishing just reprinted by SST Publications, and the horror western comic series *Wild Work* published by Antarctic Press.

He divides his time between Los Angeles and Wyoming, with his wife Meredith.

Mr. Red's website is: www.ericred.com.

His IMDB page is: http://imdb.to/LyPooe.

Follow him on Facebook and Twitter.

It waits no more!

It Waits Below
© *2014 Eric Red*

In the 1800s, an asteroid carrying an extraterrestrial life form crashed to earth and sunk a Spanish treasure ship. Now, a trio of salvage experts dives a three-man sub to the deepest part of the ocean to recover the sunken gold. There, they confront a nightmarish alien organism beyond comprehension, which has waited for over a century to get to the surface. It finally has its chance.

As their support ship on the surface is ambushed by deadly modern-day pirates, the crew of the stranded sub battles for their very lives against a monster no one on Earth has seen before.

Enjoy the following excerpt for It Waits Below:

It had traveled trillions of miles through interstellar space over millions of years on a rock fragment jettisoned from its planet when it had blown up.

It didn't need to eat.

It didn't need to breathe.

The alien was sentient.

A machine not yet turned on.

It just waited.

It did not register the stars and galaxies its asteroid hurtled past on its aimless trajectory through the infinite vacuum void, did not experience wonder, or awe, or terror—it did not think or feel at all..

The being, and there were many of it inside the fissures of the meteor, did not exist unless it was another organism's guest.

It was looking for a host.

Then it could be.

Until that time, the alien rode the rock through the cosmos.

Warship Corona.
Crow's nest.
Indian Ocean.
1853

At first glance, the mizzen lookout thought it was the Northern Star, but as the light in the night skies grew brighter, the Spanish sailor was no longer certain.

The cloudless canopy of the heavens above the ocean was encrusted with countless stars sparking like jewels—a constant reminder to the sailor of the fabulous treasure stored in the hold of the *Corona* making its seaward trek toward Edo Bay. Standing on the platform high atop the ship's mast above the sails, the Spaniard marveled at the one star out of all the others that had attracted his attention.

It grew a tail.

Not a star at all, but a comet, growing larger. The mizzen lookout thought little of it, for sailors witnessed many comets of all varieties at night on the ocean.

Wrapping his layers of sweaters and overcoats around him against the frigid night air as his breath condensed in a chilly mist before him, the sailor looked over the edge of the parapet atop the main mast. Far below, past the rigging and huge canvas sails, several of the ship's officers stood watch out on deck, faces tilted upwards, observing the comet.

At least it was something to look at. Sailor First Class Santiago Rodriguez was freezing his ass off, and the darkened empty sea held little of interest. He had been on duty for four hours, hating every minute of it. The Spaniard desperately missed the warm weather of his native Barcelona, but joining the crew of the *Corona* was a great honor.

He was on the Queen's Business.

The three-masted Spanish Santa Ana class warship was the state-of-the-art military vessel in the world at the time—a 112 gun three-decker, 213 feet long, 58 feet in the beam and weighing 2,112 tons—unbeatable by any human force on land or sea. It was why the Queen of Spain had conscripted the Naval jewel in Her Majesty's Crown to carry the fortune in gold across the ocean to Japan. The *Corona* and her crew had been months at sea, embarking from Gibraltar, sailing south across the Southern Atlantic below the horn of Africa, around the tip of New Zealand, then north past New Guinea toward Japan. The ship would hold off any challenge, impervious to all but the sea around her.

Inside the hold, guarded by six soldiers armed with muskets, was a wooden chest filled with 5,000 gold coins. It was the a tribute offered by Queen Isabella II to the Tokugawa Shogunate and Emperor of Japan to allow Spanish ships access to Japanese ports. The feudal nation had been opened to the west by American Commodore Perry in the Treaty of Kanagawa a year before, and every major nation was vying for a port on the Japanese mainland.

The voyage was a secret.

Every man aboard the *Corona* was the best the Spanish Navy had to offer—battle tested, fearless, tough as nails. They had all been handpicked from the ranks of the navy's finest. Sailor First Class Santiago Rodrigo took great pride in that, as would his children and his children's children. An officer promotion surely lay in his future. And the triple salary he received for his participation on the voyage of the *Corona* would buy his family a new house when he returned in glory to Spain. Let his fellow naval men die in Trafalgar—he was safe and content on this voyage and looking forward to setting eyes on this new land in the Far East.

The sailor's mind stopped wandering as his gaze returned to the sea, the surface of which was growing noticeably brighter, cast in a strange glowing aura—there was now thirty miles visibility across the ocean where before there had been ten. Looking upwards, Santiago observed the glowing celestial body he had first mistaken for the Northern Star had grown improbably huge—its uncanny illumination was what lit up the sea in all directions.

The comet now looked as big as the moon, with a fiery tail.

That moon was falling out of the sky.

With fantastical suddenness, night became daytime.

An immense, awe-inducing, pulsing light lit up the entire ocean as far as the eye could see— blinding white, then black, white, then black, in a dreadful, ominous, pulsing strobe. The vast illumination came with the comet falling to earth.

Heading right toward them.

The man on watch had seen many comets before, often several a night, with their graceful tails shooting across the sky. But they were always distant—this one was aiming straight for them.

By now, alarmed voices and loud sounds of activity rang across the deck below—orders shouted, running feet, bodies scrambling to their posts, winches pulled, cleats squeaking, sails flapping as the crew of the *Corona* attempted to change course and evade the inevitable.

Nothing had prepared them for this.

The mizzen lookout shielded his eyes from the apocalyptic blazing pulse of the approaching comet and knew before it happened that the shooting star from the Gods would hit their vessel and sink it and that all would be lost.

Putting his hands together and kneeling on the crow's nest, Santiago prayed as everywhere the sea grew ever brighter—knowing there was no time to scale the rigging back to the deck and in seconds, there would be no deck.

He wondered if the world was ending and prayed it wouldn't.

The comet filled the sky. The throbbing glow its incendiary tail produced strobed the sea white and black and white again in a cosmic lightning. A blazing column of afterburn stretched behind it into the heavens.

The meteor's cataclysmic roar engulfed the world in a deafening obliteration of sound—an unearthly, low, thundering rumble like a thousand mountain avalanches.

The men on deck were already running for cover or diving overboard but there was no escape. The ship was a sitting target.

The mizzen lookout stared at the oncoming rock ghosted with fire as it expanded to fill his field of vision, like a cannonball fired in slow motion heading straight between his eyes, blotting out the stars forever. "Madre Dios," were the last words Santiago Rodriguez uttered.

The meteorite impacted the *Corona* amidships just behind the bow. Its velocity, rate of descent, and weight were incalculable and created a hole in the ocean a half a mile wide, sending a volcanic eruption of millions of gallons of displaced water and marine life 10,000 feet in the air. The warship was halved by the asteroid, and within ten seconds, the back of the 2,000 ton ship had flipped stern perpendicular to the ocean, the masts disintegrating like toothpicks and sails burning like tissue. A vast maelstrom swirled the sea in a quarter mile in circumference whirlpool that swept the wreckage of the greatest military ship afloat down with the sinking meteor into the bottom of deepest part of the ocean on the planet earth.

Its million-eon voyage had ended.

It did not know earth or plan to get there.

Earth just happened to be in the way.

It did not know anything.

It had never met water, until now.

As it rode on the rock ever downwards, tied in the wreckage of the Corona, it knew only one thing.

Something, many things, warm things, traveled along with it. The being moved toward its warm companion organisms.

And became guests of its new hosts.

First contact.

The Guns of Santa Sangre
© *2013 Eric Red*

They're hired guns. The best at what they do. They've left bodies in their wake across the West. But this job is different. It'll take all their skill and courage. And very special bullets. Because their targets this time won't be shooting back. They'll fight back with ripping claws, tearing fangs and animal cunning. They're werewolves. A pack of bloodthirsty wolfmen has taken over a small Mexican village, and the gunmen are the villagers' last hope. The light of the full moon will reveal the deadliest showdown the West has ever seen—three men with six-shooters facing off against snarling, inhuman monsters.

Enjoy the following excerpt for The Guns of Santa Sangre:

John Whistler reckoned he was within thirty miles of the wanted men when they lost the wheel. Now the stagecoach was out of commission, the bounty hunter stranded to hell in the bowels of the Mexican desert, with nobody but two damn do-nothing stage drivers and the Sonoma rental wench. It was the gloaming, the sky getting dark, but the edge was off the terrible heat, so he figured they'd picked a good time to break down as any.

The big mustached man in duster and ten gallon hat stood impatiently rotating and clicking the cylinder of his Colt Dragoon pistol about two hundred feet from the disabled wagon. Whistler stared out at the forbidding, craggy Durango canyon country and vast canopy of turquoise and purple and rose-streaked late evening sky. He listened to the two Wells Fargo men arguing and cussing and the sounds of banging and creaking as the men finished the repairs on the broken slats of the right rear wheel they were fitting back into place. The weathered brown carriage was tilted at an obtuse angle. The team of four horses stood bored in their harness at the front of the chassis, tails flitting at flies.

Whistler looked over the where the sweat-soaked 15 year old prostitute in the black velvet corset and petticoat stood fanning herself. She winked at him. Eyes of violet, red hair spilling down her shoulders, she smelt sweetly of rose water and sex. Her name she'd told him was Daisy and she had herself a going concern riding the stage line back and forth, servicing passengers and kicking back a few bucks to the driver. A sweet little set up. The whore had been knee to knee with him the whole trip from Sonoma in the cramped and jouncing stage, bouncing pale freckled breasts spilling out of her corset a few feet from his face on the opposite seat.

The bounty hunter took out his silver pocket watch on the chain from his vest and snapped it open. His name "John Whistler" was engraved in elegant lettering inside the lid. The hands of the clock read, "7:53." Annoyed at being behind schedule, the man gruffly closed the watch and pocketed it.

The stagecoach junction was supposed to be just twenty miles from here, the old driver told him. Damn bit of luck. Whistler would have been there already, should have made it by dusk but for the stage mishap. Hell, he had those bad men he hunted dead to rights. They might not be there tomorrow morning. No matter, he was right on their ass and would catch up with them soon enough. The bounty hunter took out the folded wanted poster in his pocket and regarded it. The crudely sketched faces of the three outlaws stared back at him from the crumpled paper in the red hue of twilight.

Samuel Tucker.

John Fix.

Lars Bodie.

Notorious names in bold block type lettering just above the $1,000.00 reward notice on each of their heads. Gunfighters and killers with lots of bodies strewn in their wake. These men were good, but he was better. The bounty hunter had gotten his lead on their current whereabouts from a Mexican ramrod who had seen them just the evening before in a small outpost thirty miles east from where Whistler now stood. The trail was coming to an end. Their bodies would be slung over saddles. Or his would.

He'd be out of Mexico one way or the other. He drew and admired his Smith & Wesson Scoffield 45. It had no trigger guard. Made it faster to draw and fire unimpeded by such inconveniences. A saguaro cactus sat like an upright fork a few hundred yards away, the tines poking black spokes against the glowing rust of the end of the day. He contemplated a little target practice on the plant to kill the time, but reckoned he better save his bullets. The formidable men he was hunting knew how to place theirs.

Mostly, he just wanted the hell out of Mexico.

From the sound of things behind him, they were getting that wheel fixed, and it was about time. He turned around to see the fat, bearded stage driver and his young Mexican shotgunner in the scarf and vest tightening the bolts on the displaced wagon wheel and using wrenches to adjust the torque on the axle. Any time now they'd be back on the road. But he'd lost a day.

"How you boys doing on that wheel?" Whistler called over.

"It's repaired, but you best settle in mister," the old stage driver grumbled. "Because we're here for the night and pulling out at dawn."

"That does not suit me."

"It doesn't matter. We're not driving this stage in the dark, not through this kind of terrain."

"But—"

"There be cliffs and ruts and ravines everywhere along the trail 'twixt here and the junction and stage could take a plunge with one wrong turn."

The four people grouped by the carriage in the failing light.

A huge full moon hung in the sky, clouded with haze.

They heard the wolves.

Not like any Whistler heard before. A keening, yipping lupine chorus came from all sides out in the canyons. The howls began low but rose in strident pitch and timber until they became a high shrieking bay. It was a sound to freeze your blood. The bounty hunter looked at the stage driver, who was looking at the Mexican guard with the shotgun, who looked like he was about to soil himself.

"Coyotes?" Whistler asked, staring out into the near total darkness that began about three hundred feet from where they stood. The desert spaces that in daylight spread so vast were now claustrophobic and invisible beyond. The full moon was high and bright, obstructed by clouds and oddly cast no light. A tiny trickle of moonlight showed a crag of mountain peak in the gloom.

"Sure," said the old Wells Fargo guy.

"*Niente*," whispered the guard.

"What then?"

The guard didn't answer.

The big wolves, or whatever they were, roared in unison, a sonic garrote of cacophonic sound tightening around them. Closing in. The hooker was shivering in fear, her eyes huge as her dainty hands covered her ears against the bellowing growls. "Something's out there. We got to get out of here," she whimpered.

"I'm with her," Whistler confronted the driver. "We best be on our way directly."

The old timer threw down, yelling in the bounty hunter's face, spattering saliva. "I told you tain't driving this rig at night on this trail or the stagecoach will crash because I cain't see!"

By now the four horses were starting to panic, pawing the ground with their hooves, long snouts whipping back and forth in their bridles and bits, eyes marbles and ears pinned back at the horrific music in the hills.

The monstrous roaring echoing around the canyons continued unabated and drew nearer and nearer. The guard, pale and face pouring with sweat, started babbling to the driver in Spanish, and the old man yelled back at him in the local tongue that Whistler barely understood. One thing was obvious. The Mexican knew what those sounds belonged to and wanted out of there. The argument became a shoving match, and the younger man won, clambering desperately up into the driver's bench by the luggage roof rack, grabbing the reins and gesturing madly for the bounty hunter and the hooker to get into the stagecoach and hurry it up.

"After you, ma'am," quipped Whistler to the tart. He opened the door and eased her into the carriage with a helpful hand up her skirt on her firm rear end. Then he put his boot on the metal step and climbed in across from her.

The old Wells Fargo driver climbed up onto the driver's seat, cursing the whole way. He shoved the guard aside, grabbing the reigns. "I'm drivin'," he shouted, "you'll put us in a damn ditch. YYEEEE—AHHH!" He cracked the reins and the team surged forwards, the stagecoach pulling out.

The carriage picked up speed, scared horses hauling the rig at a full gallop. The wagon rocked back and forth on the uneven terrain as it plunged into the desert nocturne. Whistler could still hear the howling, but they seemed to be moving away from it. All he heard were the sounds of the wooden wheels on the rocks, the squeaking of the chassis suspension and the loud pounding of the hooves. He looked across from him in the tight, trembling quarters to see the hooker frozen in the leather seat a few feet away, pale fragile face staring out the open window of the stagecoach, eyes bugging out.

"Hurry, hurry…" she murmured.

The big wolves bayed.

And gave chase.

The bounty hunter drew both pistols and gripped them in his fists, looking out the other window. The moon was waxen. Vague jagged landscape and blurred rock formations rushed past in near total darkness. The wagon was picking up speed, hurtling recklessly now, shuddering carriage violently jarred by the broken trail. It hit a big rock and rose off its wheels, slamming down on its suspension so hard it tossed him and the woman to and fro. She screamed again and held onto the leather hand straps for dear life. The bounty hunter leaned up against the window, pistols at ready and looked out, thinking he caught glimpses of big, bounding black forms keeping pace with the speeding stagecoach.

The loud dull report of a shotgun blast sounded from the roof.

Then another.

Something hit the other side of the stagecoach like a boulder, knocking the wagon into a veering fishtail.

The old man released a horrible high-pitched scream of agony as his body was dragged off the roof seat and smashed against the door in a blur of cloth and red flesh with a bone-snapping *thud bang crack*.

The hooker saw the driver torn from the carriage and was screaming hysterically now. Whistler had to slap her silly to shut her up as he crawled across the seat to look out the other window. He fired two shots blind into the blackness, hopefully at least wounding a few of the things.

With a terrible crash, something landed on the roof so heavy it cracked the wooden ceiling.

It's all about the story...

Romance

HORROR

www.samhainpublishing.com

CPSIA information can be obtained at www.ICGtesting.com
Printed in the USA
BVOW02s0643010615

402610BV00002B/14/P